YASMINI

THE INCOMPARABLE

FORGOTTEN CLASSICS OF PULP FICTION

For additional information about these books please visit muraniapress.com

YASMINI
THE INCOMPARABLE

TALBOT MUNDY

Introduction by Brian Taves

**MURANIA
PRESS**

Dover, New Jersey

First Edition — May 2019

Book Editor & Designer: Ed Hulse.
Cover Painting: Hugh J. Ward.

Reprint History:
"A Soldier and a Gentleman" originally published complete in the January 1914 issue of *Adventure*. "The Winds of the World" originally serialized in the July-September 1915 issues of *Adventure,*

ISBN 13: 978-1071329603

Murania Press, Dover NJ
For a complete list of our other publications please visit muraniapress.com.

CONTENTS

INTRODUCTION

BY BRIAN TAVES

In 1909, a tumultuous early life behind him, London-born Talbot Mundy relocated to New York with his new wife. Within a day of landing, he was mugged and robbed of the few hundred dollars with which he had hoped to begin a new life. One of the journalists who had reported his beating offered the hungry and homeless Mundy lodgings so he could pursue his lifelong dream of writing. More than a year elapsed before he finally made his first sale—a short story titled "A Transaction in Diamonds"—to *The Scrap Book*, a pulp magazine published by the legendary Frank A. Munsey. It appeared in the February 1911 issue.

Soon Mundy was selling stories and articles regularly. He became most prominently associated with *Adventure*, the most respected and literary of the pulps, most notably following the publication in February 1912 of his moving short story, "Soul of a Regiment." His first novel, *Rung Ho!*, published in 1914, was a historical tale of the Sepoy Mutiny of 1857.

Talbot Mundy united feminism and his fascination with India in the greatest character in all his writing, the remarkable, matchless Yasmini. Her creation marked the point at which Mundy advanced beyond being a routine composer of adventure tales. A devious, manipulative, and always surprising Eurasian noblewoman, she schemed to carve an empire for herself. She first appeared in two *Adventure* novelettes in early 1914, "A Soldier and a Gentleman" and "Gulbaz and the Game," and figures prominently during the next two years in *The Winds of the World* and *King—of the Khyber Rifles*. Her youthful climb to political power forms the centerpiece of Mundy's *Guns of the Gods*, while she makes her final appearance in his *Caves of Terror*, having descended from politics to become an evil seductress and head of a house of gambling and intrigue.

The idea for Yasmini's character had been born back around 1900, in India, while Talbot was standing amidst the crowded traffic of Bombay.

> There came a closed carriage with slatted windows, of the sort in which the wives of wealthy Indians take the air; it was drawn by magnificent horses and the coachman found it so difficult to keep them in control that the man on the box beside him helped him with the reins. That was excuse enough for watching: I felt sure there would be an accident. On a platform behind the carriage were two stalwart Rajput footmen, who seemed in doubt whether to keep their places or jump down and run to the horses' heads. Suddenly the horses tried to bolt; the coachman, with a rein wrapped round his waist, exerted all his strength; the carriage lurched, and the front wheel struck the curbstone within three feet of me. The shock jarred the door, which swung open. I believe there were three women in the carriage, but I had eyes for only one of them. She was unveiled; she had golden hair; she was dressed in diaphanous silks of the color of early morning in the hills; she seemed to me, in that sudden moment, to be lovelier than any pictured woman I had ever seen; and she was amused—tickled to bits by the scandalous fact of being seen by alien eyes. She laughed gayly, and I can hear her laughter now, it was so merry and full of mischief. I had hardly time to raise my hat before one of the huge footmen jumped down from his place behind the carriage, shoved me violently backward, jumped back to his little platform, yelled to the coachman—and the carriage drove away. That was all I ever saw or knew of her. . . .

Perhaps if I had known about her any facts whatever, I might have been so hampered by those facts as
to have made her tame, implausible and valueless as a
heroine of fiction."

In the first chapter of *Guns of the Gods*, Mundy supplies Yasmini with
a biography. Her father was a Rajput, Maharajah Bubru Singh, making
her kin to all the great families of Rajputana. Her mother was a Russian,
Sonia Omanoff. Sonia's first marriage had been to a prince in Moscow,
who behaved so notoriously in public that she was found guilty when he
was murdered. The Czar commuted her sentence when she expressed her
willingness to marry an Indian as part of her country's plans for the sub-
continent. Whether Sonia would have supported or avenged herself on
her homeland is unknown, since Bubru Singh died shortly after Yasmini's
birth. Rather than accept the secluded custom of widowhood when her
husband's nephew, Gungadhura Singh, succeeded to the throne, the
British arranged for Sonia to have a separate palace. There, growing up,
Yasmini was "regaled by her mother with tales of Western outrage and
ambition, and well-schooled in all that pertained to her Eastern heritage
by the thousand-and-one intriguers whose delight and livelihood it is to
fish the troubled waters of the courts of minor kings." As a princess, born
to rule, and with all the necessary cunning to gain and govern a kingdom,
Yasmini believes it is her destiny to some day rule her father's land.

In addition to her Indian and Russian heritage, Yasmini has Scan-
dinavian blood, revealed by her "glittering golden hair and eyes that are
sometimes the color of sky seen over Himalayan peaks, sometimes of the
deep lake water in the valleys. But very often her eyes seem so full of fire
and their color is so baffling that a legend has gained currency to the effect
that she can change their hue at will." She is a crucial reversal of the pro-
totypical mixed race character that dominated writing in that era; the typical formulation embodied all the worst traits. Instead, for Yasmini, her
heritage is an advantage, and her multinational ancestry sharpens her
mind: "She is of the East and West, very terribly endowed with all the
charms of either and the brains of both," Mundy writes. "Her quick wit
can detect or invent mercurial Asian subterfuge as swiftly as appraise the
rather glacial drift of Western thought; and the wisdom of both East and

West combines in her to teach a very nearly total incredulity in human virtue. Western morals she regards as humbug, neither more nor less."

Yasmini is a Circean figure, a woman who is simultaneously amusing and dangerous, and endlessly fascinating. She is enthrallingly beautiful, sensuous, but also brilliant, wise, and has a nimble wit. Yasmini gains her exquisite dancing skill from her Russian background, almost hypnotizing men: "Every move she ever made was poetry expressed . . . as no man had ever yet seen woman." Adds Mundy: —"It is her added gift of song that makes Yasmini unique, for she can sing in any of a dozen languages, and besides the love-songs that come southward from the hills, she knows all the interminable ballads of the South and the Central Provinces." She also sings songs of her own devising and only rarely the same one twice. She is impelled by a daring and mischievous spirit, "impudence arrayed in gossamer," enjoying thrills and plots for their own sake. Her only loyalty is to her friends and her own self-interest; she is liable to change sides at will. She is sure the gods of India are on her side, although she does not believe the gods are any more consequential than men.

Her gender is a source of both strength and weakness. Yasmini relies on her knowledge of Indian customs and her unique position with other women, who admire her determination to break out of the molds offered her by both local culture and British power. In addition to her beauty and charm, she has an uncanny "gift for reading men's hearts [that] has been her secret and her source of power first and last." While she bewitches men who come near her, she has no need or use for a man, unless he is part of her goals or shares her outlook. Her first love had been a success in *Guns of the Gods*, but her inability to be happily united with Athelstan King does not frustrate or doom her, and she continues plotting in opposition to him in *Caves of Terror*.

She avails herself of the weaknesses of others, but scorns those singed at her flame, savaging those who are seduced by her beauty or intimidated by her strong will. She executes any man who threatens her secrets; coming from the north, "mercy is thought weakness." Her potential for evil is symbolized by the cobras she has trained to do her bidding.

As the First World War dragged on across Europe, Talbot Mundy wondered about the effect it was having on India. *The Winds of the World*, *King—of the Khyber Rifles*, and *Hira Singh* were dominated by this question, and in the first two he dreamed of what role a character like Yasmini might play in such circumstances. Mundy's personal curiosity about the region could not be slaked by newspaper reports, and he let his imagination roam.

The title of *The Winds of the World* signifies both the temple where the climax will take place, as well as the habitation (also revealed in "Gulbaz and the Game") where Yasmini entertains, creating "a clearing house of underground political information from every corner" where the secrets of India attract plotters and their conspiracies—knowledge she in turn labels "the winds of the world."

As Mundy's second novel, *The Winds of the World* is poised at a crossroads in his work, a unique intersection of past and future concerns. On the one hand, it invokes Mundy's previous subject matter, particularly the mix of Indian and British in the army, and the devotion of the servicemen to each other and the regiment. Yet the novel also looks forward to the themes that would increasingly come to dominate Mundy's writing, with the key characters of Colonel Kirby, Ranjoor Singh and Yasmini accenting this dichotomy. Kirby is a typical military man, but unique for the esteem and trust in which he holds his native officers, no matter how formidable the apparent evidence against them. Ranjoor Singh points simultaneously to the Anglo-Indian and military axis dominating Mundy's previous stories, as well as toward the increasing emphasis on native characters and the secret service. Yasmini also emphasizes the latter aspect, and the degree to which intrigue becomes uppermost in Mundy's depiction of India. The military and secret service milieus and characters in *The Winds of the World* foreshadow his next two, very different books, the fantasy of *King—of the Khyber Rifles*, and the regimental heroism of *Hira Singh*.

Yasmini is a complex character, a very human mix of emotions and motivations. Her thirst for power impels her to many foolish actions, as she becomes consumed in the downward spiral brought about by her thwarted ambition. Over the years, she becomes a harsher person, ruthless toward those caught in her conspiracies or amoral schemes. The admiration once aroused by her daring is now overwhelmed by the impossibility of sympathizing with her actions. Unwilling to heed the consequences of her actions, she sows the seeds of her own destruction, both in Mundy's stories and as a heroine. Her evolution suggests that Mundy did not create her with greatness in mind, but her character grew upon him as a model of feminist strength and power. Eventually, perhaps, he found her overwhelming, or the ambition underlying her actions too disturbing, and he finally turned upon her.

Feminist views infused Mundy's literature, depicting, in a manner that was highly unusual for the time and genre, female characters who seldom occupied traditional roles. Frequently they were the leading players in his stories, ambitious, manipulative, yet also likable, out-thinking and dominating men. As all his life and writings make clear, Mundy never felt either threatened by or resentful towards women, and was a lifelong believer in full and complete equality between the sexes.

Like many women with whom Mundy was involved in real life, Yasmini symbolizes Mundy's measure of the ideal woman: charismatic, intelligent, independent, thinking for herself. While failing to find an enduring paradigm of Yasmini's best qualities, Mundy's search was lifelong, and many of the women he followed, created, or loved were part of this ideal. Mundy sought such women, in his real and fictional world, and although the tide would never rise quite so high again in favor of female control as with Yasmini, his commitment to gender equality and his willingness to learn from women, and to make them the key figures in his writing, persisted.

Mundy died suddenly at his home in Florida in 1940 from complications related to diabetes. However, his writing has continuously found new readers among succeeding generations, with over fifty reprints of his novels in the years since his death.

A SOLDIER
AND A GENTLEMAN

CHAPTER I.
GENTLEMEN, SIR!

THE STEAM went up, and the stink and the miasma, over green and gruesome Rajahbatkhowa; and with the frequency and fluency of horsemen to the manner born the Tail-Twisters cursed Bengal and the Bengal Government, all Bengalis, the climate, food, flies, high heaven and any minor matter on which a curse could hang.

The Tail-Twisters are not Bengalis. They—so help them—are a regiment of Bengal Cavalry, paid for by the Bengal Government, but altogether undefiled thereby.

Their officers are Englishmen, mostly younger sons, rightly and righteously possessed of an ambition to prove themselves better than the next man. Cowardice is the only cardinal sin they recognize, although there are one or two admitted indiscretions that they frown at; not being "fit," for instance, is poor form. They admit, too, that their creed would not fit cads; it is registered and patented and leased only to gentlemen.

And the men—the native officers, and the grim, black-bearded, swaggering rank and file—are the lean-ribbed, lineal descendants of fighting men from another part of India, where it is thought an honor, and not a disgrace, to salute a better fighting man—because respect begets respect.

The horses—and there are no such horses in any other army in the world—could run rings round anything on legs. The defaulter sheets were curiosities—about as necessary as a Christian chaplain; Mohammedan sons of landed gentry who are voluntary soldiers do not get into clink. The Regiment was clean five ways, and ready, and aware of it.

But it stood in tented lines and swore and sweated, and its language was infinitely more abominable than that of the army which once swore in Flanders. The men's tongue, made for swearing and enriched with military terms, could evolve profanity beyond the ken of even steam shovel drivers or Billingsgate fish porters; and it worked both watches under.

The Mess did its best, and led the blasphemy in clean clipped English—all, that is to say, but Colonel Stapleton. He swore only in action and then seldom.

Nobody swore at the police because they, of course, are beyond the pale or reach of anything the human mouth can compass. The Mess was civil to the District Superintendent, and avoided all reference to his trade—they would not have dreamed of calling it profession—they were sorry for him and, when he looked in on them every third day or so they made him drunk. But they could have done the same thing to the Devil or a Russian, had he turned up.

The Colonel would ask him once and only once, in just so many words, "Situation beyond you yet?"

He would answer: "No. Not yet, sir."

Then the Mess would sigh in unison and talk volubly of other things.

Day after steamy, sweltering day they exercised their horses, ate the awful chicken of the country and the more than awful goat, and wished all the luck there is to the dacoits. The only thing that cheered them was the intermittent news of fresh atrocities—of a village sacked, of some one crucified on an anthill near a crossroads, of a baboo held to ransom, or of a policeman who had been too active in the hunt, captured and cut to pieces and left in baskets at the police camp entrance. Then there would be a thrill of pleasure through the lines. Some trooper would take his saber to the squadron swordsmith to have imaginary dints smoothed out, and the officers would look to revolver mechanisms.

But the upshot was invariably the same; the police (with three European officers to a district of eight hundred square miles) still thought that they could handle the dacoits without the military, and the Tail-Twisters ate their heads off still—hot, scornful and impatient.

Gopi Lall was out and on the rampage. Gopi Lall was a sportsman, according to his lights, and a man of acumen. He could have given the Tail-Twisters a ride and a fight that would have satisfied even them. There was a price on his head; there had been a dozen murders proved against him personally, half a hundred against his followers. He had looted, blackmailed and run away until the District writhed; so he was fair, clean quarry.

The Tail-Twisters would have cheerfully surrendered the blood money to the police, and five times that much in addition, subscribed among themselves, for a two-day chance at him. But the horses pawed along their lines in vain, and Gopi Lall continued to bribe the native police with one hand, terrify them with the other, and feather his undiscoverable nest among the jungle-clad hills with other people's property.

The police officers still proclaimed their faith in their men's integrity and skill, the Governor of a Province held his hand, the native press grew daily more volubly indignant, and Gopi Lall laughed at all of them until the clean, sunlit barracks back at Balibhum seemed after all like paradise that had been left behind. The Tail-Twisters had been glad to come away but they were soldiers; they objected to being merely "a measure of precaution," and they would have been overjoyed now to get their marching orders back again.

"The trouble is, you see," said Colonel Stapleton, when the cloth in the stuffy Mess tent had been withdrawn from the trestle table and the Madeira was going round the same way as the sun, "that policemen—police officers, I mean—are forced to handle men" who know everything that's crooked. They deal with crooks—I mean the men do, not the officers—and they become crooked. That reacts on the officers again. It doesn't make them crooks, for thank God a gentleman remains a gentleman under any circumstances. But it makes them in the end ignore things that they shouldn't overlook. It blunts their finer feelings."

He looked round the table, not for approval—for the Colonel of a Regiment says what seems good to him and that again is law—but for attention. He had it. The eight who sat with him were men who, each in turn, was almost worshiped by a native officer and a hundred stiff-chinned soldiers, who wasted no worship or respect on anything else less manly than themselves. But when Colonel Stapleton laid down the law, the eight would listen as shaven friars to their abbot.

"Now God forbid that we soldiers should become policemen! Let us remain soldiers before everything! The proudest boast that England has to her name is the raising of such regiments as this. Is there another nation that could call on native gentlemen, pay them nothing, or practically nothing, ask them to clothe and horse and feed themselves, form them into regiments, swear them in for three years and keep them for thirty, discipline them, let them officer their own troops, but put our own officers over theirs; and in spite of a difference in religion, language, customs and point of view produce such regiments? No, gentlemen! England stands alone in that particular, and long may she stand alone!"

"I wish he wouldn't preach!" whispered young Boileau—he who won the Guzerat pig sticking cup the season before, and took everything for granted except money. He mostly had to borrow that.

"They should pick native gentlemen to be policemen too," continued the Colonel. "Failing that, in a case of this kind they ought to make use of us promptly. As for being conversant with the despicable details, why the very fact that we know nothing of them is in our favor! Dirt and the ruts it lies in should be handled at the lance point. The police hunt rats like ferrets; they go in after them and defile themselves. Rats should be smoked out into the open and then killed off. The Government of this country is making a terrible mistake."

"Wish to the deuce the Government 'ud muzzle him!" whispered Boileau, and Stapleton caught what he said.

"Captain Boileau—stand up, sir!"

Boileau flushed and did as he was told. The Madeira had scarcely more than started on its rounds; they had toasted the Queen perhaps ten minutes before, so the glass in front of him was not more than his second. Hence the flush was due to either shame or irritation.

"I overheard your remark, sir. I prefer to believe that it did not refer to me. Let me remind you, though, that there are no circumstances under which a soldier can not remain a gentleman—no conceivable circumstance, sir. A gentleman is deferential to his seniors. A gentleman is courteous and polite. A gentleman does not make irreverent and irrelevant remarks in undertones at a time when his senior is speaking. Sit down, sir; but remember that your calling is the highest, without exception, that there is, and that there is no excuse—not even momentary forgetfulness—for diverging from that rule."

He suppressed his impatience with an effort.

"As I was saying, gentlemen, I name no names, but the Government is making a mistake. The police serves a certain purpose and is a necessary evil. But when dacoity breaks out it is a serious error of judgment to employ any but gentlemen to extinguish it. To set a thief to catch a thief is wrong. To round up thieves one needs men who are incorruptible and who will stoop to nothing that is beneath a soldier's dignity. I have said as much in my letter to his Excellency; I put it strongly, and there may be results. The dawn may see the beginning of the end of Gopi Lall."

He had hardly finished speaking—he had barely more than waved away the decanter that was passed to him—when he and the rest of them sat bolt upright and listened hard.

"Oh, only a policeman," ventured Boileau.

But policemen do not ride as a general rule as this man rode. They could hear him some distance off but his horse seemed scarcely to touch the ground, and he was coming like an arrow.

"Shod horse!" said Colonel Stapleton. "Ah! There's the challenge."

"Yes, and barely a pause. He's coming on—at a trot now. No, he's galloping again. Despatches, by the Great Lord Harry!"

"It's our man," swore Colonel Stapleton. "It's Dost Mohammed."

"Can't be, sir. He only left us the day before yesterday at noon."

"It's Dost Mohammed. A trooper would draw rein. It's Dost Mohammed with good news; else why in a hurry?"

There was a sound outside as of a cataclysm—brought to sudden sparking halt. A saber clattered, a pair of loose-roweled spurs jangled, and a deep voice growled. Then suddenly, framed against the outer darkness, Dost Mohammed stood in the tent door and saluted.

"Rung Ho, Bahadur!"

They made room for him, to let him sit beside the Colonel. British and native officers neither eat together nor discuss their women; but in all save creed and caste they are blood brothers, whose Regiment is father, mother, honor and religion to them all. Dost Mohammed was a man of men—a born soldier, proved out, and more than welcome. But he stood first before the Colonel, holding out a letter.

"I bring good news, Huzoor!"

The Colonel seized what he brought and tore it open.

"Gentlemen!" he said. "It is as I told you. His Excellency has seen reason. He has ordered us to move at once to put an end to the dacoity. We will start after Gopi Lall at dawn."

CHAPTER II.
A GENTLEMAN DOES HIS DUTY

CRIME, of course, is geographical. So is virtue. And Yasmini was a heroine. Heaven—who gave her eyes unfathomable—knows too the unfathomable secret of her name and origin; for she was not of Bengal near of Madras. She was of India, and all India knew of her, though none knew whence she came.

Some said she was a high caste woman; others that a Maharaja once had brought her from the Hills, to be a plaything in the death-watched depths of his zenana. That story added that the Maharaja died. And all who knew her, or knew of her, said that her little slender wrists could force a dagger home as artfully as her little jeweled ankles danced, or as her eyes could lure; and they sang songs about her eyes from Peshawur to Cape Cormorin. She herself sang some of them, and they were not at all moral songs, as morals are expounded in the West.

Art was the essence of her. She was suppleness and subtlety and studied grace in every attitude and word. And she was not married; for marriage, in the East at all events, would have been the sepulcher of artistry like hers. None knew whence her money or her jewels came, and none dared ask—just as none dared question her prerogative of dwelling in the Panch Mahal or her right to call it by that name. She could even change a language. She did exactly as she chose, and what she chose was mostly unexpected.

India, which of all the countries of the world alone could produce a Yasmini, alone has other wonders to unfold—old cities, undismantled, un-crumbled, uninhabited, and unexplained; cities in whose streets the jungle fights for room between the ton piece granite curbstones and the lords of the jungle make their lairs in latticed palaces.

There had been such a city once, close to Rajah-batkbowa, and a hundred thousand men all armed with axes might have cleared it still to shine in the jungle coaxing sun. But only one piece of it stood in the open—carved and painted, cupolaed and domed; a wonder building round a courtyard where fountains used to play in long forgotten ages; and there lived Yasmini. She called the place the Panch Mahal; and that, in a lan-guage of the cleaner, braver North, means "the playground of the ladies."

The North-born troopers under Colonel Stapleton's command knew well the meaning of the words; and they knew to a big, thigh-booted gen-tleman the road that led through twisted jungle to the building she had named. Through the long hot afternoons there were often ten or twenty of them chatting in the latticed windows on the upper floor, or testing their soldier wits against the readier, trained repartee of Yasmini's hand-maidens. She herself paid little heed to them, and less respect; she conde-scended only to sufficient courtesy to keep them coming there, and made her women keep them well supplied with cigarettes and strange, wonder-scented brands of sherbet.

But every now and then a native officer would swagger, spur jingling and saber clanking, underneath the arch to call on her; and then there would be a fluttering in the nest above, and Yasmini herself would come almost but not quite as Cleopatra came to Antony. She would stand at the stair head auraed in some pale blue muslin stuff, and she would greet him as the dawn greets night. Like night, his strength and resolution and conceit would vanish. But Cleopatra was in love with Antony.

Yasmini would dance for him, talk to him, bring him sherbet with her own amazing hands and sing a song or two that punned and played subtly round his warriorhood, her womanhood, and paradise where both might sit enthroned. Then while the troopers drew away into the corners in envious obedience, the officer would whisper to her things he should not have whispered, in return for promises that she did not intend to keep.

When evening came—for those were evenings of the eve of martial law, and darkness had to find the Regiment prepared—she would send him off, flattered and fooled; fierce-bearded, as empty of secrets as an egg the crows have found, to chew the bitter cud of recollection until memory of her overcame remorse, and his servant polished up his spurs for him and he threw discretion to the winds and came again.

Always the troopers came and were entertained and given sherbet. Now and then the native officers would jingle in, and be shown a glimpse of what Allah has provided for the truly brave and good in paradise. And daily, sometimes hourly, Gopi Lall, up in his fastness in the hills, received news of the Regiment's intentions, and was told how long yet he might dare to loose his following, red- handed, on the countryside.

The tastes and the inclinations of Yasmini would be as difficult to follow as the movements of her twinkling feet. Her eyes were laughing pools of mystery; her tongue an instrument of subtly woven, smothered, underhand intrigue; and her beauty could, and did, procure for her the ab-ject slavery of any man on whom she had designs. She could pick the wearer of her favors from among the best spurred and booted bloods of India. Yet——

Gopi Lall was a Bengali, while she was from the North, where they despise his nationality and creed and speech and habits as a hadji hates a giaour. And at that, he was a Bengal outcast. His one sound eye was baleful, lit by greed and overhung by a lid devoid of lashes. His lips were slit and scarred where once a knife that he carried in his mouth had been hammered inward by an intended victim's fist. His hair—for he did not shave his head—was a shock of black, bewildering beastliness, uncombed, unoiled, unwashed. And his creed was the worst of him:

"I am the enemy of all the gods—of virtue, pity, charity, faith, mercy, love. I am the friend of fear and hate and hell. I have no human friends; who are not my servants are my enemies."

She had drifted with her entourage of waiting women from a hatchery of treason on the outer wall of Delhi to her present strange abiding place, and Gopi Lall had sent her soon afterward one love missive—through the window. It was gory, and the blood was barely dried. Its eyes, wide opened, had been forced into a squint when dead, or during death from torture; and the lips had been attended to as only a dacoit's imagination could direct. It was not easy to recognize the once alluring face of Yasmini's particular pet handmaiden; but then Yasmini, too, had imagination beyond the ordinary. She buried the mistreated head and sent no word of it to the police.

Her answer had been unexpected, as nearly all that she directed was. She sent another maid, an innocent, sweet featured girl who had not seen the horror tossed in through the window; she sent her with a note to wait where Gopi Lall's men were known to pass occasionally. The note read:

*Here is another. And if my lord would deign to visit
me there are more than a dozen who are at his service.*

The second girl had come back, well frightened, but alive, and with an answer. It was not in writing, nor on paper; but Gopi Lall's thumb mark done in blood on a piece of calico was a known passport on that countryside. It meant leave to live, and it was never violated while its holder had it; should he relinquish it through fear or at the feel of torture too devilish to name, that would entail no breach of faith by Gopi Lall. He had been known to keep one of his thumb print licensees alive for fourteen days, and then to let him go because the suffering wretch swallowed what he would not willingly surrender.

While she had that piece of calico, then, Yasmini was free to dwell in what she called her Panch Mahal, and she used her freedom to send messages by devious routes and unsuspected hands to the butcher who had thinned down her establishment. But Gopi Lall never came to her himself.

Up in some hell-stained aerie, Heaven knew where among the hills, he ruled a thousand outlaws. Perhaps a dozen of them, more or less, knew Gopi Lall. They were his Generals of rapine, who handed down his orders to the rest. Each of his Generals held in hand a horde of other ruffians who, oftener than not, were peaceful countrymen, to all appearance living decent lives in unsuspecting villages, befriended by their victims' relatives, and known to the police and to the courts as honest men.

When one of these paid a chance visit to the house of Yasmini and sold a cord of wood perhaps, or brought trapped wild fowl or a bunch of jungle flowers as his tribute to her beauty, there was neither suspicion nor excuse for it. It was nothing but the ordinary, decent, humble way of rustic simpletons, who—as their betters did less innocently—might surely worship at the shrine of loveliness.

But, through channels undiscoverable, Gopi Lall became aware of all the news and of every move that the police might contemplate against him; and he knew, too, that the soldiers were still doomed to inactivity. And all the clue there was as to who might be in league with him was that certain villagers grew strangely rich—for villagers. That and one other thing.

Yasmini—bejeweled and beguiling, very much besought, ever coaxing information from strong men self-trained in secrecy, and giving neither explanation for her presence in fever-fouled Bengal nor rewarding any man with more than smiles and promises—watched daily for a man who did not come and talked long and often with the villagers who drifted in to pay her their respects, or sell something or bring her flowers.

Soon a rumor grew that she loved this one-eyed monster of the hills. Soon it became common knowledge that she loved him. The story spread and grew by spreading, until even Europeans heard of it. Some said that she had loved him in another part of India, had seen him once in passing and had lost her heart to him; that she had followed, and had placed herself deliberately where he could come and seize her and carry her away.

Others said that she had only heard of him, and that, tigress-like, she had loved at a distance a fabled, visionary Gopi Lall, described to her as an outlaw, but the flower of chivalry. These swore that, had she seen him, she would have recoiled in horror from the thought of being wooed or won by such a bloody, revolting brute.

And there was Colonel Stapleton. He was the last to hear the rumors, and he let his officers believe whatever ribald impropriety they chose. He, first among soldiers, and soldier among gentlemen, believed the version that was mildest, and diluted even that with gallantry. To Stapleton it was unthinkable that any woman could love or let herself be loved by the real Gopi Lall. Therefore she had heard false stories of him. Therefore—it followed as the night the day—it was his duty to do something in the matter.

Her propriety or lack of it; her right to claim the treatment accordable to women of less questionable standing; her creed, if she had any; her caste, color, history, or hopes were nothing to him. She was a woman, he a gentleman. The rest was obvious.

To send for her would be impossible, even had he more than humor for his reason; for in India even ladies such as Yasmini observe sufficient of the purdah law to preclude visits to a European officer. And, should he send a native officer alone, he doubted that his message would reach her worded and delivered just as he intended—gallantly, without a hint of impropriety or interference.

He decided, after quite a lot of thought, to go himself, accompanied by a native officer. And since Dost Mohammed was the man of all his eight commissioned charges whom he trusted most, the Colonel took him—weary after his two-day ride, but unreluctant.

"You see, Dost Mohammed," he explained, "we leave at dawn. This is the apparent duty of gentlemen. We don't know how much harm this Gopi Lall may do before we round him up, so we'll warn her now—you and I together—before it's too late. "

"As you say, Huzoor," growled Dost Mohammed. And because of that ban on discussing women folk, he saw fit not to tell his Colonel certain things he might have told. It was little that Dost Mohammed knew, except some fragmentary history; but even that much might have saved the trip.

So Dost Mohammed rode beside him to the gilded dwelling on the jungle edge, and waited in the courtyard listening to the murmurings and gigglings above, and watching the shifting lights and shadows passing. And after an interminable wait Yasmini herself came down, close-veiled as if all the virtues of the East and West alike were concentrated in her loveliness.

Speaking in Hindustani, the lingua franca of India, Colonel Stapleton told her what he had to say of Gopi Lall, and of the rumor that she loved him. Yasmini thanked him, bowing low as a woodland fairy might have bowed to Oberon. With a little titter of embarrassment she disclaimed all knowledge of and certainly all love for the outlaw. She professed profound horror of him, and the pious hope that such a monster among men might meet a quick-found slow-drawn Nemesis.

She satisfied the Colonel; but when he and his fierce coadjutor had ridden off—almost before the hoofbeats had died down in the steamy night mist—Yasmini laughed long and merrily; laughed with the tinkling cadence of a peal of fairy bells; lay on a cushoned divan and laughed; laughed as her maidens undressed her; and later, laughed herself to sleep.

"Are all men fools?" she laughed. "Nay. Find me another word! Princes and priests and statesmen—they are fools: But soldiers, Englishmen—oh, women, soothe me; rub my ribs; pray Hanuman, the monkey god, to find a word for them!"

CHAPTER III.
THE OLD MAN LANDS ON BOILEAU

GOPI LALL, like other bandits of less visionary latitudes, had a half developed, half mocking notion of his own almost divinity. And, as greater men have done before him, he left his own country with neither following nor prospects, and came back to it an all-crowned king. The price put on his head by another Province had wrought the change for him.

He was certainly a humorist, in his own grim way. Three thousand rupees—at which a smarting and indignant Government valued him— was a fortune in itself; and, when he came back with policemen on his trail to his own Bengal, he was penniless. So he decapitated the first tax paying villager he could find whose size and general ugliness were something like his own, doctored the head with a knife, removed one eye, dried out the socket, and sent the resulting horror in a basket to police headquarters by the hand of a trusted lieutenant. He also sent a dozen witnesses to identify the thing and lay low himself until the blood reward was paid.

Of course feud followed, for the lieutenant claimed one-third of the money, and the witnesses all clamored for their share as well. As the logical result all thirteen men lay pegged out one afternoon on anthills, and to cap his quaint conceit Gopi Lall sent their heads to the police, with an accompanying homily, laboriously written out in blood. It was typically babooese, and it ended with a moral such as Æsop might have penned, but the gist of it was, "Such should be the end of all dishonest men!"

So the Government, which has no sense of humor, loved him, and did its ceaseless best to capture him, that it might hug him properly— with a slip knot and a hempen rope. And since Bengal breeds Bengalis, as well as snakes and jungle fever and the Indian Penal Code, Gopi Lall had ample opportunity to exercise his wit. If any knew where his hill-and-jungle-hidden ærie was, none dared tell of it; and, as for the native press, it used him as political ammunition, treating him one day as a national hero in revolt against bureaucracy, and the next as proof of crass incompetence on everybody's part.

The police, of course, used him as a scapegoat, and gave him warning of their moves whenever their three English officers were indiscreet enough to drop a hint. They robbed right and left, and gave Gopi Lall the credit for it. But credit was not passed on and taken at its mere face value. When a robbery occurred that he had had no hand in, his share of it had to be left in some hiding place where he knew where to look for it, or else a dead policeman would be found within a day or two, staring up at the sun without his eyelids. He was not afraid of the police, and he was at much pains to make the fact apparent.

But the Tail-Twisters were another matter altogether. The man who can buy, blackmail, coax away, or steal the honor of a Rajput gentleman who wears a regimental crest could bribe high Heaven; and that Regiment, pawing and perspiring in its tented lines, was something that made Gopi Lall afraid. He took no liberties with it, and sent no greased night creepers to steal the horse feed and accouterments. Nor did he waylay the troopers who swaggered now and then along the jungle paths.

But he worked hard and quickly in an opposite direction. He made a levy on the villages to the north of him that exceeded all of his previous exactions, and with the money thus extorted he bribed the native press of eight cities to declaim against the Government for ordering out troops. For that once, the police became national heroes, or very nearly so, and even the Governor in person was denounced as an iconoclast for contemplating such a thing as the supersession of the "honorable constabeels."

Lithographed one-thousand-copy circulations hummed with indignation at the thought of turning loose a thousand "predatory horsemen" on the suffering countryside. So the Government of India, which always listens for a while before it acts and then smites hard and fast, kept the "brutal and licentious soldiery" in camp.

And Yasmini sang songs to her guitar, and danced, and melted strong men's hearts. And Colonel Stapleton wrote letters. And young Boileau— "Bandobust Boileau," who could lead a squadron like a gray wolf on a breast high scent, but who could not hold his tongue—talked just a little bit too loudly in his tent of "old women in the Service nowadays," and of "Don Quixotes who should be at home in padded cells."

So at dawn one morning when the Tail-Twisters swooped like a jingling whirlwind out of camp to round up Gopi Lall, in a tent that thrummed already with the morning heat sat Boileau, with a pile of documents in front of him that would keep him busy for a dozen days—him and the baboo. When the Colonel of a regiment does need to tame the rising flood of youthful insolence, there are always plenty of blue indent forms, and payment vouchers that need auditing, and other things even less interesting to the military type of wit.

He sat and watched the dust go up above the Regiment; saw the glittering lance heads rise, and dip, and vanish; heard the thunder of the hoofs die down; and then faced the task in front of him. He realized that the fault was his, and that the more quickly the red-tape- tied routine was waded through, the sooner he would lead his men again; but he felt like a schoolboy kept in after hours, with the sting of temporary ostracism added to the drudgery.

"Must admit the old man landed on me where I'd feel it," he told himself. "Did it neatly, too. 'Captain Boileau, I have to leave one officer behind to attend to details. I've selected you.' Cuss him! Left me to think out the reason for myself, and—blast his stateliness!—let the men think what they liked, too!"

A man, whose job, and honor, and promotion all depend on making sons of the sons of soldiers regard him as a demigod is vulnerable where he keeps his pride.

He toiled at the maddening "returns in triplicate" until the flies drove him from the tent. In spite of the netting and the squeaky improvised punkah, even the ink pot was full of flies, and even the baboo gave up regarding them as essential elements like air and earth.

He went to the gloomy, empty Mess tent, where a solitary servitor provided him with curried goat and flies.

There were more flies in his whisky peg and in the butter, and even the boy he sent for to stand behind his chair failed to keep the still uncooked ones from promenading on his cheek.

So he went back to the office tent again and tried to drown his consciousness of the hot, pestilential loneliness in hard work.

But the official office working hours in salubrious Bengal are limited, and the Bengali baboo, who has his uses, is a man who also knows his rights. The clerk had gone without his noonday two-hour snooze in deference to Boileau's wishes, but, as he expressed it, he was "theoreticallee antagonistic, sir, to policy of working overtime without increased emolument."

So Boileau cursed him thoroughly and let him go at three o'clock. He did not see the force of borrowing money, at sixty odd percent, from the baboo's relatives to spend even fractions of it on the baboo.

For the next few hours he sat and swore and read the three-weeks-old Home newspapers alternately. Then he went out and looked his horses over. Then the thought of dinner all alone again, with mosquitos this time instead of flies, swept over him, and for a while nostalgia had him in its depressing maw. And after that, of course, the particular red devil who sits on tree tops all over India and beckons to the lonely European drew nearer and held converse with him.

Youth called, and the fire of youth that leads the Anglo-Saxon into mischief. Mischief he must have, or see, or do within an hour or two, or else weep; and no soldier has any hankering for tears. Besides, for what is mischief, unless for the amusement of men of stamina?

"Who is this Yasmini?" he asked of the first native he could find.

The man waxed interminably eloquent, after the eloquence which belongs to the East alone.

"What language does she speak?"

"All languages; the language of love, sahib, is a common tongue."

"Does she make love in English?"

"Nay, sahib. Who could? Neither does she make love, ever. The gods, who made her, made that unnecessary. When she lacks love, men bring it to her."

"She sounds amusing."

"Sahib—she is Yasmini."

"Um-m-m! D'you think she would receive me?"

"Who knows, sahib?" responded the native. "He who can tell the color of an unborn infant's eyes might know perhaps what Yasmini will do. There be dead men, sahib, who might tell, too, what good they had from her—none other!"

"Then, babooji, you wouldn't care to call on her, eh?"

"Sahib, have you seen a serpent hypnotize a bird? Would you be that bird? Have you ever watched a moth that fluttered round a lamp, and envied him?"

"I've seen the moths at it, baboo. But how about the notion of skating over thin ice?"

"Yasmini and ice, sahib, are as different as Kin-chinjunga from the Plains."

"Which is the nearest way to where she lives? You've got me interested, babooji. I'll call on the lady."

"Nay, God forbid, sahib! I have warned you. I will not direct you to your undoing! There are women of the countryside in hundreds who—"

"Chup!" commanded Boileau. So the baboo held his tongue.

But fifteen minutes later Boileau's servant came to him, carrying his Panama to replace the helmet that in that climate in the daytime a man must wear even inside his tent.

"D'you know the way to Yasmini's?" he asked.

And the wicked, wrinkled old Abdullah grinned.

"I'll not bother about dinner. As soon as it's dark bring a lamp and lead me to her."

"Will the sahib dress?" he asked deferentially.

"Um-m-m-n-yes. She's a—ah—a—er—she's what we white men call a lady, isn't she?"

"Sahib, she is Yasmini. There is no woman like her in the world!"

"Yes, I'll dress as though for dinner. And—ah—Abdullah——"

"Sahib?"

"Hold your tongue!"

Abdullah grinned again.

CHAPTER IV.
A VILLAGER EARNS HIS SALT

COLONEL STAPLETON was not a man to inveigh against policemen and then adopt their tactics or avail himself of their assistance. Nor had he risen to the rank of Colonel in a regiment that admitted no superior on earth without being a soldier in every courtly inch of him. The Stapleton of drawing rooms and mess tables—if the truth were known, of somewhat prosy platitudes, and rather too fastidious ideas—was another person than the Stapleton who led the Tail-Twisters when their lances rippled in the open, and their chargers strained behind him and the trumpeter.

He was still courtly. A lone woman would have picked him still of all his Regiment as the right man to apply to for protection. But a general of division, too, would have picked him to lead a rally, or a quick-sent charge to turn the tide of battle in a crisis—him and his Regiment.

He led his Regiment now—at an easy canter to take full advantage of the morning cool—straight toward the hazy line of hills where Gopi Lall was currently supposed to have his lair. The District Superintendent of Police, warned of the change in the direction of affairs too late to interfere, wore out an Arab pony in pursuit of him, and brought him to a momentary halt within a mile of the ragged foothills.

"I understand, sir, that you have been placed in charge of things," he panted, wiping off the perspiration.

"Yes sir. You have not been misinformed."

"Then don't you want the police to cooperate?"

"No, sir."

"But——"

"I prefer to act independently. I won't deprive you or your policemen of any credit that may accrue to you. If I interfered with your plans, or availed myself of your men, it might be said afterward, if your men captured him, that my Regiment had done the work."

He started to ride on.

"But, Colonel Stapleton——"

"Well, sir?"

"You won't be able to ride right up to him like that! Why, he's certain to have had notice of your start already; this country's honeycombed with spies. He'll be miles away by the time you get to where he may have been last night."

"At least I'll find his buzzard's roost," said Colonel Stapleton, "and make it a bit too hot to hold him for some time to come! I suppose you know where his headquarters are?"

"Nobody seems to know exactly. I know about within ten miles."

"I'm going to know exactly, and within two hours. If he bolts, look out for him and if you catch him, you do it to your own advantage. I'll set him moving, and keep him on the run, but no man of my Regiment will claim the reward unless one of my men bags him."

"Will you wait one hour, sir, while I ride back and telegraph? He'll bolt toward the north, I'm sure of it. He's probably on his way now. I'd like to get a cordon of my men in place to intercept him."

"D'you mean to tell me that you haven't had a cordon drawn these three weeks past?"

"Yes, but I'd like to warn the men."

"Through a—ah—baboo telegraphist?"

"How else?"

The Colonel smiled at him.

"I'll wait for no one, sir. Good morning!"

Before the sun was two hours up the Tail-Twisters were in among the foothills, split up troop by troop, and scouring every trail that led toward the center of the hills. And a half troop under Dost Mohammed was busily rounding up outraged, expostulating villagers. They tried on him the tactics that for months past had foiled or fooled or suited the police. But he found a way to change their attitude; lances and sabers, fierce eyes and upbrushed beards and blunt directness, warhorse-carried, did what the police had failed in signally. Soon Dost Mohammed rode with a prisoner up behind him who knew Gopi Lall's nest and the road to it, and dared not refuse to show the way.

What threats the grim Mohammedan growled to him as they rode were never entered in the Regimental history; but they seemed to be fierce enough, and backed with enough reality nearly to scare the soul out of the wretch. For, as they rode nearer in an ever narrowing arc of troops, to where a ring of trees stood on a dome-shaped hill, the prisoner showed signs of fright such as it is not exactly good to watch.

Time and again he begged to be left behind. Over and over he swore that from now on the road was straight and easy. But to his prayers and oaths the native officer answered nothing that any save the prisoner could hear. Had the Colonel heard, he might have felt disposed to deny the statement, given on the honor of a soldier, that he, Stapleton, was infinitely worse, more cruel, more ingenious, and less amenable to reason than the bloodsome Gopi Lall himself!

After a while, though, even that inducement lost its spur. The prisoner argued that he knew from grim experience what Gopi Lall was capable of doing, whereas the Colonel's tendencies were hearsay. He threw himself down from Dost Mohammed's horse and lay where he fell, shuddering on the ground. He would not rise, even when they urged him with a lance butt. He swore that he preferred death there to the chance of what might happen should Gopi Lall see who had led his enemies.

So, lest Gopi Lall recognize him, they tore two eye-holes in his loin cloth and wrapped that round his head, and put him on the horse again and started on.

"The Government will pay me for my cloth?" he wailed.

"Hold, Colonel sahib!" called the native soldier. "This black fellow of the foothills is playing with us!"

"What makes you think that?"

"He is not so frightened as he seems."

They formed a ring round the trembling prisoner; he was trembling now in earnest.

"I will more than terrify him, Colonel sahib, if I may."

"No, Dost Mohammed!"

"Huzoor, we——"

"We are not policemen, even if we are doing policeman's work! I'll have no dog's tricks here."

At the word "dog's tricks" the soldier glowered, for it was hovering dangerously near an insult; Mohammedans and dogs are not associable, even in metaphor.

"If he's not afraid, why is he shamming fear?"

"I know not, Colonel sahib. A dog might smell the reason."

The native officer had chosen the wrong moment to display resentment at imaginary insults, as he divined on the instant. If Colonel Stapleton was courtly and considerate on every possible occasion, he was a stickler, too, for deference to himself and fully capable of enforcing it. His eye alone, when he was roused, was quite enough to cow most ordinary men. The native officer changed his tune in a hurry, before the Colonel could have time to speak.

"It was but a soldier's joke, Huzoor. Let this man hunt, as a dog hunts, quartering the ground while the Regiment waits. I will soon see what he knows. If he wishes salt let him earn it."

That was a pun that either in English or the native language might have had several meanings; the Colonel ignored all of them. He was in a hurry to get on, and too impatient to read riddles.

"Ride on with him," he ordered. "You and ten men."

So Dost Mohammed rode with him, feeling in his saddle bag to make quite certain that he had what he needed. He and his ten rode over a ridge, and down into the dip beyond; and then he called halt unexpectedly, and threw the prisoner to the ground.

"Bind him!" he ordered; and without a word, or even a look of astonishment, the troopers trussed him and cross trussed him with their hobble ropes. Then Dost Mohammed reached into his saddle bag again. He did not dismount himself.

"A pinch or two will serve," he ordered, passing a little package to the nearest trooper. Another trooper forced open the prisoner's jaws, and the first man took the package and poured something into the gaping mouth.

"Be careful lest he swallow it too quickly, and see that he spit out none!"

They squeezed the wretch's throat to prevent his swallowing, and one man stuck a finger on his tongue and rubbed the dose well over it.

"So! Now let him rise. Kick him up. So—now!"

He legged his horse up beside the prisoner, and watched him with blazing eyes.

"Thou hast thy salt. Now pay for it. Salt without water is payment for thy service in advance. There will be water when we reach the den of Gopi Lall."

The troopers mounted, and for two minutes sat in a half circle, watching the varying emotions play across their prisoner's face. Their own faces were immovable, like the masks of Fate. The prisoner looked at the trees above him, and the hills around, and at the ground between his feet. Then he began to swallow hard, and next his eyes fell on a little tinkling stream that ran winding fifty yards away. He made a dash to reach it, but a trooper spurred his horse, and a drawn saber flashed between him and the stream.

"There will be water—cool water—in the den of Gopi Lall!" said Dost Mohammed.

The man went on his knees, but no answer came from the troopers. They sat and waited for the quite inevitable. He threw his tied hands up in an attitude of piteous appeal; not daring to speak, for fear of getting more salt saliva down his throat. But the troopers waited.

"Lead us to Gopi Lall," said Dost Mohammed.

Another minute the prisoner sought for a way out. Then he surrendered. He came to Dost Mohammed's saddle bow, and waited to be lifted up, for he could not mount alone with his hands tied. A trooper reined in beside him and seized him under the arms and swung him up behind the officer. Then:

"Fours—right about! Trot! Canter!" ordered Dost Mohammed. Within fifteen minutes from the start they were back to where the Colonel waited.

But the punctured loin cloth was over the prisoner's head again, and nobody could see that the wretched man was undergoing torture.

"Why is he tied?" demanded Colonel Stapleton.

"He tried to escape, Huzoor."

"Oh. What did you discover?"

"He was acting fear, to throw us off the scent. To make us believe that we were nearing Gopi Lall's headquarters, he pretended that he was more and more afraid. He will now show us the true road. Shall I lead on, Huzoor?"

So, extended to twenty horses' lengths apart, the Regiment wheeled and rode back at a canter ten miles along the road by which they came. Then, at a sign from the hooded prisoner—he gave it with his leg, for he could neither move his hands nor speak—Dost Mohammed wheeled and swung uphill suddenly along a track that was cleverly concealed by scrub. No trumpet sounded; but at a sign from Colonel Stapleton the troops split up, and snooped in different directions to surround the knoll above the jungle to which the track quite evidently led. And one troop and Colonel Stapleton himself followed Dost Mohammed and his ten.

The track wound and twisted almost on itself, through blind, black jungle; it was so narrow that for nearly all the way they had to ride in single file. Half way up Dost Mohammed rode into a string stretched above the path. A blunderbuss fixed in a near-by tree burst the same instant; and although it burst from overloading, scattering the slugs and nails harmlessly, the noise it made would have been enough to alarm the Seven Sleepers.

"Ride!" roared Colonel Stapleton from behind. "Crack on the pace, Dost Mohammed!"

But the native officer had spurred and settled down to ride in deadly earnest even before the instant order came. With a crash that set the jungle thundering as if a herd of elephants were stampeding through it, the troop whirled on until it reached a clearing—checked for an instant—swung out into line—and swept forward at a gallop.

"Halt!" roared Stapleton.

Before them was a fort, or something like one, made only of thin mud walls and rough stones here and there, but pierced for rifle firing. There was no flag above it, and no sign to show whether those who held it were outlaws or peaceful citizens. Only a babel from the interior proved that panic reigned inside. A minute later crash after crash resounded from eight different directions, and from four ways at once troop after troop, torn and bleeding from the jungle thorns, broke out into the open. The fort was surrounded, and retreat cut off.

"Order them to bring out Gopi Lall."

Dost Mohammed rode ahead, still with his prisoner up behind him, and engaged in altercation at the gate. A moment later the gate swung open, and a weird procession came out sheepishly—fifteen men, a dozen women, two children, and a native pony, lame and saddle-galled.

"Line them up and look them over."

There were no weapons in the whole procession, and there surely was no Gopi Lall. Dost Mohammed dropped his prisoner and let him drink deep at a spring that bubbled from the ground before the gate.

"What made that man so thirsty?" asked the Colonel.

"Fear, Huzoor."

"Um-m-m!"

He stared very hard at Dost Mohammed for a minute, but the Rajput's eyes did not so much as quiver.

"Well—we're wasting time."

He took a troop himself, and searched the whole fort thoroughly.

The troopers drove their lances or their saber points into every crack and cranny; they probed the stamped earth floor and prodded in among the beams and around the eaves. But there was neither sign of Gopi Lall nor hidden loot.

The prisoners admitted readily enough that the fort was Gopi Lall's headquarters, and that he had slept there overnight; but more than that they would not say. Two among them were the bandit's captives, held for ransom; but, with truly Eastern logic, they were the least communicative. They had had trouble enough, and did not intend to risk the outlaw's vengeance by betraying anything they knew.

There was scarcely any evidence there worth preserving, and no clue whatever to Gopi Lall's present whereabouts. A few old blunderbusses and some native swords were found in corners, but they showed no signs of recent use. The soldiers carried these into the open and stacked them and later made the prisoners carry them. But first the Colonel ordered fire set to the fort thatch.

"At least I'll spoil his rendezvous," he swore. "And if there's anything we didn't find there, he won't have the use of it."

When the flames had burst, and blazed, and were beginning to die down again, he called his troop commanders to him.

"Now separate," he ordered. "Divide the whole country into sections, and scour it thoroughly. Don't leave a single nook or cranny or hut or hiding place unsearched. And don't trust to the police cordon to the north. In other words, don't dally. Ride him down. The brute was here last night, so he can't have got far. Overtake him.

"And, in case he doubles back, or hides in the jungle, keep on scouring the country until you get him. Take any food you want and give vouchers for it; I'll cash the vouchers back at Rajabatkhowa. Send in reports to me there."

There was no place for the Colonel of a regiment then except headquarters, with the gleeful men split up in detachments and no possibility of centralized control.

So, a little sadly, he took one half troop as an escort and for camp guard duty, rounded up his prisoners, and started back to where young Boileau was supposed to be concentrating all his powers on writing up the Regiment's "returns."

CHAPTER V.
BOILEAU RUNS A RISK

THE fireflies danced like a myriad fairy lights; the jungle beside them whispered weird night sounds through the steaming dark, and their footfalls on the rotted leaves were like the creeping of conspirators, as Boileau and his servant took the ax-cleared, winding path that led to Yasmini's. The servant went ahead, swinging the lantern to betray the tree roots.

Boileau, a dozen yards behind, felt guilty; and the sense of guilt brought him a thrill he had not experienced since Aurang Zeb, his charger, ran away with him and brought up all standing on the railway line in front of the Bombay Mail Express. He knew too much of Indian caste and custom to expect to be received, even where the men of his own troop might lounge; but he vaguely guessed that Yasmini and Adventure and himself were all three mates that night.

Abdullah, grinning, set the lantern down on the courtyard tiles and went to scrabbling with his fingers on a narrow door. It was newer than the carved stone niche it fitted, and looked like one of Yasmini's precautions, for it was strongly reinforced with bars of iron and flat-headed nails.

No more than one man could have entered through it at a time. Soon Abdullah started whispering, and Boileau—with a strange impatience in his veins, and a stranger sense of standing on the edge of every thing—looked up and watched the shadows flitting by the window. There seemed to be excitement up above, if nothing else.

"What's happening, Abdullah?" he asked, after many minutes of hissed argument through a little hole that opened in the panel. The hole was not square; no lance could have been thrust through it, and its outer end was too small for an eye to look through it over a pistol barrel. It closed, like a bunghole, with a peg.

"Patience a little, sahib. She is considering."

"Is that the famous Yasmini beyond that hole?"

"Nay, sahib, but her maid. She went once and returned again, and now she is gone for the second time."

"What's all the trouble?"

"No trouble, sahib. Yasmini would know."

"Know what?"

"Whether she confers an honor or receives one."

"'Pon my soul, I'd give a month's income to know the same thing!" laughed Boileau to himself. And then the door opened grudgingly and Abdullah beckoned to him and bowed him through, and squatted on the step outside with the dog- like patience of the Indian native servant.

Inside were darkness, and the smell of musk—black darkness, made blacker yet by a curtain at the stair head. Some one whom he could not see replaced the peg in the peephole; and an unseen soft hand that trembled at his touch but did not draw away, took his.

"Lead on, McDuff!" said Boileau, throwing off his sense of helplessness, and kicking out to find the bottom step. But his dress spur caught in gauzy drapery and something ripped. He stood on one leg, and tried to free himself, but the wearer of the gauze pulled, too, to free it. He felt his balance going and kicked out again, and fell. A second later he was struggling on the ground with a giggling woman, laughing from sheer appreciation of the unforeseen, but expecting every second to feel a long knife in his ribs.

Then before he could regain his feet the curtain parted at the stair top and a radiance appeared in the middle of it—Yasmini herself.

There was no doubt—she must be Yasmini. He had thought of her as black, or dull olive color at the best. He saw an ivory and old rose tinted damsel, who might or might not be twenty years of age. He had thought of black hair, drawn back in straight lined waves. He saw a mass of burnished copper-gold, that fell in curling cataracts from crown to knees. He had thought of thin, cruel lips, dyed blue perhaps, and even of a nose ring. What he saw were features that would be May-crowned in the West, and lips—-red lips, uncarmined; lips that a shaven anchorite would have fought half the world to kiss.

She stood forward on the step and smiled down at him, framed in an aura of gold light between black curtains. He could see her feet, pale pink and ivory, encased in gilded slippers. Above them, some pale-blue filmy stuff encircled her as mist enfolds the morning, hinting at loveliness and making it far lovelier—by concealment. He could neither speak nor laugh now, nor find his feet. He lay spellbound, looking upward at her, until his eyes met hers. And he had thought of almond eyes, brown or perhaps hazel!

No man that ever lived could tell the secret of the color of her eyes. Few dared look into them longer than to bear away a memory of smoldering loveliness—of molten jewels, lovelit under drooping lids. But Boileau was a man whose every breath of life was daring, and he stared—and stared—and forgot the power of speech.

Yasmini spoke first and what she said, in a velvet voice that sounded vaguely like the love call of a nightingale, was in a language Boileau did not understand. But the maid understood it and found her feet at once; and Boileau guessed. However purred, through lips however sweet, the tongues of the ancient East are apt at framing comment on such matters as a man and a maiden in the dark.

"What did she say?" asked Boileau, feeling the blushes rise from somewhere down his neck and race beneath his hair until his ears glowed crimson. But the girl only giggled and pushed him toward the stairs.

So up went Boileau, swaggering to get his self-possession back, letting his spurs clank handsomely and twirling at his waxed mustache. And Yasmini made way for him, bowing before him mockingly—half, he suspected, to let him realize her supple grace, and half because she really was amused. Eight maids—all dark-skinned contrasts to the queen of this strange jungle bower—attended her, and seemed to know her thoughts. They piled the cushions high on a long, low divan by the window, and motioned Boileau to it; and, feeling like an idiot, he sat on it, and sank deep down among the soft embroidery. It was impossible to sit; he sprawled, and felt more like an idiot than ever.

But Yasmini herself came over and sat near him on a pile of cushions, pushing out one slippered foot so that he could see the greenish veins under the transparent skin. And he began to forget his awkwardness in amazed contemplation of what the curtained East could lay bare whenever it chose.

A maid extinguished most of the lamps, and left only half a dozen hanging, jeweled lights that glowed mysteriously, multicolored, through faint blue sandal smoke. Two maids sat near her. One fanned her, for the heat was stifling; one watched. Another maid bent over the divan and wafted air at Boileau with a fan of peacock feathers. Yasmini, showing little even pearls of teeth, smiled like the soul of early morning, leaned on her elbow and began to talk.

She spoke now in Hindustani, which Boileau understood. For all its other qualities that is a language that can sound, and be, like honey on the lips of loveliness.

"What ails my lord?"

She purred it, as though it were an overture to love itself.

"Nothing ails me. I think I am singularly favored."

"You seem displeased. Is aught lacking?"

"Miss Yasmini, I think there is nothing lacking when you are at hand!"

He could not for the life of him bring himself to call her Yasmini without some prefix. It sounded ridiculous, but he, too, felt ridiculous— until he looked into her eyes again. Then he forgot himself and everything except her eyes.

"My lord is pleased to joke with me?"

"'Pon my soul!"

English was the only tongue that suited his dilemma. With her eyes on him, he could not think unless he thought aloud, and he had a foolish notion that if his thoughts were in English she might not understand.

"Does anybody ever joke with you?" he asked in Hindustani.

Her eyes changed—not in color, but as if the light behind them glowed a little more.

"Not often. One did—once. My lord has not yet deigned to tell the cause of the honor that he pays me."

That was a stumper. She waited for his answer as a suppliant waits, pillowed at his feet and looking up at him. There was not a hint of laughter in her eyes, nor the vaguest, least suggestion that she thought him an intruder or a boor, or anything except what he had thought himself an hour ago—a spurred and righteous lord of what he looked at.

"I had heard of you, that's all."

"And came to see me? Why? Why at this hour?"

"'Pon my soul, I——"

"To laugh at me?"

"On my honor, no!"

"To order me away?"

She looked at his spurs and at his military mess jacket; and if she were not afraid she gave a very good imitation of concern.

"I don't suppose there's a man living who would order you away from anywhere!"

"Then I have leave to stay on here?"

"So far as I can give it you have leave to stay here till the crack of doom. I'd hate to see you go. I want to see a lot more of you. I——"

He cursed the unresisting pillows that prevented him from sitting upright. No white man—least of all a soldier—can collect his wits and fence with words reclining in a nest of scented clouds. Besides, a soldier's garments are not made for it; he looks ridiculous.

"Then why at this hour, Heavenborn?"

The last thing that Boileau had expected was to be snubbed for breach of etiquette.

"It isn't so late as all that, is it?" he stammered awkwardly. He felt for his watch, but had none. He did not want to go, but for the life of him he could think of no excuse for staying. And Yasmini continued to look up at him like a little girl suppliant, awaiting explanations.

"Why—ah—" he twirled at his mustache and tried to seem at ease—"I was busy all day long and—ah—my native servant said——"

"What did he say?"

"Said that he knew the way here and that you might receive me—said he wasn't sure, but he thought you might."

"And is that your servant—he who sits below there at the door?"

There was a world of wonder in her voice, and she watched him now through eyelids almost closed; he could no longer see the pools of fire that glowed behind them.

"Yes."

"Then the way of the sahib log is to ask questions of their-low caste servants—" she shuddered, but even that movement was all suppleness and grace "and to follow their advice in matters pertaining to their visits?"

"Abdullah isn't a low caste man. He's——"

"No?"

Boileau remembered then that there are castes within castes, and that even Mohammedans are not without a caste law of their own, so he said nothing.

"And that man—that creature of the devil—said that I would receive you? No wonder that you came! Will the Heavenborn partake of sherbet?"

"No thanks," said Boileau. "I'm sorry you've gathered such a false impression. I—ah—wouldn't have offended you for worlds—ah—I'll take my leave now and ah—call—again, perhaps tomorrow, at a more reasonable hour. Didn't want to meet my own troopers here, you know," he added, as an afterthought, by way of mild retaliation.

"Have your troopers, too, said strange things of me?"

"Not to me, at all events. We—ah don't discuss—ah—ladies."

Yasmini smiled, and he might take her smile to mean exactly what he chose. He rose, and she rose languidly, taking her maid's hand. She might have been smiling at his tight-kneed effort to escape with dignity from the embracing divan. Whatever the cause of it, her smile bewildered him exactly as his first sight of her had done, and he could not find words as she bowed in front of him, with the same mock worship, and the same lithe grace and led him to the stair.

He went down the stair feeling like an idiot—glad of the darkness—going sidewise to prevent his spurs from catching in the carpet; but in spite of it his spurs did catch and he fell down nearly to the bottom. And his feelings were still further tortured by the sound of peal on peal

of tinkling, silvery laughter from the room above, that started immediately the maid opened the narrow door for him. A chorus of laughter
from the maids was the last sound that he heard as the door slammed
tight behind him.

He walked back like a man in a stupor, stumbling once or twice in
spite of Abdullah's care to hold the lamp over each protruding tree root.
He could see Yasmini's eyes in the dark, but every time he tried to gaze at
them, they moved and when he tried to follow them they moved again.

"I've not been drinking," he muttered to himself. "It must be liver.
Yes, it's liver. But ye gods and little fishes, what a woman!"

"Been trying to get cool, Boileau?" said a voice, as he passed down
the lines to his own quarters, and he nearly jumped. It was only by a miracle that he recalled his nerve in time. He turned into the tent whence the
voice came, and saw his Colonel sitting in a camp chair smoking.

"Didn't expect you back so soon, sir. Any luck with Gopi Lall?"

"No. Found his nest. Got him on the run, that's all. The troops are
after him. Any cooler out in the jungle there?"

Boileau laughed. "I got a cool reception, sir," he answered. "I called
on Yasmini."

"The very deuce you did! What's she like?"

"She's a wonder, sir. Couldn't describe her—no man living could."

"Beautiful?"

"Have to find a new word, sir."

"Gave you a cool reception did she? I wonder she admitted you. Did
you get the least idea as to why she's here?"

"None whatever."

"Is she—ah—I mean—what about her morals?"

"Judging by the way she treated me, sir, I would say she was——"

"Well, what?"

"That she belies her reputation. She's a native, of course, and there's
no means of judging them, any more than a man can tell how the stories
about her started. But she's chaperoned more thoroughly than a seventeen
year old débutante at home, and she's as dignified—for all her witchery—
as the deuce himself."

"Um-m-m! I'd keep away if I were you. I'm not giving orders, but—
well—it's good advice. If any trouble came of it—she's a native woman,

mind—you'd run the risk of being neither officer nor gentleman. A deuce of a nasty risk to run! Turning in? Good night."

CHAPTER VI.
DOST MOHAMMED GOES ON A STILL HUNT

ALL that the Tail-Twisters, working troop by troop, unearthed was evidence of police complicity and supineness. They found misguided natives who mistook them for policemen, thinking that anything in uniform was some sort of a "constabeel," and from these they learnt surprising things; as, for instance, that the flood levy had been paid that month to Gopi Lall, and therefore the police would find themselves in trouble if they trespassed.

At first there would be disillusionment, for a trooper of the Bengal Horse is not exactly flattered by being likened to a civilian, and to a policeman least of all. The butt of a lance thrust with an oath of explanation at the erring rustic's stomach would bring acknowledgment of error. But once it was known that they were troops, and not police, the channels of information dried, so after awhile they pretended to be a new brand of "constabeel" whenever the pretense was possible.

From time to time they came on villagers who offered them rupees; and he who has tried to tip a Bengal cavalryman for service rendered may have a good idea of what reception that met. They will loot, those fierce, black-bearded troopers, in time of war—none more readily or thoroughly; but gratuities, in money or in kind, are rather more to be withheld than verbal insult. Their pride is not of the made-for-show description.

Whether hunting through the tangled thickets where thatched huts were hidden in tiny clearings, or scouring on a chance-encountered trail from village to hill village, they found evidence in plenty of the outlaw's doings and of the terror he had established, but never a sign of Gopi Lall himself.

"Where is his woman?" demanded Dost Mohammed twenty times a day at least. And the answer was always the same—often in the same words:

"Huzoor, what woman dare refuse him?"

"Which woman loves him most?"

"None love him. All fear him!"

"Which, then, does he most love?"

"Huzoor, does a he wolf love the sambur? Does a tiger love the village buffalo?"

Then, "May Allah rip the vitals out of every Jungli in Bengal!" Dost
Mohammed would swear, and spur his charger on to the next village.

Cross quartering the country they searched, as eagles search,
minutely, for signs of any guard that might betray the whereabouts of the
robber's hidden loot; but either he had trusted nobody to guard or else the
men he trusted were too shrewd to show that they were watching.

They made prisoners who led them along half hidden trails to where
the outlaw once had been; and once thus guided they discovered underneath a waterfall a secret cave, where possibly his loot had once been hidden. There was one rupee there, fallen in a crack between the rocks; a
trooper forced it out with his saber point. But there was neither other loot
than that one coin there, nor track of Gopi Lall.

Once they fell in with a posse of police, who grinned at them and
asked what they had done with the outlaw's head. That nearly brought
about a fracas, and it was only the timely arrival of their English officers
that stopped them from teaching the "constabeels" how a charger-and-
Rajput-driven lance point feels. The police, under questioning from the
officers, swore that Gopi Lall had left the country and would not return.

They began almost to believe that Gopi Lall had been a myth, and
several officers became converts to the theory that he was in reality a syn-
dicate of robbers, who had taken one collective name for the sake of mystery and convenience. Acting on that suggestion they began the search all
over again, rounding up the inhabitants of every village and making the
headmen give an account of each. But still there was no result worth men-
tioning. They succeeded in corroborating the fact of an actual, single, Gopi
Lall's existence, but nothing more.

Then Dost Mohammed became possessed of an idea, and asked for
leave to hunt alone.

"Why, Dost Mohammed?" The senior Major lacked not a little of
the Colonel's tact. "For the reward?"

The Rajput flushed under his dark skin. "Because thus I will hunt
better, sahib."

The Major pulled out a copy of the printed proclamation from his saddle bag and looked it over.

"'The reward is offered to any person or persons who procure or bring such information as shall lead to the arrest and conviction of the outlaw known as Gopi Lall.' That means, Dost Mohammed, that the first man to hand in the information gets the money."

Dost Mohammed sat his horse in silence, glaring.

"It says, too, at the bottom, 'in addition to the above named reward for information, a sum of rupees three thousand will be paid to whomsoever shall produce the head or body or both of the above named Gopi Lall.' That would be five thousand rupees all told—nothing much to divide among a Regiment, but a tidy little sum for any one man; what?"

"Since when, sahib, has an officer of this Regiment been subject to suspicion such as recruits for the Regulars merit?"

"You say you have a private clue. If you followed it and found the man you would be within your rights if you claimed the whole reward."

"I said nothing of a private clue, sahib, nor of a clue at all, nor of my rights. I said that I had an idea, and a good one, that I could best carry out alone. All the rights I claim are the right to be treated as a man of honor. As for the reward——"

He leaned slightly from the saddle and spat, with a gesture that was eloquent.

"Then if I let you go alone, you'll only claim one share in any case?"

"You had no need to ask, sahib. I will neither claim nor accept one copper piece of the reward!"

"I have to consider the Regiment, Dost Mohammed."

"And I, sahib, who have served her Majesty but twenty years as yet, thought naturally only of the money! Have I your leave to go?"

"Look here, Dost Mohammed, I had no intention of offering you an insult, and you know it. You've no right to take my remarks that way. You're hovering dangerously near a breach of discipline."

The native officer saluted and sat still.

"D'you understand that I was taking an ordinary elementary precaution on the other men's behalf?"

"I understand, sahib, that you misunderstood me."

"And you me. Very well then."

The Mohammedan did not answer, but he did not have either the air of a man who had not understood his superior officer.

"You'd better tell me what this plan of yours is."

"Sahib, you would only laugh at me."

"I give you my word of honor I will not."

"Neither will you agree, sahib, if I tell you."

"You want me to take both you and your plan on trust, eh? Very well. I'll prove my faith in you. You have leave. Now, tell me."

"I will be Gopi Lall."

"You!"

"I, sahib."

"How—why—what the——?"

"Sahib, on this countryside there are dozens—there must be—who are his friends; who know which way he would run; probably who know which way he did run—who advised him or would advise him——"

"But man alive! Dost Mohammed! You don't look in the least like Gopi Lall. You couldn't make yourself look like him even if you plucked one eye out."

"And sahib, would Gopi Lall—with a hue and cry behind—travel undisguised? His ugliness is a byword even where he is not known. Men know that he has but one eye and tangled hair that never knew the comb, and lips that are like sun-cracked pollution. Would he journey with his name and number on his face for all the world to see, as a trooper wears his crest?"

"But—what language does he speak?"

"From choice? Bengali."

"And you?"

"I speak it too, as well as he."

"It's a deuce of a risky sort of plan, Dost Mohammed!"

"The risk is mine, sahib."

"I hardly know what to say. You see, you're an officer; it seems hardly the proper work for a commissioned man. It 'ud hardly be creditable to the Regiment if you got knifed or shot or run through by one of our own men while disguised as a murdering thief."

"Will it be a credit to the Regiment, sahib, to go back to the lines without his head; to do no better than the rascally police; to have even the little children ask us where are the soldiers, since the Bengal Horse became constabeels?"

"Why not let a trooper try it?"

"Because I already have permission, sahib!"

"True. You hold me to my word? Very well. Go then, and good luck to you. But for the love of goodness be careful, Dost Mohammed."

"Sahib, I will be careful at least to live until I track down Gopi Lall."

CHAPTER VII.
BOILEAU CALLS AGAIN

NOW, Captain Fitzherbert Cholmondeley Boileau was something of a devil of a man. There was no mistake about that, and nobody doubted it, least of all himself. He deliberately cultivated the impression. There was nothing really vicious, of course, in his whole makeup or he could neither have come by a commission in the Tail-Twisters, nor, once in the Regiment, have retained it. But he liked to be considered daring, and he was always on the lookout for an opportunity.

The blood that ran in his veins was the same sort that makes a brave and efficient officer of ordinary clay in any country; but in his case it ran rather more racily than usual, and the thought of danger to be courted, and above all of a dangerous woman to be courted, was like ozone to his nostrils.

Yasmini was dangerous. He had been warned against her by more than one native, by his brother officers on various occasions, and by his Colonel. And Yasmini had snubbed him and laughed at him. Therefore— the corollary was obvious—he and Yasmini were destined to cross foils at least once again.

The clerical work of the Regiment grew no less irksome to him as the sultry days wore on, and now that the Colonel had come back, and there was little chance of his getting a ride with the Regiment in any case, his ambition to get the red tape business over and done with died down in him. And he recalled most distinctly how the Colonel had been careful to advise, and not to order, him with reference to Yasmini.

It took him next to no time to make up his mind. On the third af-ternoon following his evening adventure at the Panch Mahal he got into civilian clothes and set off to Yasmini's strange jungle nest, this time un-accompanied.

She received him on this occasion without keeping him waiting, and with no exhibition of surprise. She seemed almost to have expected him. Evidently he had been seen approaching, for he had not stood for one minute before the little iron-studded door before the same maid that had admitted him the last time swung it open for him again, and smiled a warm welcome.

Yasmini came as before to the head of the narrow stair to meet him, and bowed again low to him as if he were the lord of all the East and she his handmaiden. But wonder of wonders in the East!—she provided a European chair on which he could sit, and even cross his knees, with dignity.

When he came before, she had deliberately tried to make him ill at ease by studied mockery. Now, though, she did exactly the opposite. Without asking him, she sent for sherbet, took the scented, colored stuff from the maid who brought it, and gave it to him with her own little jeweled hands. He drank it from pure politeness and wished immediately that he hadn't; but she betrayed no amusement at his efforts to straighten out his face and seem appreciative.

She was neither amused, nor yet suppliant. Her raiment was the same—as gorgeous and as wonderful—though slightly modified in color in artful regard to the altered light. It was she who had changed. She wore a look and manner of artless, ingenuous camaraderie.

"I want you to come here often," she smiled at him, standing before him for a minute, then subsiding with amazing grace among the billowy cushions by the window. He saw no waiting maids in evidence; but he did see that a curtain to her right moved gently, and he guessed that they were neither unseen nor unheard.

"That's awfully good of you, I'm sure." He would have liked to kick himself the moment he had said it; but with her eyes on him, even when in her present mood, he could voice nothing but mechanically ready platitudes. Yet he was the Tail-Twisters' one expert in the game of flirting, just as he was their only Adonis, and the only white-skinned wrestler in the Regiment.

Captain Boileau was no one-sided, overbalanced ladies' man, but an all around soldier, with sporting instincts, ready wit, and steel wire nerve.

But Yasmini—perhaps a hundred pounds of her—could hold him at her mercy! He did not understand the circumstance. On his way to her he had walked with the gait and buoyancy of youth in search of fresh adventure. In her presence he could only sit and let his ears grow red and finger his mustache.

"Are there no other officers whom you could bring with you?" she purred.

That, for the moment, brought him to his senses.

"No. Thank goodness, there are not. I'm full of the idea of enjoying your acquaintance all to myself for the next day or two."

She smiled, and drooped her eyelids. Suddenly she clapped her hands and called for cigarettes. When the maid brought them she lit one, and ordered the rest set down between herself and Boileau.

"Are you then all alone?" she asked.

"No. There's the Colonel sahib."

"And he? Could he not come?"

"He could. He might. But why? Why ask him? Won't I do?"

"You? You are only one—and young and——"

She blew great rings of cigarette smoke and if she finished the sentence Boileau, at all events did not catch the words.

"And the Colonel sahib," he aswered, "is old—and stiff mannered—and pompous—and——"

"The others?"

"Won't be back for days, most likely. There's no knowing when. They're after Gopi Lall."

She reminded him of a snake the second he said that, though he could not have told why. There was nothing snake-like in her attitude, nor in her eyes; they glowed. He thought it must be something passing in her mind that reached him telepathically. After a few years in the East even the most materialistic, incredulous of men come to believe implicitly in things that savants of the West call foolishness.

"And where do they look for Gopi Lall?"

"Everywhere."

"How?"

"Oh, by quartering the country and asking questions, and keeping a bright lookout."

"And, should they fail to find him——?"

"They won't fail."

Now, she really did seem amused, and made no effort to conceal it.

"Will they find him because the men who look for him are mostly Rajputs, or because their officers are English?"

"For both reasons, I expect. But, tell me, why do you want all the other officers to call on you?"

Her eyes changed again, and the momentary display of amusement left her. Now it was a look of almost business acumen that stole across her face; she was a partner all at once, exchanging confidences.

"Because—because people in these parts, strangers to me, who know nothing of me and of whom I know nothing, have been saying things that they have no right to say."

"What sort of things?"

"Bad things. That I plot against the government."

Boileau whistled.

"I hadn't heard of it."

"And if the officers of your famous Regiment should visit me from time to time, and see what passes here, and know what company I keep, whom I receive, of what they speak, then—then men will still talk, for no woman's tongue is the equal of a man's at slandering! But they will talk to little purpose."

"What harm could that kind of gossip do to you in any case?"

"Much harm. I want to stay here. I choose to stay here. I like this place."

She was almost vehement.

"But none can buy this house or the ground it stands on, since it has no owner. What, then, could I do were the police to come and order me away? Could I argue with them, or have I friends more powerful—yet? But if your officers should come, and come often, then the police would not dare interfere with an honored friend of theirs."

"Well, since you put it that way—mind you, I think you're needlessly alarmed—I'll ask Colonel Stapleton sahib to call on you."

"Will you? Please!"

"I suppose that means I sha'n't get another opportunity of seeing you alone?"

He was recovering his nerve, now that she betrayed symptoms of not being quite at ease herself.

"We are not alone."

He eyed the curtain, that still moved gently from time to time.

"No? But—the maids are yours—an order——"

She raised her eyebrows very slightly, but enough to warn Boileau that he was what he would have called "running wide."

"Do your memsahibs receive our native gentlemen alone?" And that was an argument that was unanswerable.

"You're the most beautiful woman I ever saw," he said quite truthfully, but with a soldier's motive. He had of course the cavalryman's ingrained belief in flank tactics.

"Yes?"

She seemed scarcely interested.

"That is why you called a second time?"

"That is why I want to see you alone—why I don't want to bring the Colonel sahib or the others."

"You need not bring the others——"

He started almost to his feet.

"You could send them, one by one or two by two, whichever would be better, and come yourself some other time."

"Some evening? I am busy in the daytime."

"Some other time. You will be welcome. You will all be welcome."

She was eying him very narrowly now, and he was conscious of it. He knew perfectly well, too, that she was fencing with some definite end in view, quite different from the one she had professed. It needed little knowledge of the East to divine that much. Nothing in the East is ever done directly, least of all love making. Boileau remembered, then, that he was a very handsome man; and next, he realized again that she was eying him through lowered lids. With a flash of intuition it occurred to him that one English officer on the calling list of a native lady would be likely to cause scandal, whereas the better part of a dozen, calling constantly, would silence it. The rest would be a most effective blind. The one would—

"I begin to understand," he said, working away at his mustache.

She smiled at him bewitchingly, and he felt the blood go mounting to his temples. But he could not guess whether she was laughing at him, or was in love with him, or was approving his ready recognition of her subtlety.

"Then bring the Colonel sahib as a beginning," she said, nodding sagely. "Later, when the others come from seeking Gopi Lall, send them here also."

"Send the Colonel sahib now, you mean today?"

"Why not today? Will the sudden summons disconcert him?"

Boileau laughed aloud at the idea of anything—of even a woman, however lovely—disconcerting Colonel Stapleton; he knew his Colonel from experience as being a man with a polite speech and a precept and a plan for every possible occasion.

"Is he very fierce? Is he unmannerly? I have seen him from a distance; his mustaches go like this."

She imitated, very prettily, the motions of a military gentleman attending to the dressing of his upper lip.

"You'll find him courtlier than even your own native Princes when they come to ask favors of our Viceroy."

"Then bring him. Send him."

"Very well. But, Yasmini—"

"My lord?"

"Don't, for the love of goodness, make eyes at him. He'd get young again! We want him to grow old; he's standing in the way of promotion."

"I? I make eyes at him?"

She bowed him out with a dignity that somewhat undermined his sense of intimacy. But she smiled at him as he started down the stairs.

CHAPTER VIII.
"GOPI LALL"

FEW natives of the North of India would find it difficult to change their appearance, so far as their heads are concerned. Under their turbans they wear long black hair, that can be twisted and tangled into knots or let fall disheveled. It took Dost Mohammed less than half a minute to make himself look like a devil, or a fakir—which is much the same thing—or anything he chose to call himself, except a soldier. He made the change, though, well out of eyesight of the Regiment, for his own pride's sake.

A patch over one eye was easily arranged, and a cloth wrapped round his mouth prevented anyone from knowing whether or not his lips were horrible. But his clothing was a different matter. So was his horse.

Two things were certain. Gopi Lall had not taken with him, and could not have obtained, a charger such as Dost Mahommed's; and Dost Mohammed would not ever think of starting on any kind of hunt without his horse.

The problem would have beaten any ordinary man. He did not dare, for instance, to borrow clothing from a villager, or to take it by main force, for news of such extraordinary conduct would have spread like wildfire, and if Gopi Lall should happen to be hiding anywhere within a radius of forty miles he would know within a day or less that an officer was after him disguised. Dost Mohammed had to find another way than that.

First, he let the troop ride out of sight of him. Then he picketed his horse in a hollow down among some trees, where he could not be over-looked. Nobody had troubled to ask him why he kept back a live goat from the tiny flock the Regiment had bought for sustenance, but now he proceeded to kill the beast, slicing off its head with one clean blow of his saber. Next he removed his stirrup irons and smeared them thoroughly with blood, and put more blood on the horse's withers and on his mane. Then he smeared plenty of the blood about himself, and eyed the whole result.

It was good. Anyone might reasonably think that he had slain the horse's rider and ridden off on him. He stripped off his uniform and cached it together with his scabbard; but the saber itself he kept, smearing it with blood and holding it naked in his hand.

After a cautious look around him, he mounted and spurred out of the hollow at a gallop, careering like a man possessed, and giving a good imitation of a rider frightened of his horse, or not at ease on him.

He drew the horse up on his haunches at the first hut he came to, left him standing, and sprang like a lunatic, bare legged and blood-smeared, to the hut door, which he proceeded to hammer with his saber hilt until the frightened owner came. The man was speechless from sheer amazement—Dost Mohammed speechless for reasons of his own.

Instead of speaking, he began to tear the loin cloth from the man's middle, hitting him a smart rap on the head with the saber hilt when he resisted. He had donned the loin cloth, leaped on his horse again, and ridden off before the man had time to more than realize that he had been attacked. Dost Mohammed left in the opposite direction to that his troop had taken, with the certainty in his mind that whether Gopi Lall were in the neighborhood or not the rumor of his being there would scatter broadcast within an hour.

He rode, now, to another hollow, and hid there until evening, with the double purpose of giving the rumor time to percolate, and the darkness a chance to hide what was probably a very poor resemblance to the robber. In the dark, with the story of his coming on ahead of him, he anticipated little or no risk of detection.

When the low moon rose above the tree tops and the jungle noises had begun to greet the night, he rode out again, but this time far more leisurely, taking little care to look about him, but keeping his ears open for the sound of forage parties from his own Regiment. Before he had ridden twenty minutes at a walk, a woman slipped out of the scrub beside him and brought him a cooked chicken, with the whispered information that the troopers were in camp for the night, many miles away.

He seized the chicken, broke off a leg, and devoured it hungrily.

"Where is she?" he demanded, taking care to growl surlily from behind his mouth cloth, and looking anywhere but at her.

"She waits at home."

That was enough for the first try. This woman evidently knew Gopi Lall, and might possibly detect the disguise; but he had established one fact. There really was a particular one woman.

"So-ho!" thought Dost Mohammed. He drove his spurs in and decamped, cantering away without a word of thanks. He ran no risk in assuming that the real outlaw was a mighty ungrateful gentleman.

But "at home" was a vague direction, and soon he began almost to despair of ever getting nearer to the mark. No more women came to him surreptitiously, and the few shadowy forms he did see vanished the moment that he challenged them. He chased one man for nearly a quarter of a mile, only to lose him in the darkness—a piece of clumsiness for which he cursed himself soundly. Gopi Lall had a reputation for absolutely never missing anything or anybody, and, if he wanted to live on the outlaw's record for a while, it seemed he would have to be less punctilious.

He had determined to ride down and run through the next man who failed to halt when challenged, instead of trying to capture him; but the next man seemed to guess his thougths, and threw up his hands, and went down on his knees, begging for mercy.

"Where is she I seek?" growled Dost Mohammed.

"Sahib—Heavenborn—Prince of dacoits—how should I know?"

"Answer, or——"

"Honorable one! Mercy! What have I done? What have I not done? I saw her but an hour ago, and she was yet there. But how do I know that she is there now?"

"Thou liest!"

"Nay, nay, Heavenborn! Tiger of the hills! How should I lie, who truly fear thee? I say I saw her—I say truth."

"I say thou liest!"

"If I lie, oh Gopi Lall——"

It was well! The disguise had worked so far at all events, and the rumor had spread, and there really was a woman!

"Harken! It is not my view to let men lie to me unpunished. Lead on! In case she be not there, pray to thy gods on the way thither, Jungli!"

"But, Heavenborn, I was going home—but a little way from here—my children wait—my little ones—my——"

"Lead on!"

"But, Prince of plunderers, let me go just one little minute to my home. I would warn my children; then I will go with thee willingly."

The saber whistled round the wretch's head, close enough to have shaved him had his beard been two days older. No Gopi Lall, nor any other expert, could have performed that feat better. The man's complaints came to a sudden end. He turned and settled down to run in front of the horse.

Under the cloth that hid his mouth, Dost Mohammed chuckled to himself; but he rode carefully, with his saber pointing downward to the peasant's back and with his ears and eyes on the alert. Three times they passed other men walking homeward, and because he did not challenge them, they made profound obeisance instead of running. One man even lay face downward on the path and beat the earth with flattened hands.

"The Colonel sahib was right," swore Dost Mohammed. "Too much honor is not good! As a soldier and a man of honor no man ever treated me to this."

For the best part of an hour they moved into the darkness as fast as the frightened peasant could run, Dost Mohammed noting his bearing carefully with the aid of the compass that every true fighting man should carry in his head. They were moving in a direction at right angles to that the extended troops had taken; before long, he calculated, he would cross a line between the Tail- Twisters and their quarters at Rajahbatkhowa.

They reached a clearing in the jungle, and there Dost Mahommed chose to stop and feed his horse.

"But, Heavenborn, why do this here? With but a quarter of a coss to go, and safety there, why wait?"

"An excellent reason!" thought Dost Mohammed. "Allah knows what will happen when I get there! Chup!" he growled aloud.

"The Heavenborn knows best."

"Chup! I ordered. Black earthworm!"

Twenty minutes later they went on again, and in less than five minutes after that they emerged into another clearing where a hut loomed darkly in the misty moonlight.

"There, Prince of plunderers! Said I not so? She waits!"

"Then go thy way and thank thy jungle gods!"

The man was gone more quickly than a frightened jackal; he turned, tucked his head down, and was gone. Dost Mohammed, with the cloth about his face drawn even higher yet, rode on.

"Oh, Gopi Lall?" It was not a soft voice.

"Quietly!" growled the Rajput.

He dismounted by a low fence, and stood waiting on the near side of his horse, fumbling with the stirrup.

"There are none here who listen. Thou mayest trust me! The troops—may Allah whelm them—are miles away. Oh, Gopi Lall, thou greatest fool of fools! You trust that woman, who is naught but a tigress and an enemy, while I, who truly love thee, wait alone. Come—eat, beloved."

"How knowest thou where I have been?" He answered huskily, and stood behind the horse where the moonlight could not fall on him.

"They have harmed thee? Thy throat? My Prince of——"

"Silence! The hurt is nothing. I asked, how knowest thou where I have been?"

"How! Hear him! Who sent thee all those messages? Who waits for thee always? Who but Yasmini? Sahib—Heavenborn—my lord! Trust not that tigress instead of me! She will slay thee in the dark, or hand thee over. She is thine enemy—naught else!"

Dost Mohammed, wondering what the real outlaw would have done if given such advice, took a chance and laughed. It seemed he had guessed right, for the woman behaved as if she quite expected it.

"Aye, laugh! Laugh on! Did she laugh, think you, when you slew her lover? Think you she forgot? Think you she came here from the distant North to sing you love songs? Bah! Thou art a madman, Gopi Lall! Thy head is turned by flattery. When did I ever flatter thee? Therefore, I who love thee wait alone, while she, who lies and lies and lies again, gets thee ever tighter in her clutches! Thou fool of fools!"

But Dost Mohammed knew enough. His thoughts came quick as lightning. The Regiment was twenty miles away, and in the wrong direction. To Rajahbatkhowa was roughly forty miles, and his charger was fresh enough to make the distance; for all his height the Rajput was a lightweight, and he could ride as only a born horseman of the North can. He was mounted and away, and thanking God that he had fed his horse, before the woman knew that he was starting; and a minute later he was down tight in the saddle, headed straight for the mess tent where his Colonel ought to be.

Ten minutes after he had gone, a dozen troopers burst in from the jungle and made the woman prisoner. They had with them the trembling peasant who had served as guide for Dost Mohammed.

"Where is thy man, Gopi Lall?" they demanded. But they might as well have asked the dead. Now the woman understood why he had galloped off without a word, and more than ever she idolized her robber lord, who could hear and see with his one eye so infinitely better than the eagles! She only prayed that he had not ridden off to Yasmini.

They questioned and cross-questioned the woman for some fifteen minutes, and threatened her with coarse military-Rajput oaths; but all her answers were denials.

"Good for thee," said a Rissaldar at last, turning to the trembling guide, "that we found thee on our way to camp, and not twenty miles from here! We would have hanged thee else. Go!"

And with that they booted him and spurred him and lance-pummeled him and chased him to the roadway.

CHAPTER IX.
THE PANCH MAHAL'S BACK DOOR

COLONEL STAPLETON proved difficult in the matter of calling on Yasmini that evening, but Boileau stuck to his point. His private reason, of course, was that he wanted an excuse for going back again at once, but the reason he gave was one calculated to work on the Colonel's well known gallantry.

"Of course, sir, it's unusual, I know. But there you are. She's a lone woman, and she's frightened. She has a strange idea that the police will order her away unless we show we're friendly."

"But if she's up to no mischief, why on earth should she be afraid of the police?"

"You said yourself, sir, not so very long ago that the police lose all sense of decency, or words to that effect. They could make things pretty uncomfortable for an unprotected woman. You'd never believe, sir, how anxious she was for me to bring you along."

"I advised you not to go there again, you'll remember."

"I know you did, sir. I can only say I'm glad those weren't orders. I'd like you to see for yourself what kind of woman she is. Then you'd understand my calling there again."

The Colonel leaned back in his chair and looked hard at him for half a minute. "I understand that much, at least, perfectly!" he answered. "Well—I'll go, since she's so anxious. But I shall give her plainly to understand that I can offer her no protection from the consequences of any action of her own, and I shall advise her to go away from here."

"Will you come this evening?"

"Yes, I'll come now and get it over."

So the Colonel called for his horse, and he and Boileau rode together to the Panch Mahal, with a trooper behind and a lantern bearer in front and a great display of dignity.

"It's a deuce of a strange hour to go calling on a native woman, Boileau, and I must confess I don't at all like it."

"You'll find she'll receive us well enough, sir."

That prophecy proved justified. Yasmini outdid herself. She was coquetry, and subtlety, and dignity and grace in one; and though she left no stone unturned to win her way to Colonel Stapleton's good graces, she let Boileau see that she was deeply in his debt for having brought him. If Boileau chose to misinterpret some of the soft glances that she sent him, that was understandable at least; and he was too overcome by Yasmini's spell, and too amused by the Colonel's evident amazement, to reason like a man of sense.

He forgot for the time being the gulf that separates the Englishman and native women of far lower caste than Yasmini; forgot that though the purdah might be absent for the once the rule of centuries remained the same; and remembered only that he was a very handsome man and she a lovely woman.

The Colonel told Yasmini what he had said he would. But he put it so delicately, in punctilious and perfect Hindustani, that all of the sting was taken out of it; he sounded more like a courtier assuring her of everlasting homage than a cavalry colonel declining his moral and material support.

"You see," he said, "it's no business of mine to ask you why you happen to be here. Any man with half an eye can see at a glance that you are charming, and as clever as you are beautiful. Therefore, madam, if you'll excuse my saying so, people are quite justified in wondering why you don't look for more healthful quarters. The neighborhood of this jungle can not be too wholesome; now, can it?"

"I have good reasons for being here—very good ones, Colonel sahib. Colonel sahib, may not a woman have her little secrets—or her big ones?"

"Certainly she may—and always does."

"But she must not blame mere man for wondering what those secrets are," he added.

He rose to go, but she begged him not to. She offered him refreshment, entertainment, anything; she called for her maids to dance and play on their guitars, and then, because he still persisted with his air of courteous but unpersuadable dignity, she drew him aside and whispered to him.

"I would like to tell you why I stay here, Colonel sahib; but it must be only for your ears. Then you will understand, and will protect me."

"I can promise you nothing," he warned. "Nothing, that is to say, more than is due to any woman from any man."

"But I must tell it to you alone."

"You'd better go, Boileau!" he said across his shoulder.

He was facing Yasmini, looking down into her eyes, and beginning to feel her spell. Boileau got up, bowed, and started for the stairs, but she left the Colonel and came over to him.

"He won't remain," she whispered. "I am sure he won't. But I am frightened. I must have some one here this evening. Will you return?"

"I'll do anything you say!"

"Then do you go straight home—straight home—" she laid one light hand on his shoulder, and he thrilled—"and when he returns, ride back again to me!"

"Why straight home?" wondered Boileau. "What earthly difference can that make to her?"

He did ride straight home; but when he reached his tent he was still wondering.

"Is she up to mischief with the Colonel now, I wonder? Can't be! Still—I took him there, and I'm responsible."

He called for his horse again, and then countermanded the order and sent for his personal servant, who came running with a lantern. Then he once more changed his mind, took the lantern himself and started off.

Before he had gone a quarter of a mile he saw another lamp, and caught sight of the Colonel's charger; he turned almost instinctively into a narrow track that led to the right of the main path. He felt ashamed of himself a moment later, but continued since he did not care to let the Colonel know that he had sought concealment and then changed his mind. He suspected that the narrow path that he had taken must come out eventually near the Panch Mahal, since there were no other buildings near to which a used track could lead.

His surmise proved correct. After half an hour of stumbling through the pitchy blackness, shuddering at the thought of snakes, he came out of the jungle at a corner of the Panch Mahal that he had never seen before, and stood still for a moment looking at it. It was not the exact rear of the building, but a wing that projected to the right of the rear in the direction of the thickest jungle, and there were no lights in the windows up above to prove that that part of the building was occupied. He could see the wall; though, clearly, for it was white, and he could make out the shape of the open windows.

The next thing he noticed was that a thick, knotted rope hung down from the top window nearly to the ground, swaying gently in the breeze. Then he heard a voice, and listened. The words were Hindustani, and the voice beyond doubt Yasmini's.

"Any sign of him yet?"

"Not yet."

He remembered then that two of Yasmini's maids were from Madras, and that she had to use the common tongue of India to communicate with them. All the same, he wondered why he listened, and thought no better of himself for doing so.

"Go further, then, and see if he is coming. There must be at least one white man here tonight!"

"Now, what in blazes is the game?" thought Boileau.

He was not without brains, and, once his suspicions were aroused, not at all easy to trick. He much more than suspected now that Yasmini's desire to see him was not actuated by any admiration. His cavalry training, too, had seeped into his system and made action—prompt, unexpected action—an essential remedy for doubt. He stooped, loosed the straps beneath his insteps that held his trousers tight, and pulled off his spurs. Then he saw some one, whom he took to be Yasmini herself, come to the window, haul up the rope, and hang the coils on some projection. But when she went away the rope fell down again. She had left the window open.

Adventure—and excitement—and something primitive he could not have named—mystery and the lure of it—began to call to Boileau. The military were in charge now of operations against the outlaw, and as an officer he remembered that he had the right to investigate suspicious circumstances. Too—and that was not to be overlooked—his sudden appearance through a window might appeal to Yasmini's feeling for romance. And then, he wanted to; that was a good enough reason in itself. All those arguments left out of account a feeling deeper down that told him there was danger near at hand. Danger never called to Boileau unanswered.

He walked up and seized the rope and jerked it. It was made fast at the top. A moment later he was shinning up it, as fast as a native would have done, and thanking Heaven that he had left his spurs behind.

He vaulted lightly through the window, and landed on something nearly solid that was on a divan underneath. A second later the something grunted, and an arm like a black snake licked out of the darkness, and he felt the sting of a knife that seared his cheek. Quicker than thought itself he gripped the wrist he could not see, wrenched at it, and sent the knife spinning; he heard it fall some distance away on wood. Next he was locked in a native wrestler's hold that was something new in his experience. Not a word was said nor another sound made but heavy breathing. He was fighting for dear life against a slippery antagonist, who stank enough to sicken him, but whom he could not see!

CHAPTER X.
THE COLONEL RETRACTS A STATEMENT

COLONEL STAPLETON sat before his tent, gasping in the stuffiness and trying to forget the spell that Yasmini had cast on him in common with every other man who came within the radius of her eyes. He lit a cigar, and swore at himself—gently, because unless the Colonel of a Regiment respects himself, his men will not respect him—but comprehensively. "I ought to be a long way from my second childhood yet!" he muttered. Then he pricked his ears.

"Headed this way, by gad! Shod horse—tired, too, and ridden hard! News from one of the troops, I'll be bound."

With an outlaw on the rampage, and military stores worth stealing under tents, even a General of Division would have been made to halt and give an account of himself. None but members of the Regiment knew the password. But he heard the challenge and the answer, and no even momentary check. It was surely news from the scene of operations.

A foaming horse reeled out of the blackness and stopped, heaving and sobbing, before his tent. From his back a figure leaped who looked like a devil fresh from Tophet—who held a naked saber in his hand—whose long black hair was loose and tangled—but who brought the saber up to the salute like a soldier and a swordsman.

"Rung ho, Bahadur! Again I bring good news!"

"Why, Dost Mohammed! What in Heaven's name?"

"Gopi Lall, Huzoor, is near——can be taken alive—at Yasmini's!"

"Are you straight from there?"

"No, sahib."

The Colonel sprang to his feet, stepped up to Dost Mohammed, and looked straight into his eyes.

"Are you sure you're sane?" he asked.

"Sane, sahib, and not a little weary—but we lose time!"

"I myself left Yasmini's less than an hour ago—much less. She invited me, and she did her best to prevent my leaving."

"None the less, sahib, Gopi Lall is there."

"What makes you think so?"

"Sahib, is there time for argument? I tracked him—I found his woman in the hills—I listened to her. Colonel sahib, I did not ride like this for the fun of it!"

"But, man alive, if Gopi Lall is really there, why should she ask me of all people not to go away?"

"Proof, Huzoor, if proof were lacking! With your Honor in her house, who would dare suspect her? With you in charge of operations against Gopi Lall, would any dare look for him in the house where you were? Would a woman of the race and caste of Yasmini—under your favor, sahib—consent to receive an European in her house on any terms or for any motive not dishonest? Think, Colonel sahib—think and hasten!"

"Dost Mohammed, we must have other evidence than this. She's a woman—a defenseless woman. I can't on mere hearsay invade her house and search it, and put her to shame and inconvenience. I can have the house watched, surrounded; I've plenty of troopers here for that. But enter the house, accuse her, without evidence? I think not!"

"Colonel sahib, have I run this risk, put on this shame of a disguise, found his trail, and ridden thus, for nothing? Know you aught of Yasmini? Know you aught of me? Is a high caste woman, who lets down the purdah and receives Europeans, to weigh more in the balance than I? Am I a soldier, or a carrier of nurses' tales? My record—is that nothing?"

He threw his hands up in a gesture of despair—but Colonel Stapleton had come to a decision.

"Orderly!" he called.

A man appeared, like an armed ghost from the shadows.

"Turn out the guard!"

Half a minute later the clank of sabers told that the order had been obeyed.

"Have you a spare uniform where you can get it, Dost Mohammed?"

"Yes, Colonel sahib."

"Then put it on. Hurry. Take command of the men and start at once. Surround the house unseen and unheard if possible. I will ride to the front door and ask admittance."

The native officer saluted and made off, leading his foundered horse and talking to it caressingly. Colonel Stapleton went back into his tent and picked up a copy of the Indian Penal Code. He turned over the pages hurriedly.

"I always did say," he ground his teeth as he muttered, "that police work is no business for a gentleman. Orderly!" he called. "Send Captain Boileau sahib here to me."

"Ne hai, sahib."

"What? Not in camp? What d'ye mean? When did he go?"

The orderly told of Boileau's return on horseback, and of his setting out again on foot.

"That must have been his lantern I saw. He's back there, is he?"

He was growing puzzled, and rather more suspicious than he cared to feel. At the moment he heard the guard ride off, so he called for his own charger and started after them, growing every second more resentful of the circumstances that could put such distasteful duty in his path. He rode alone to Yasmini's little door and tied his horse outside; and Yasmini, alone, admitted him.

"The Colonel sahib—back—again—so soon?"

There were wonder and amusement, but mostly gladness, in her voice. She seemed to think that this was a sending of the gods.

"Madam," he said with dignity (only he used the statelier native word that means 'mistress of many servants'), "I am in receipt of information that has made this visit necessary."

Her eyes opened wide, but she showed no sign of embarrassment—only interest and curiosity.

"Why wait here at the door? Will not the Heavenborn———?"

Instead of finishing the sentence, she floated up the stairs ahead of him. He could have sworn that her little gilded slippers did not touch the carpet. He could have sworn, too, much more positively, that though there was no maid there to close it the studded door slammed tight behind him.

He refused to sit. She reclined, cushioned and languorous, on a divan and lit a cigarette. But there were no maids to protect her, and the Colonel was a man of manners. He stood before her, at least four yards away.

"I am told that the outlaw Gopi Lall is in your house!"

She laughed at him. It was silvery, fairy laughter, spontaneous, musical, irresistible—sheer, frank amusement. He was laughing too before he knew it—laughing and twisting his mustache, and fighting with the tendency to run away.

"Surely that is a wonder of a joke. Who is the wit? Name him, Colonel sahib."

"A man of my own Regiment, mistress of many servants—a man whose word I must respect, at least to the extent of trying at all events to verify it. I have reason to suppose, too, that an officer of mine—the Captain Boileau whom you know—is also here."

This time Yasmini was not amused. Her eyes changed and she clenched her little hands on a cushion in indignant anger.

"By what right—on whose honor—to what end—do you—dares anyone say that?" She snarled it like a tigress, and curled up on one elbow looking—all lovely though she was—like an animal about to spring.

"Curse!" muttered the Colonel to himself.

"Do I, then, keep a trysting place for British officers?"

"As I have already said, madam, I don't know what you keep here, what you do here, or why you stay. You must excuse me if I feel obliged to say that it is hard to believe what you told me this evening. That story about hidden treasure is—ah—well—ah—is—I would like to believe it! Won't you help me to?"

"You mean?"

"I mean that it is necessary that I should see for myself who or what is in this house. No one could regret the necessity more than I, but such is the fact."

"You can not! You dare not!"

Now she was on her feet.

"It is against all custom—contrary to law!"

"The law is, madam, that I must ask admittance, then ask leave to search. If, after a reasonable time for reflection, that leave is refused me, I then have the right to use force if necessary."

"That is not the law!"

She faced him with her chin up, eyes ablaze; and he felt his heart melting inside him at the sight of outraged womanhood.

"Go, sir! Leave me! You are insolent!"

"Madam, I shall be very glad to go when I am satisfied that you have no one hidden here. I have a most unpleasant duty to perform—one that you could make much easier for me if you would."

"You shall not!"

Yasmini stamped her foot and looked lovelier angry than when she purred. "How dare you to search my house!"

"And I unfortunately must insist, much though I regret it."

It was a deuce of a predicament for a man whose creed was courtesy! He had to keep reminding himself that a soldier was a man who did his duty under any circumstances.

"Are you a man of honor?"

Those amazing, blazing eyes seemed able to read into his mind! She saw that she had made a home thrust, but—cleverer than many of her kind—instead of following it up until the wound was numb, she changed her tactics instantly.

"Colonel sahib!"

Now she was pleading with him—with the pathos in her voice of a cruelly ill treated child. Reproach, petition, dumb questioning unbelief shone out of her eyes, and her movement even was in part.

"It was truth I told you. There is, there must be, treasure hidden here. I am here to find it, that is all. If I told what I know, the half of India would be here with pick and shovel to forestall me."

"I am here to look for Gopi Lall, not treasure," answered Stapleton. "If he is not here, my search can do no harm."

"No harm? An insult to your honor is no harm, eh, Colonel sahib? Are all soldiers, then, outragers of women's privacy—or are some soldiers better than the rest?'"

He pulled himself together with an effort, remembering that the sooner this beastly business was over and done with the better for him and her.

"Once more, madam, I ask your permission to search this house."

"And I refuse it!"

"And I am a soldier and a gentleman!" thought Stapleton. Aloud he said to her, "Then I must fall back on my authority, and search without your leave."

He stepped to the nearest door, which was hidden by a curtain to his left and to her right—nearer by two yards to him than her. But she was there before him. Those who had ever seen her dance could have believed anything of her, but to him her movement seemed to have been almost supernatural. She faced him, back against the door, with arms folded on her heaving bosom and her whole blue, gauzy dress vibrating with the passion that possessed her.

"Now! I dare you!"

"Madam, this house is surrounded. No one can get away unseen—not even you or I. There is no sense in trying to prevent me. Why, I could whistle and call up forty troopers to enforce my orders."

"Do it, then! I dare you!"

She was a better hand than he at reading minds. If she were bluffing, she was certainly disposed to go the limit. Was he? Was he prepared to order in half a troop of cavalry, to trample through her house and upset things, and do by force what he could do so delicately? Not while he had one slim chance left of avoiding it!

His suspicions, of course, were thoroughly aroused by this time. No maids, no Boileau, no leave to search, Dost Mohammed's positiveness, Yasmini's concern—there were too many circumstances to explain away. Search he must, and would, although he hated himself more each instant. He reached past her, and felt under the curtain for the fastening of the door. In an instant she was at his throat!

No tigress ever sprang more quickly or more savagely. He felt her grip—and Heavens! how strong her little fingers were! He saw her free hand go to her bosom. Like a flick of light he caught the sheen of steel. So he set his throat muscles, and used both hands and all his strength and energy in the effort to obtain the knife. But she held it out, away from him, and her strong, lithe fingers gripped his throat until he had to spare one hand in the effort to wrench them loose.

Then the knife slithered for his ribs, and he guarded with his forearm only just in time. He seized her around the waist, raised her off her feet—she weighed almost nothing—and swung her round and round and round, hoping to lay her on her back. But her fingers still dug in and the supple, graceful little tigress drew in—in—in along his arms until her face touched his, then writhed, and twirled, and tripped him—him! The six-foot Colonel of a regiment of Bengal Horse lay struggling on his back, with a slip of a woman who weighed a hundred pounds his master!

She had lost the throat grip in the sudden fall, but would he shout for help? Would he let his troopers see him at the mercy of a dancer? Or let them see him fighting with a woman? He saw the gleam of the knife again, and seized her, and crushed her to him, and got the wrist at last. The fight that followed was the worst in his experience.

Even then, he would not hurt her willingly. He wanted the knife; with that in his possession, or tossed out of her reach, he had no doubt of what the end would be. But he could not get the knife. She seemed to want his lifeblood, and fought for it with the ferocity of a tiger-cat—although no animal that ever breathed would have shown half of her brain and courage. Her dancer's muscles were as strong as his, and far more active; her very smallness placed him at a disadvantage, to say nothing of his gentlemanly fear of hurting her. She showed no fear of hurting him!

She tried to get her fingers in his eyes. Her hair was down and round her shoulders, and time and again she used it as a weapon of offense, shaking her head until it fell in waves over his eyes and blinded him. Then the wrist that held the knife would jerk spasmodically, and he would save himself by nothing else than sheer, brute strength. He held on tight to her slender wrist, but it felt like a steel wire hawser gloved in satin; a hold on the lance of a charging enemy would have been as easy!

They fought all over the floor of the room, up on their feet, then down again. His breath came short now, in labored gasps, and he doubted whether he could have shouted loud enough to make the troopers hear, even if he had cared to try. But she had begun to smile, through lips that had grown strangely cruel, and her breath came evenly. She would dance away from him, swoop in again and try to trip him, and dance away.

Once she all but got her wrist free, but he followed and held on; then she came in toward him like a flash of blue light, and tangled herself between his legs and threw him. He reeled to the floor with a crack that brought the sparks.

He heard her chuckle, saw the flash of steel again, collected all his strength for one more effort to draw her in and crush the breath out of her—when, "Hold!" cried a voice he knew. A second later Boileau had her in his arms, tight pinioned from behind, and held her helpless.

"I have the honor to report, sir, that I've just killed Gopi Lall, or somebody who answers his description."

The Colonel rose to his feet, rubbing his head, and wishing he could rub a dozen places all at once. He noticed then that Boileau was panting too, that his mess jacket was blood soaked and torn in ribbons, and that there were bruises on his arms. He stepped up to Yasmini, and took her knife. She surrendered it quite readily.

"I can not fight two gentlemen!" she said, with the accent very strongly on the last word.

"Confound it, Boileau! This is a deuce of an unpleasant business! What did you say? Killed Gopi Lall? Where? How? Hold her! Hold that woman!"

"He need not hold me!" she answered scornfully. "I am helpless. I surrender."

"Hold her wrists for the present!" commanded Stapleton. "Where did you say you killled him?"

"In the room at the end of that passage, sir."

"Come and show me. Bring her, too."

The Colonel took one wrist, and Boileau the other. Between them they led Yasmini along the passage.

"A neat way of repaying hospitality!" she sneered.

But her manner changed the moment that she saw what Boileau had to show.

He had lit two lamps before he left the room, and by their dim light they could make out what the room contained.

On the floor, by the divan near the window, in the room which Boileau had entered by means of the knotted rope, there lay a one-eyed monster of a man, stone dead. His one sound eye was starting from its socket, and the tongue protruded through scarred and ghastly blue-dyed lips. Both arms were curled—fists clenched, above his head in an attitude of dying agony, and from between them foul, greasy, black locks of hair protruded like a nest of snakes.

"Choked him, sir. Had to. Tried to knife me in the dark; then got a brand new hold on me, and tried to break my neck."

His explanation was cut short by Yasmini. She shrieked, tore her hands loose, then threw her head back and wailed. It sounded like a love song, or a death chant—or else a chant about the death of love. And then she shrieked again. Boileau made a move to seize her wrists.

"Leave her alone!" commanded Stapleton.

Together they stood still and watched her, dry-eyed and terrible in grief—disheveled, and a dozen times more beautiful than ever. There was a knife in the dead man's cummerbund, but neither of them noticed that.

Suddenly she sprang, seized the knife, and drew it. Stapleton and Boileau jumped on the defensive, ready to disarm her, but she took no notice of them. Instead, she knelt, and stared down at the dead man's one protruding eye. Then, with a curse that raised the hair of both who watched, she plunged the long knife deep into the eye, and drew it out and plunged it in the body—drew it out and plunged it in again—again!

"By gad, I can't watch that!" swore Stapleton.

"Shall I——?"

"No. Don't touch her. Yasmini!"

She stopped, and looked up. Then she rose and glared at both of them. They stepped forward, but she threw down the knife and stood with her bloody hands beside her, so they both stepped back again.

"Dogs! Devils! Rob me, would you, of revenge? You might have taken jewels—money—clothes—I would have laughed! Revenge was all I asked, or sought or lived for! Officers! Lords of India: Mouthers about honor! You have taken my honor from me. What is left?"

She was silent for a minute, fighting back her sobs; but if ever dumb eyes swore, hers blazed blasphemy. "See—robbers of a woman's honor!— I will show you."

Drawing a key from her bosom, she went to another door, opened it, and motioned them to come and look. So they stood beside her and peered in, feeling like men about to pry on some one's sacred secrets.

"I had that ready for him—for tonight! Until midnight my maids were to have watched, lest the police should get on his trail and interfere. I had no fear of soldiers, only the police. Had they come, I had another plan ready—another place to lure him to. You fools—you honor-robbers—were but meant to allay police suspicions; they have watched this house from time to time of late. See! See what you have saved that murderer by slaying him!"

There was little in the stone-floored room except an iron chair, but the purpose of that was evident. It had twisted wire straps made fast to it; a man could have been bound in the chair with their aid so that he could not move. Beside the chair were braziers, heaped with charcoal; and by them pincers, and little rods of steel, and tiny awls, and lengths of wire, and needles—a complete assortment of instruments of torture!

"He would have lived three days, or more, under my hand!" hissed Yasmini between set teeth.

"But why? What had you got against the man?" Colonel Stapleton was more bewildered now than ever.

"I? Because that pig of pigs, that one-eyed plunderer of offal heaps, that carrion, slew my lover, my Maharaja, the one love of my life! He ran! The rat-louse ran! He made suspicion fall on me. But I followed—I, with only a dozen maids to help me. I tricked him. I trapped him. I had a bone to pick with Gopi Lall! I would have picked it, but for you!"

"But how did you get him here?"

"The mad, conceited swine imagined that I loved him—as certain other dogs have done!"

She looked a little too hard at Boileau, when she said that, for his peace of mind.

"Sahib!" called a voice. "Huzoor! Colonel sahib!"

Stapleton walked over to the window and leaned out.

"Is that you, Dost Mohammed?"

"Aye. Have you found him, sahib?"

"Yes. He's here. He's dead."

"Who killed him?"

"Captain Boileau."

"Present my compliments to Captain Boileau sahib. Tell him that his hands will be undefiled when they are washed."

"You'd better send two troopers up here, Dost Mohammed, to take charge of the body and watch until morning. Come up with them. Have you seen anything of the maidservants?"

"They are here, sahib, all here; they were watching in the jungle. We came on them before they could give the alarm."

"Let them come up, then, to wait on their mistress."

Twenty minutes later Colonel Stapleton and Boileau started camp-ward side by side.

"Let this be a lesson to you, Boileau my boy! How did you come to be up there?"

"Saw a rope, sir, and climbed up through a window."

"A bally ungentlemanly thing to do!"

"It put an end to another gentleman's career, sir!"

"Yes. And for that, and another reason, I won't refer to it again. But, as I said, let this be a lesson to you. If ever you get to be the Colonel of a regiment, don't ever—on any grounds at all—insist on helping the police!"

"I'll try to remember it, sir."

"I feel as if I'd robbed that woman, though that's absurd of course. If anybody'd told me that once—ever in my life—I would lay hands on a woman, even in self-defense, I would have thought him mad. And here I've actually fought a woman. I had thought, and I have said repeatedly, that there are no circumstances under which a soldier can not be a gentleman. I retract it. There is one. When engaged on police duty he runs a very serious risk!"

CHAPTER XI.
(Which has no title to head it, but which leaves the reader with a feeling that he would like to read more of Yasmini.)

THE Tail-Twisters rode back to Balibhum after another week had passed, and left the police behind them to gnash their teeth and curse their luck. There were five thousand good rupees not in police pockets that a grudging Government had paid by way of reward for Gopi Lall.

What made the police so angry was not so much the fact that the Regiment had "wiped their eye" for them, for the native Indian policeman has neither shame nor sportsmanship nor anything but criminal ideas.

Nor was it so much that they did not get the money. It was who did get it that annoyed them.

There were something like a thousand native gentlemen and sixteen officers entitled to a share in that reward. Dost Mohammed had the lion's claim, but he had sworn to touch no copper piece of it. Therefore there were in the neighborhood of five rupees a head to be divided up among the host. And, five rupees is, say, a dollar and two thirds.

The British officers, of course, declined their share, and the native officers all followed suit in Dost Mohammed's wake. It was down to the troopers, then, to make fair division of the spoil; and they took a vote on it.

They had many or them lounged, and smoked, and listened up at Yasmini's. They had all eye-worshipped her, and some had heard her sing. Some, even, had seen her dance. The rest all wished that they had done these things, and some pretended that they had.

The vote, then, was unanimous. They took the lot to her, in hundred-rupee Bank of India notes, on a salver carried on crossed sabers. And she danced for them in the middle of the courtyard, while they sat their horses in appreciative silence. When the police came a few days later to make trouble, and to order her away, and (perhaps) receive a little blackmail, Yasmini was gone.

For years after that it was the fashion among subalterns, and civilians, and others who were stony broke but visionary and believing, to ask for leave and travel to Rajahbatkhowa where the Panch Mahal and the hidden jungle city is. There they would hunt for the fabled hidden treasure that was said to have brought Yasmini so far.

They never found a trace of it, though the architectural societies and antiquarians had reason to be thankful—which goes to show how practical the gods who make men mad can be.

But, many years later, long after the sporadic search for hidden treasure had died a natural death and the jungle had covered up again the traces of it, there was a woman up at Delhi who would tell strange stories in the evening, when the fancy seized her, and there were listeners enough. She had once been maid to Yasmini.

She told the story with a thousand varying details—for who wants to listen to the same plain tale twice over?—of the outlaw's death, and of the officer who killed him with his hands, and of the Colonel sahib who fought with Yasmini and got the worst of it. But she added other things that at the time the story happened would have been of most absorbing interest to the police. They had been among the greediest hunters for the fabled hidden treasure; but they had hunted too, and far more thoroughly, for something else.

Where had the outlaw's loot gone? It was commonly computed at a lakh of silver coin, and though a tenth of that would have been quite a considerable sum for an outlaw to amass in such a district, still the estimate increased as years rolled on, and every one believed it. Surely it was hidden somewhere!

But the former maid of Yasmini's would tell how, night after night for three nights, Gopi Lall would come beneath the window of the Panch Mahal, and how she and Yasmini would lower down a rope, and draw up heavy burdens, close-wrapped in cloth. She had no notion what was in the packages, nor yet had anyone—but Yasmini.

And Yasmini, who wove herself most diligently into the inner history of India, never seemed to lack for capital, nor sense to hold her tongue.

THE WINDS
OF THE WORLD

Ever the Winds of the World fare forth
(Oh, listen ye! Ah, listen ye!),
East and West, and South and North,
Shuttles weaving back and forth
Amid the warp! (Oh, listen ye!)
Can sightless touch—can vision keen
Hunt where the Winds of the World have been
And searching, learn what rumors mean?
(Nay, ye who are wise! Nay, listen ye!)
When tracks are crossed and scent is stale,
'Tis fools who shout—the fast who fail!
But wise men harken—Listen ye!

—Yasmini's Song

CHAPTER I.

A watery July sun was hurrying toward a Punjab sky-line, as if weary of squandering his strength on men who did not mind, and resentful of the unexplainable—a rainy-weather field-day. The cold steel and khaki of native Indian cavalry at attention gleamed motionless between British infantry and two batteries of horse artillery. The only noticeable sound was the voice of a general officer, that rose and fell explaining and asserting pride in his command, but saying nothing as to the why of exercises in the mud. Nor did he mention why the censorship was in full force. He did not say a word of Germany, or Belgium.

In front of the third squadron from the right, Risaldar-Major Ranjoor Singh sat his charger like a big bronze statue. He would have stooped to see his right spur bettor, that shone in spite of mud, for though he has been a man these five-and-twenty years, Ranjoor Singh has neither lost his boyhood love of such things, nor intends to; he has been accused of wearing solid silver spurs in bed. But it hurt him to bend much, after a day's hard exercise on a horse such as he rode.

Once—in a rock-strewn gully where the whistling Himalayan wind was Acting Antiseptic-of-the-Day—a young surgeon had taken hurried stitches over Ranjoor Singh's ribs without probing deep enough for an Afghan bullet; that bullet burned after a long day in the saddle. And Bagh was—as the big brute's name implied—a tiger of a horse, unweakened even by monsoon weather, and his habit was to spring with terrific suddenness when his rider moved on him.

So Ranjoor Singh sat still. He was willing to eat agony at any time for the squadron's sake—for a squadron of Outram's Own is a unity to marvel at, or envy; and its leader a man to be forgiven spurs a half-inch longer than the regulation. As a soldier, however, he was careful of himself when occasion offered.

Sikh-soldier-wise, he preferred Bagh to all other horses in the world, because it had needed persuasion, much stroking of a black beard—to hide anxiety—and many a secret night-ride—to sweat the brute's savagery—before the colonel-sahib could be made to see his virtues as a charger and accept him into the regiment. Sikh-wise, he loved all things that expressed in any way his own unconquerable fire. Most of all, however, he loved the squadron; there was no woman, nor anything between him and D Squadron; but Bagh came next.

Spurs were not needed when the general ceased speaking, and the British colonel of Outram's Own shouted an order. Bagh, brute energy beneath hand-polished hair and plastered dirt, sprang like a loosed Hell-tantrum, and his rider's lips drew tight over clenched teeth as he mastered self, agony and horse in one man's effort. Fight how he would, heel, tooth and eye all flashing, Bagh was forced to hold his rightful place in front of the squadron, precisely the right distance behind the last supernumerary of the squadron next in front.

Line after rippling line, all Sikhs of the true Sikh baptism except for the eight of their officers who were European, Outram's Own swept down a living avenue of British troops; and neither gunners nor infantry could see one flaw in them, although picking flaws in native regiments is almost part of the British army officer's religion.

To the blare of military music, through a bog of their own mixing, the Sikhs trotted for a mile, then drew into a walk, to bring the horses into barracks cool enough for watering.

They reached stables as the sun dipped under the near-by acacia trees, and while the black-bearded troopers scraped and rubbed the mud from weary horses, Banjoor Singh went through a task whose form at least was part of his very life. He could imagine nothing less than death or active service that could keep him from inspecting every horse in the squadron before he ate or drank, or as much as washed himself.

But, although the day had been a hard one and the strain on the horses more than ordinary, his examination now was so perfunctory that the squadron gaped; the troopers signaled with their eyes as he passed, little more than glancing at each horse. Almost before his back had vanished at the stable entrance, wonderment burst into words.

"For the third time he does thus!"

"See! My beast overreached, and he passed without detecting it! Does the sun set the same way still?"

"I have noticed that he does thus each time after a field-day. What is the connection? A field-day in the rains—a general officer talking to us afterward about the Salt, as if a Sikh does not understand the Salt better than a British general knows English—and our risaldar-major neglecting the horses—is there a connection?"

"Aye. What is all this? We worked no harder in the war against the Chitralis. There is something in my bones that speaks of war, when I listen for a while!"

"War! Hear him, brothers! Talk is talk, but there will be no war until India grows too fat to breathe—unless the past be remembered and we make one for ourselves!"

There was silence for a while, if a change of sounds is silence. The Delhi mud sticks as tight as any, and the kneading of it from out of horse-hair taxes most of a trooper's energy and full attention. Then, the East being the East in all things, a solitary; trooper picked up the scent and gave tongue, as a true hound guides the pack.

"Who is *she*?" he wondered, loud enough for fifty men to hear.

From out of a cloud of horse-dust, where a stable helper on probation combed a tangled tail, came one word of swift enlightenment.

"Yasmini!"

"Ah-h-h-h!" In a second the whole squadron was by the ears, and the stable-helper was the center of an interest he had not bargained for.

"Nay, sahibs, I but followed him, and how should I know? Nay, then I did not follow him! It so happened. I took that road, and he stepped out of a *tikka-gharri* at her door. Am I blind? Do I not know her door? Does not everybody know it? Who am I that I should know why he goes again? But—does a moth fly only once to the lamp-flame? Does a drunkard drink but once? By the Guru, nay! May my tongue parch in my throat if I said he is a drunkard! I said—I meant to say—seeing she is Yasmini, and he having been to see her once—and being again in a great hurry—whither goes he?"

So the squadron chose a sub-committee of inquiry, seven strong, that being a lucky number the wide world over, and the movements of the risaldar-major were reported one by one to the squadron with the infinite exactness of small detail that seems so useless to all save Easterns.

Fifteen minutes after he had left his quarters, no longer in khaki uniform, but dressed as a Sikh gentleman, the whole squadron knew the color of his undershirt, also that he had hired a *tikka-gharri*, and that his only weapon was the ornamental dagger that a true Sikh wears twisted in his hair. One after one, five other men reported him nearly all the way through Delhi, through the Chandni Chowk—where the last man but one nearly lost him in the evening crowd—to the narrow place where, with a bend in the street to either hand, is Yasmini's.

The last man watched him through Yasmini's outer door and up the lower stairs before hurrying back to the squadron. And a little later on, being almost as inquisitive as they were careful for their major, the squadron delegated other men, in mufti, to watch for him at the foot of Yasmini's stairs, or as near to the foot as might be, and see him safely home again if they had to fight all Asia on the way.

These men had some money with them, and weapons hidden underneath their clothes; for, having betted largely on the quail-fight at Abdul's stables, the squadron was in funds.

"In case of trouble one can bribe the police," counseled Nanak Singh, and he surely ought to know, for he was the oldest trooper, and trouble everlasting had preserved him from promotion. "But weapons are good, when policemen are not looking," he added, and the squadron agreed.

It was Tej Singh, not given to talking as is rule, who voiced the general opinion.

"Now we are on the track of things. Now, perhaps, we shall know the meaning of field exercises during the monsoon, with our horses up to the belly in blue mud! The winds of all the world blow into Yasmini's and out again. Our risaldar-major knows nothing at all of women—and that is the danger. But he can listen to the wind; and, what he hears, sooner or later we shall know, too. I smell happenings!"

Those three words comprised the whole of it. The squadron spent most of the night whispering, dissecting, analyzing, subdividing, weighing, guessing at that smell of happenings, while its risaldar-major, thinking his secret all his own, investigated nearer to its source.

CHAPTER II.

Yasmini bears a reputation that includes her gift for dancing and her skill in song, but is not bounded thereby, Her stairs illustrated it—the two flights of steep winding stairs that lead to her bewildering reception-floor; they seem to have been designed to take men's breath away, and to deliver them at the top defenseless.

But Risaldar-Major Ranjoor Singh mounted them with scarcely an effort, as a man who could master Bagh well might, and at the top his middle-aged back was straight and his eye clear. The cunning, curtained lights did not distract him; so he did not make the usual mistake of thinking that the Loveliness who met him was Yasmini.

Yasmini likes to make her first impression of the evening on a man just as he comes from making an idiot of himself; so the maid who curtsies in the stair-head maze of mirrored lights has been trained to imitate her. But Ranjoor Singh flipped the girl a coin, and it jingled at her feet.

The maid ceased bowing, too insulted to retort. The piece of silver—she would have stooped for gold, just as surely as she would have recognized its ring—lay where it fell. Ranjoor Singh stepped forward toward a glass-bead curtain through which a soft light shone, and an unexpected low laugh greeted him. It was merry, mocking, musical—and something more. There was wisdom hidden in it—masquerading as frivolity; somewhere, too, there was villainy-villainy that she who laughed knew all about and found more interesting than a play.

Then suddenly the curtain parted, and Yasmini blocked the way, standing with arms spread wide to either door-post, smiling at him; and Ranjoor Singh had to stop and stare whether it suited him or not.

Yasmini is not old, nor nearly old, for all that India is full of tales about her, from the Himalayas to Cape Comorin. In a land where twelve is a marriageable age, a woman need not live to thirty to be talked about; and if she can dance as Yasmini does—though only the Russian ballet can do that—she has the secret of perpetual youth to help her defy the years. No doubt the soft light favored her, but she might have been Ranjoor Singh's granddaughter as she barred his way and looked him up and down impudently through languorous brown eyes.

"Salaam, O plowman!" she mocked. She was not actually still an instant, for the light played incessantly on her gauzy silken trousers and jeweled slippers, but she made no move to admit him. "My honor grows! Twice—nay, three times in a little while!"

She spoke in the Jat tongue fluently; but that was not remarkable, because Yasmini is mistress of so many languages that men say one can not speak in her hearing and not be understood.

"I am a soldier," answered Ranjoor Singh more than a little stiffly.

" 'I am a statesman,' said the viceroy's babu! A Sikh is a Jat farmer with a lion's tail and the manners of a buffalo! Age or gallantry will bend a man's back. What keeps it straight—the smell of the farmyard on his shoes?"

Ranjoor Singh did not answer, nor did he bow low as she intended. She forgot, perhaps, that on a previous occasion he had seen her snatch a man's turban from his head and run with it into the room, to the man's sweating shame. He kicked his shoes off calmly and waited as a man waits on parade, looking straight into her eyes that were like dark jewels, only no jewels in the world ever glowed so wonderfully; he thought he could read anger in them, but that ruffled him no more than her mockery.

"Enter, then, O farmer!" she said, turning lithely as a snake, to beckon him and lead the way.

Now he had only a back view of her, but the contour of her neck and chin and her shoulders mocked him just as surely as her lips were making signals that he could not see. One answer to the signals was the tittering of twenty maids, who sat together by the great deep window, ready to make music.

"They laugh to see a farmer strayed from his manure-pile!" purred Yasmini over her shoulder; but Ranjoor Singh followed her unperturbed.

He was finding time to study the long room, its divans and deep cushions around the walls; and it did not escape his notice that many people were expected. He guessed there was room for thirty or forty to sit at ease. Like a pale blue will-o'-the-wisp, a glitter in the cunning lights, she led him to a far end of the room where many cushions were, There she turned on him with a snake-like suddenness that was one of her surest tricks.

"I shall have great guests tonight—I shall be busy."

"That is thy affair," said Ranjoor Singh, aware that her eyes were seeking to read his soul. The dropped lids did not deceive him.

"Then, what do you want here?"

That question was sheer impudence. It is very well understood in Delhi that any native gentleman of rank may call on Yasmini between midday and midnight without offering a reason for his visit; otherwise it would be impossible to hold a salon and be a power in politics, in a land where politics run deep, but where men do not admit openly to which party they belong. But Yasmini represents the spirit of the Old East, sweeter than a rose and twice as tempting—with a poisoned thorn inside. And here was the New East, in the shape of a middle-aged Sikh officer taught by Young England.

He annoyed her.

Ranjoor Singh's answer was to seat himself, with a dignity the West has yet to learn, on a long divan against the wall that gave him a good view of the entrance and all the rest of the room, window included. Instantly Yasmini flung herself on the other end of it, and lay face downward, with her chin resting on both hands.

She studied his face intently for sixty seconds, and it very seldom takes her that long to read a man's character, guess at his past, and make arrangements for his future, if she thinks him worth her while.

"Why are you here?" she asked again at the end of her scrutiny.

Ranjoor Singh seemed not to hear her; he was watching other men who entered, and listening to the sound of yet others on the stairs. No other Sikh came in, nor more than one of any other caste or tribe; yet he counted thirty men in half as many minutes.

"I think you are a buffalo!" she said at last; but if Ranjoor Singh was interested in her thoughts he forgot to admit it.

A dozen more men entered, and the air, already heavy, grew thick with tobacco smoke mingling with the smoke of sandal-wood that floated back and forth in layers as the punkahs swung lazily. Outside, the rain swished and chilled the night air; but the hot air from inside hurried out to meet the cool, and none of the cool came in. The noise of rain became depressing until Yasmini made a signal to her maids and they started to make music.

Then Yasmini caught a new sound on the stairs, and swiftly, instantly, instead of glancing to the entrance, her eyes sought Ranjoor Singh's; and she saw that he had heard it too. So she sat up as if enlightenment had come and had brought disillusion in its wake.

The glass-bead curtain jingled, and a maid backed through it giggling, followed in a hurry by a European, dressed in a white duck apology for evening clothes. He seemed a little the worse for drink, but not too drunk to recognize the real Yasmini when he saw her and to blush crimson for having acted like an idiot.

"Queen of the Night!" he said in Hindustani that was peculiarly mispronounced.

"*Box-wallah!*" she answered under her breath; but she smiled at him, and aloud she said, "Will the sahib honor us all by being seated?"

A maid took charge of the man at once, and led him to a seat not far from the middle of the room. Yasmini, whose eyes were on Ranjoor Singh every other second, noticed that the Sikh, having summed up the European, had already lost all interest.

But there, were other footsteps. The curtain parted again to admit a second European, a somewhat older man, who glanced back over his shoulder deferentially and, to Yasmini's unerring eye, tried to carry off prudish timidity with an air of knowingness.

"Who is he?" demanded Ranjoor Singh; and Yasmini rattled the bracelets on her ankles loud enough to hide a whisper.

"An agent," she answered. "He has an office here in Delhi. The first man is his clerk, who is supposed to be the leader into mischief; they have made him a little drunk lest he understand too much. I have sent a maid to him that he may understand even less."

The second man was closely followed by a third, and Yasmini smothered a squeal of excitement, for she saw that Ranjoor Singh's eyes were ablaze at last and that he had sat bolt upright without knowing it. The third man was dressed like the other two in white duck, but he wore his clothes not as they did. He was tall and straight. One could easily enough imagine him dressed better.

His quick, intelligent gray eyes swept over the whole room while he took two steps, and at once picked out Yasmini as the mistress of the place; but he waited to bow to her until the first man pointed her out. Then it seemed to Ranjoor Singh—who was watching as minutely as Yasmini in turn watched him—that, when he bowed, this tall, confident-looking individual almost clicked his heels together, but remembered not to do so just in time. The eyes of the East miss no small details. Yasmini, letting her jeweled ankles jingle again, chuckled to Ranjoor Singh.

"And they say he comes from Europe selling goods," she whispered. "The fat man who is frightened claims to be a customer for bales of blankets. Since when has the customer been humble while the seller calls the tune? Look!"

The second arrival and the third sat down together as she spoke; and while the second sat like a merchant, nursing fat hands on a consequential paunch, the third sat straight-backed, kicking a little sidewise with his left leg. Ranjoor Singh saw, too, that he kept his heels a little more than a spur's length off from the divan's drapery.

"Listen!" hissed Ranjoor Singh.

Yasmini wriggled closer, and pretended to be watching her maids over by the window.

"That man who came last," said the risaldar-major, "has been told that thou art like a spider, watching from the middle of the web of India."

"Then for once they have told the truth!" she chuckled.

"In the bazaar he asked to be shown men of all the tribes, that he might study their commercial needs. He was told to come here and meet them; and these were sent for from the caravanserais. Is it not so?"

"Art thou thyself for the Raj?" asked Yasmini.

"I lead a squadron of Sikh cavalry," said Ranjoor Singh, "and you ask me am I for the Raj?"

"The buffalo that carries water for the office lawn is for the Raj!"

"Then he and I are brothers."

"And he, yonder—what of him?" She was growing impatient, for the tune was nearly at an end, and it would be time presently for her to take up the burden of entertainment.

"He will ask, perhaps, to speak with a Sikh of influence."

"Sahib, 'to hear is to obey,'" she mocked, rising to her feet.

"Listen yet!" commanded Ranjoor Singh. "Serve me in this matter, and there will be great reward. I, who am only one, might die by a dagger, or a rope in the dark, or ground glass in my bread; but then there would be a squadron, and perhaps a regiment, to ask questions."

"Perhaps?"

"Perhaps. Who knows?"

He spoke from modesty, sure of the squadron that he loved so much better than his life, but not caring to magnify his own importance by claiming the regard of the other squadrons, too. But Yasmini, who never in her life went straight from point to point of an idea and never could believe that anybody else did, supposed he meant that one squadron was in his confidence, whereas the rest had not yet been sounded.

"So speaks one who is for the Raj!" she grinned.

Playing for profit and amusement, she never, never let anybody know which side she had taken in any game. Therefore she despised a man who showed his hand to her, as she believed Ranjoor Singh had done. But she only showed contempt when it suited her, and by no means always when she felt it.

The minor music ceased and all eyes in the room were turned to her. She rose to her feet as a hooded cobra comes toward its prey, sparing a sidewise surreptitious smile of confidence for Ranjoor Singh that no eye caught save his; yet as she turned from him and swayed in the first few steps of a dance devised that minute, his quick ear caught the truth of her opinion:

"Buffalo!" she murmured.

The flutes in the window wailed about mystery. The lights, and the sandal-smoke, and the expectant silence emphasized it. Step by step, as if the spirit of all dancing had its home in her, she told a wordless tale, using her feet and every sinuous muscle as no other woman in India ever did.

Men say that Yasmini is partly Russian, and that may be true, for she speaks Russian fluently. Russian or not, the members of the Russian ballet are the only others in the world who share her art. Certainly, she keeps in touch with Russia, and knows more even than the Indian government about what goes on beyond India's northern frontier. She makes and magnifies the whole into a mystery; and her dance that night expressed the fascination mystery has for her.

And then she sang. It is her added gift of song that makes Yasmini unique, for she can sing in any of a dozen languages, and besides the love-songs that come southward from the hills, she knows all the interminable ballads of the South and the Central Provinces. But when, as that evening, she is at her best, mixing magic under the eyes of the inquisitive, she sings songs of her own making and only very rarely the same song twice. She sang that night of the winds of the world which, she claims, carry the news to her; although others say her sources of information speak more distinctly.

It seemed that the thread of an idea ran through song and dance alike, and that the hillmen and beyond-the-hills-men, who sat back-to-the-wall and watched, could follow the meaning of it. They began to crowd closer, to squat cross-legged on the floor, in circles one outside the other, until the European three became the center of three rings of men who stared at them with owls' solemnity.

Then Yasmini ceased dancing. Then one of the Europeans drew his watch out; and he had to show it to the other two before he could convince them that they had sat for two hours without wanting to do anything but watch and listen.

"So *wass!*" said one of them—the drunken.

"Du lieber Gott—schon halb zwolf!" said the second.

The third man made no remark. He was watching Ranjoor Singh.

The risaldar-major had left the divan by the end wall and walked—all grim straight lines in contrast to Yasmini's curves—to a spot directly facing the three Europeans; and it seemed there sat a hillman on the piece of floor he coveted.

"Get up!" he commanded. "Make room!"

The hillman did not budge, for an Afridi pretends to feel for a Sikh the scorn that a Sikh feels truly for Afridis. The flat of Ranjoor Singh's foot came to his assistance, and the hillman budged. In an instant he was on his feet, with a lightning right hand reaching for his knife.

But Yasmini allows no butcher's work on her premises, and her words within those walls are law, since no man knows who is on whose side. Yasmini beckoned him, and the Afridi slouched toward her sullenly. She whispered something, and he started for the stairs at once, without any further protest.

Then there vanished all doubt as to which of the three Europeans was most important. The man who had come in first had accepted sherbet from the maid who sat beside him; he went suddenly from drowsiness to slumber, and the woman spurned his bullet-head away from her shoulder, letting him fall like a log among the cushions. The stout second man looked frightened and sat nursing helpless hands. But the third man sat forward, and tense silence fell on the assembly as the eyes of every man sought his.

Only Yasmini, hovering in the background, had time to watch anything other than those gray European eyes; she saw that they were interested most in Ranjoor Singh, and the maids who noticed her expression of sweet innocence knew that she was thinking fast.

"You are a Sikh?" said the gray-eyed man; and the crowd drew in its breath, for he spoke Hindustani with an accent that very few achieve, even with long practice.

"Then you are of a brave nation—you will understand me. The Sikhs are a martial race. Their theory of politics is based on the military spirit—is it not so?"

Ranjoor Singh, who understood and tried to live the Sikh religion with all his gentlemanly might, was there to acquire information, not to impart it. He grunted gravely.

"All martial nations expand eventually. They tell me—I have heard—some of you Sikhs have tried Canada?"

Ranjoor Singh did not wince, though his back stiffened when the men around him grinned; it is a sore point with the Sikhs that Canada does not accept their emigrants.

"Sikhs are admitted into all the German colonies," said the man with the gray eyes. "They are welcome."

"Do many go?" asked Ranjoor Singh.

"That is the point. The Sikhs want a place in the sun from which they are barred at present—eh? Now, Germany—"

"Germany? Where is Germany?" asked Yasmini. She understands the last trick in the art of getting a story on its way. "To the west is England. Farther west, Ameliki. To the north lies Russia. To the south the *kali pani*-ocean. Where is Germany?"

The man with the gray eyes took her literally, since his nation are not slow at seizing opportunity. He launched without a word more of preliminary into a lecture on Germany that lasted hours and held his audience spellbound. It was colorful, complete, and it did not seem to have been memorized. But that was art. He had no word of blame for England. He even had praise, when praise made German virtue seem by that much greater; and the inference from first to last was of German super-virtue.

Some one in the crowd—who bore a bullet-mark in proof he did not jest—suggested to him that the British army was the biggest and fiercest in the world. So he told them of a German army, millions strong, that marched in league—long columns—an army that guarded by the prosperous hundred thousand factory chimneys that smoked until the central European sky was black.

Long, long after midnight, in a final burst of imagination, he likened Germany to a bee—hive from which a swarm must soon emerge for lack of room inside. And he proved, then, that he knew he had made an impression on them, for he dismissed them with an impudence that would have set them laughing at him when he first began to speak.

"Ye have my leave to go!" he said, as if he owned the place; and they all went except one.

"That is a lot of talk," said Ranjoor Singh, when the last man had started for the stairs. "What does it amount to? When will the bees swarm?"

The German eyed him keenly, but the Sikh's eyes did not flinch.

"What is your rank?" the German asked.

"Squadron leader!"

"Oh!"

The two stood up, and now there was no mistake about the German's heels; they clicked. The two were almost of a height, although the Sikh's head—dress made him seem the taller. They were both unusually fine—looking men, and limb for limb they matched.

"If war were in Europe you would be taken there to fight," said the German.

Ranjoor Singh showed no surprise.

"Whether you wanted to fight or not."

There was no hint of laughter in the Sikh's brown eyes.

"Germany has no quarrel with the Sikhs."

"I have heard of none," said Ranjoor Singh.

"Wherever the German flag should fly, after a war, the Sikhs would have free footing."

Ranjoor Singh looked interested, even pleased.

"Who is not against Germany is for her."

"Let us have plain words," said Ranjoor Singh, leading the way to a corner in which he judged they could not be overheard; there he turned suddenly, borrowing a trick from Yasmini.

"I am a Sikh—a patriot. What are you offering?"

"The freedom of the earth!" the German answered. "Self-government! The right to emigrate. Liberty!"

"On what condition? For a bargain has two sides."

"That the Sikhs fail England!"

"When?"

"When the time comes! What is the answer?"

"I will answer when the time comes," answered Ranjoor Singh, saluting stiffly before turning on his heel.

Then he stalked out of the room, with a slight bow to Yasmini as he passed.

"Buffalo!" she murmured after him. "Jat buffalo!"

Then the Germans went away, after some heavy compliments that seemed to amuse Yasmini prodigiously, helping along the man who had drunk sherbet and who now seemed inclined to weep. They dragged him down the stairs between them, backward. Yasmini waited at the stair—head until she heard them pull him into a *gharri* and drive away. Then she turned to her favorite maid.

"Them—those cattle—I understand!" she said. "But it does not suit me that a Sikh, a Jat, a buffalo, should come here making mysteries of his own without consulting me! And what does not suit me I do not tolerate! Go, get that Afridi whom the soldier kicked—I told him to wait outside in the street until I sent for him."

The Afridi came, nearly as helpless as the man who had drunk sherbet, though less tearful and almost infinitely more resentful. What clothing had not been torn from him was soaked in blood, and there was no inch of him that was not bruised.

"Krishna!" said Yasmini impiously.

"Allah!" swore the Afridi.

"Who did it? What has happened?"

"Outside in the street I said to some men who waited that Ranjoor Singh the Sikh is a bastard. From then until now they beat me, only leaving off to follow him hence when he came out through the door!"

Yasmini laughed, peal upon peal of silver laughter—and of sheer merriment.

"The gods love Yasmini!" she chuckled. "Aye, the gods love me! The Jat spoke of a squadron; it is evident that he spoke truth. So his squadron watched him here! Go, *jungli!* Go, wash the blood away. Thou shalt have revenge! Come again tomorrow. Nay, go now, I would sleep when I have finished laughing. Aye—the gods love Yasmini!"

CHAPTER III.

The colonel of Outram's Own dropped into a club where he was only one, and not the greatest, of many men entitled to respect. There were three men talking by a window, their voices drowned by the din of rain on the veranda roof, each of whom nodded to him. He chose, however, a solitary chair, for, though subalterns do not believe it, a colonel has exactly that diffidence about approaching senior civilians which a subaltern ought to feel.

In a moment all that was visible of him from the door was a pair of brown riding-boots, very much fore-shortened, resting on the long arm of a cane chair, and two sets of wonderfully modeled fingers that held up a newspaper. From the window where the three men talked he could be seen in profile.

"Wears well—doesn't he?" said one of them.

"Swears well, too, confound him!"

"Hah! Been trying to pump him, eh?"

"Yes. He's like a big bird catching flies—picks off your questions one at a time, with one eye on you and the other one cocked for the next question. Get nothing out of him but yes or no. Good fellow, though, when you're not drawing him."

"You mean trying to draw him. He's the best that come. Wish they were all like Kirby."

The man who had not spoken yet—he looked younger, was some years older, and watched the faces of the other two while seeming to listen to something in the distance—looked at a cheap watch nervously.

"Wish the Sikhs were all like Kirby!" he said. "If this business comes to a head, we're going to wish we had a million Kirbys. What did he say? Temper of his men excellent, I suppose?"

"Used that one word."

"Um-m-m! No suspicions, eh?"

"Said, 'No, no suspicions!'"

"Uh! I'll have a word with him." He waddled off, shaking his drab silk suit into shape and twisting a leather watch-guard around his finger.

"Believe it will come to anything?" asked one of the two men he had left behind.

"Dunno. Hope not. Awful business if it does."

"Remember how we were promised a world-war two years ago, just before the Balkans took fire?"

"Yes. That was a near thing, too. But they weren't quite ready then. Now they are ready, and they think we're not. If I were asked, I'd say we ought to let them know we're ready for 'em. They want to fight because they think they can catch us napping; they'd think twice if they knew they couldn't do it."

"Are they blind and deaf? Can't they see and hear?"

"*Quem deus vult perdere, prius dementat*, Ponsonby, my boy."

The man in drab silk slipped into a chair next to Kirby's as a wolf slips into his lair, very circumspectly, and without noise; then he rutched the chair sidewise toward Kirby with about as much noise as a company of infantry would make.

"Have a drink?" he asked, as Kirby looked up from his paper.

"Ginger ale, please," said Kirby, putting the paper down.

A turbaned waiter brought long glasses in which ice tinkled, and the two sipped slowly, not looking at each other.

"Know Yasmini?" asked the man in drab silk suddenly.

"Heard of her, of course."

"Ever see her?"

"No."

"Ah! Most extraordinary woman. Wonderful!"

Kirby looked puzzled, and held his peace.

"Any of your officers ever visit her?"

"Not when they're supposed to be on duty."

"But at other times?"

"None of my affair if they do. Don't know, I'm sure."

"Um-m-m!"

"Yes," said Kirby, without vehemence.

"Look at his beak!" said one of the two men by the window. "Never see a big bird act that way? Look at his bright eye!"

"Wish mine were as bright, and my beak as aquiline; means direct-ness—soldierly directness, that does!"

"Who is your best native officer, supposing you've any choice?" asked the man in the drab silk suit, speaking to the ceiling apparently.

"Ranjoor Singh," said Kirby promptly.

It was quite clear there was no doubt in his mind.

"How is he best? In what way?"

"Best man I've got. Fit to command the regiment."

"Um-m-m!"

"Yes," said Kirby.

The man in drab sat sidewise and caught Kirby's eye, which was not difficult. There was nothing furtive about him.

"With a censorship that isn't admitted, but which has been rather obvious for more than a month; with all forces undergoing field training during the worst of the rains—it's fair to suppose your men smell something?"

"They've been sweating, certainly."

"Do they smell a rat?"

"Yes."

"Ask questions?"

"Yes."

"What do you tell them?"

"That I don't know, and they must wait until I do."

"Any recent efforts been made to tamper with them?"

"Not more than I reported. You know, of course, of the translations from Canadian papers, discussing the rejection of Sikh immigrants? Each man received a copy through the mail."

"Yes. We caught the crowd who printed that. Couldn't discover, though, how it got into the regiment's mail bags without being post-marked. Let's see—wasn't Ranjoor Singh officer-of-the-day?"

"Yes."

"Um-m-m! Would it surprise you to know that Ranjoor Singh visits Yasmini?"

"Wouldn't interest me."

"What follows is in strict confidence, please."

"I'm listening."

"I want you to hear reason. India, the whole of India, mind, has its ear to the ground. All up and down the length of the land—in every bazaar—in the ranks of every native regiment—it's known that people representing some other European Power are trying to sow discontent

with our rule; and it's obvious to any native that we're on the watch for
something big that we expect to break any minute. Is that clear?"

"Yes."

"Our strongest card is the loyalty of the native troops."

"Yes."

"Everybody knows that. Also, this thing we're looking for is most
damnably real—might burst today, tomorrow—any time. So, even with
the censorship in working order, it wouldn't be wise to arrest a native officer merely on suspicion."

"I'd arrest one of mine," said Kirby, "if I had any reason to suspect
him for a second."

"Wouldn't be wise! You mustn't!" The man in drab silk shook his
head. "Now, suppose you were to arrest Ranjoor Singh—"

Kirby laughed outright.

"Suppose the Chandni Chowk were Regent Street!" he jeered.

"Last night," said the man in drab silk, "Risaldar-Major Ranjoor
Singh visited Yasmini, leaving six or more of the men of his squadron
waiting for him in the street outside. In Yasmini's room he listened for
hours to a lecture on Germany, delivered by a German who has British
naturalization papers, whether forged or not is not yet clear.

"After the lecture he had a private conversation lasting some minutes
with the German who says he is an Englishman, and who, by the way,
speaks Hindustani like a native. And, before he started home, his men
who waited in the street thrashed an Afridi within an inch of his life for
threatening to report Ranjoor Singh's presence at the lecture to the authorities."

"Who told you this?" asked Colonel Kirby.

"The Afridi, Yasmini, and three hillmen who were there by invitation. I spoke with them all less than an hour ago. They all agree. But if
Ranjoor Singh were asked about it, he would lie himself out of it in any
of a dozen ways, and would be on his guard in future. If he were arrested,
it would bring to a head what may prove to be a passing trifle; it would
make the men angry, and the news would spread, whatever we might do
to prevent it."

"What am I to understand that you want, then?" asked Kirby.

"Watch him closely, without letting him suspect it."

"Before I'd seriously consider orders to do that, they'd have to come through military channels in the regular way," said Kirby, without any emotion.

"I could arrange that, of course. I'll mention it to Todhunter."

"And if the order reached me in the regular way, I'd resign rather than carry it out."

"Um-m-m!" said the man in drab silk.

"Yes," said Kirby.

"You seem to forget that I, too, represent a government department, and have the country's interests at heart. Do you imagine I have a grudge against Ranjoor Singh?"

"I forget nothing of the kind," said Kirby, "and imagination doesn't enter into it. I know Ranjoor Singh, and that's enough. If he's a traitor, so am I. If he's not a loyal gallant officer, then I'm not either. I'll stand or fall by his honor, for I know the man and you don't."

"Uh!" said the man in drab silk.

"Yes," said Colonel Kirby.

"Look!" said one of the two men at the window. "Direct as a hornet's sting—isn't a kink in him! Look at the angle of his chin!"

"You can tell his Sikh officers; they imitate him."

"Do I understand you to refuse me point—blank?" asked the man in the drab suit, still fidgeting with his watch—guard. Perhaps he guessed that two men in the window were discussing him.

"Yes," said Kirby.

"I shall have to go over your head."

"Understand me, then. If an order of that kind reaches me, I shall arrest Ranjoor Singh at once, so that he may stand trial and be cleared like a gentleman. I'll have nothing done to one of my officers that would be intolerable if done to me, so long as I command the regiment!"

"What alternative do you suggest?" asked the man in gray, with a wry face.

"Ask Ranjoor Singh about it."

"Who? You or I?"

"He wouldn't answer you."

"Then ask him yourself. But I shall remember, Colonel Kirby, that you did not oblige me in the matter."

"Very well," said Kirby,

"Another drink?"

"No, thanks."

"Who won?" asked one of the two men in the window.

"Kirby!"

"I don't think so. I've been watching his face. He's just the least bit rattled. It's somebody else who has won; Kirby's been fighting another man's battle. But it's obvious who lost—look at that watch-chain going! Come away."

CHAPTER IV.

Of course an Afridi can be depended on to overdo anything. The particular Afridi whom Ranjoor Singh had kicked was able to see very little virtue in Yasmin's method of attack. Suckled in a mountain-range where vengeance is believed as real and worthy as love must be transitory, his very bowels ached for physical retaliation, just as his skin and bones smarted from the beating the risaldar-major's men had given him.

He was scoffed at by small boys as he slunk through byways of the big bazaar. A woman who had smiled at him but a day ago now emptied unseemly things on him from an upper story when he went to moan beneath her window. He decided to include that woman in his vengeance, too, if possible, but not to miss Ranjoor Singh on her account; there was not room for him and Ranjoor Singh on one rain-pelted earth, but, if needs must, the woman might wait a while.

As nearly all humans do when their mood is similar to his, he slunk into dark places, growling like a dog and believing all the world his enemy. He came very near to the summit of exasperation when, on making application at a free dispensary, his sores were dressed for him by a Hindu assistant apothecary who lectured him on brotherly love with interlarded excerpts from Carlyle done into Hindustani. But the climax came when a native policeman poked him in the ribs with a truncheon and ordered him out of sight.

With a snarl that would have done credit to a panther driven off its prey, he slunk up a byway to shelter himself and think of new obscenities; and as he stood beneath a cloth awning to await the passing of a more than usually heavy downpour, the rotten fibers burst at last and let ten gallons of filthy rain down on him.

From that minute he could see only red; so it was in a red haze that two of the troopers from Ranjoor Singh's squadron passed the end of the lane. He felt himself clutching at a red knife, breathing red air through distended nostrils. He forgot his sores; forgot to feel them.

As he hunted the two troopers through the maze of streets, he recognized them for two of the men who had thrashed him; so he drew closer, for fear they might escape him in the crowd. Now that he no longer wandered objectless, but looked ahead and walked with a will and a purpose, street-corner "constabeels" ceased to trouble him; there were too many people in those thronged, kaleidoscopic streets for any but the loafers to be noticed. He drew nearer and nearer to the troopers, all unsuspected.

But the pace was fast, and they approached their barracks, where his chance of ramming a knife into them and getting away unseen would be increasingly more remote; and he had no desire to die until he had killed the other four men, Ranjoor Singh himself, and the woman who had spurned his love. He must kill these two, he decided, while yet safe from barrack hue and cry.

He crept yet closer, and—now that his plan was forming in his mind-began to see less red. In a minute more he recognized a house at a street corner, whose lower story once had been a shop, but that now was boarded up and showed from outside little sign of occupation. But he saw that the door at the end of an alley by the building was ajar, and through a chink between the shutters of an upper story his keen northern eyes detected lamp-light. That was enough. He set his teeth and drew his long clean knife.

Wounds, bruises, pain, all mean nothing to a hillman when there is murder in his eye, unless they be spurs that goad him to greater frenzy and more speed. The troopers swaggered at a drilled man's marching pace; the Afridi came like a wind—devil, ripping down a gully from the northern hills, all frenzy.

Had he not seen red again, had only a little brain—work mingled in his rage, he would have scored a clean victory and have been free to wreak red vengeance on the rest. As it was, rage mastered him, and he yelled as he drove the long knife home between the shoulders of one of the troopers in front of him.

That yell was a mistake, for he was dealing with picked, drilled men of birth and a certain education. The struck man sank to his knees, but the other turned in time to guard the next blow with his forearm; he seized a good fistful of the Afridi's bandages and landed hard on his naked foot with the heel of an ammunition boot. The Afridi screamed like a wild beast as he wrenched himself away, leaving the bandages in the trooper's hand; and for an instant the trooper half turned to succor his comrade.

"Nay, after him!" urged the wounded man in the Jat tongue; and, seeing a crowd come running from four directions, the Sikh let him lie, to race after the Afridi.

He caught little more than a glimpse of torn clothes disappearing through the little door at the end of the alley by the boarded shop, and a second after he had started in pursuit he saw the door shut with a slam and thought he heard a bolt snick home.

The door, though small, looked stout, and, thinking as he charged to the assault, the Sikh put all the advantage he had of weight, and steel-shod boots, and strength, and speed into the effort. A yard from the door he took off, as a man does at the broad jump in the inter-regimental sports, landing against the lower panel with his heels two feet from the bottom.

The door went inward as if struck by a blast of dynamite, and the Sikh's head struck a flagstone. Long strong arms seized him by the feet and dragged him inside. Then the door closed again, and this time a bolt really did shoot home, to be followed by two others and a bar that fitted vertically into the beam above and the floor beneath.

Outside, thirty feet from the street corner, the crowd came together as a tide-race meets amid the rocks, roaring, shouting, surging, swaying back and forth, nine-tenths questioning at the limit of its lungs, and one-tenth yelling information that was false before they had it. Those at the back believed already that there were ten men down. In the next street there was supposed to be a riot. And the shrill repeated whistle of the nearest policeman summoning help confirmed the crowd in its belief, besides convincing it of new atrocities as yet unguessed.

Only one man in the crowd had wit enough to carry the tale to barracks where it might be expected to produce action. He was a Bengali
babu, bare of leg and fat of paunch, who had enough imagination to conceive of a regiment in receipt of the news, and the mental picture so appealed to him that he held his protruding stomach in both hands while
he ran down-street like a landslide, his mouth agape and his eyes all but
popping from his head.

He reached the barrack gate speechless and breathless, just as Ranjoor Singh rode up on Bagh, mud-plastered after an afternoon's work
teaching scouts. He clung to the risaldar-major's stirrup, and was dragged
ten feet, slobbering and bubbling incoherencies, before the savage charger
could be reined in and made to stand.

"What is it, oh, *babuji?*" laughed Ranjoor Singh. "Are the Moslems
out after your temple gods?"

"Aha! Run! Gallop! Bring all the guns!" This in English, all of it.
"Blood in the gutter—blood like water—twentee policemen are already
dead, and your men have done it! Gallop quicklee. *Jaldee, jaldee!*"

"Go and get twenty more policemen to wipe away the blood!" advised
Ranjoor Singh, sitting back in the saddle to get a better look at him, and
reining back the impatient Bagh. "I am no constabeel; I am a soldier."

"Aha! Yes. You better hurry. All your men are underneath—what-
you-call-it?—bottom dog. You better hurry like slippery! One Afridi is
beginning things, and where is one Afridi with a long knife are many
more kinds of trouble!"

The babu was recovering his breath, and with it his yearning to be-
hold a regiment careering through the barrack gate to the rescue. He still
clung to the stirrup, and since he would not let go, Ranjoor Singh proceeded to tow him, with a cautious, booted right leg ready to spur Bagh
away to the left should the brute commence to kick.

"You are hard-hearted person, and your fate is forever sealed if you
refuse to listen!" wailed the babu. "The blood of your men lies in street
calling aloud for vengeance!" A university education works wonders for
babu vocabulary. "I tell you it is a riot, and most extremelee serious affair!"

That was the wrong appeal to make, as the babu himself would have
known had he been less excited. In time of riot the place for a Sikh officer
would be at the regiment's headquarters, in readiness for the order from

a civil magistrate without which interference would cost him his commission. But the babu was beside himself, what with breathlessness and disappointment. He decided it was expedient to strengthen his appeal, and his imagination was still working.

"There will be two regiments of Tommees—drunken Tommees, presentlee. They will take your men to jail. The Tommees are already on the way. Should they get there first your men will be everlastinglee disgraced as well as muleted. You should hurry."

Ranjoor Singh ceased from frowning and looked satisfied. If there were trouble enough in the bazaar to call for the despatch of British soldiers to the scene, then nothing in the world was more certain than that any men of his who happened to be in danger would be rescued with neatness and speed. If there was no trouble yet, there would very likely be some swearing when the soldiers got there. In the meantime he was wet through, both with rain and perspiration. The thought of a bath and dry clothes urged him like the voice of a siren calling; and he had shown the babu all the courtesy his Sikh creed and profession demanded.

So he clucked to Bagh, and the big brute plunged into a canter, just as eager for his sais and gram as his master was for clean dry clothes. For two strides the babu clung to the stirrup, wrenching it free from the risaldar-major's foot; then the horse grew savage at the unaccustomed extra weight, and lashed out hard behind him, missing the babu twice in quick succession, but filling him full to the stuttering teeth with fear. Ranjoor Singh touched the horse with his right spur, and in a second the babu lay along on his stomach in the mud.

He lay for a minute, believing himself dead. Then he cried aloud, since he knew he must be broken into pieces. Then he felt himself. At last he rose, and after a speechless glance at the back of the risaldar-major, started slowly along the street toward where the "riot" was.

"It is enough," he said in English, since he was a "failed B.A.," "to try the patience of Job's comforter. This militaree business has corrupted even Sikh cavalry until they no longer are dependable. Yes. It is time! It is time indeed that German influence be felt, in order that British yoke may be cast off for good and all. Now I take it a German soldier would have arrested everybodee, and I would have received much *kudos* in addition to cash reward paid for information. In meantime, it is to be seen whether or not—yes, precisely—a pencil is mightier than a sword, which means that a babu is superior in wit and general attainments. Let us see!"

He began to run again, at a truly astonishing pace, considering his paunch and all-round ungainliness, getting over the ground faster than many a thin man could have done. As he ran his lips worked, for though he had no breath to spare for speech, his brain was forming words that crowded for expression.

"The Sikhs!" he screamed, as he came within earshot of the milling crowd, through which four small policemen were trying to force a path. "The Sikhs! They ride to the rescue!"

"The Sikhs!" yelled somebody on the edge of the crowd, who had more breath but not enough imagination to ask questions. "The Sikhs are coming! Run!"

"The Sikhs! The Sikhs!"

The crowd took it up. And since it was a crowd, and there was nothing else to do; and since it had had protection but no violence at Sikh hands ever since '57; and since the babu really did look frightened, it shouted that the Sikhs were coming until it believed the news and had made itself thoroughly afraid.

"Run, brothers!" shouted some man in the middle who owned a voice like a bull-buffalo's. And that being a new idea and just as good as any, the whole crowd took to its heels, leaving the four policemen staring at the body of a dead Sikh, and the fat babu complacently regarding all of them. Presently a European police officer trotted up on a white pony, examined the body, asked a dozen questions of the four policemen, wrote in his memorandum book, and ordered the body to be taken to the morgue.

"Come here, you!" he called to the babu.

So the babu waddled to him, judging his salaam shrewdly so that it suggested deference while leaving no doubt as to the intended insult.

"What do you know about this?"

"As peaceful citizen in pursuance of daily bread and other perquisites, I claim protection of police! While proceeding on way was thrown to ground violentlee by galloping horse whose rider urged same in opposite direction. Observe my deshabille. Regard this mud on my person. I insist on full rigor of the law for which I am taxed inordinately."

"What sort of a horse? Who rode it? How long ago?"

"Am losing all count of time since being overwhelmed. Should say veree recently, however. The horse was ridden by a person who urged it vehemently. It was a brown horse, I think."

"Which way did he go?"

"How should I know? He went away, knocking me over in transit and causing me great distress."

"Was he armed?"

"Two arms. With one he steered the animal. With the other he urged him, thus."

The babu described in pantomime an imaginary human riding for his life, whom not even the adroitest police officer could recognize as Ranjoor Singh, even had he been acquainted with the risaldar-major.

"Had he a weapon of any kind?"

"Not knowing, would prefer to say nothing about that. It was with the horse—with the rump of the animal that he hit me, and not with a sword of any kind."

"Well, you had better come with me to the office, and there we'll take down your deposition."

"Am I arrested?"

"No. You're a witness."

"On the contrary, I am prosecutor! I demand as stated formerly full rigor of the law. I demand capture and arrest, together with fine and imprisonment of party assaulting me, failing which I shall address complaint to government!"

"Come along. We'll talk about that at the office."

So the babu was escorted to the stuffy little police office, where he was made to sit on a bench beside ten native witnesses of other crimes; and presently he was called to a desk at which a native clerk presided. There he was made to recite his story again, and since he had had time in which to think, he told a most amazing, disconnected yarn that looked even more untruthful by the time the clerk had written his own version of it on a sheet. To this version the babu was required to swear, and he did so without a blink.

Then there was more delay, while somebody was found who knew him and could certify to his address, and it was nearly evening by the time he was allowed to go.

It was also nearly evening when a messenger arrived at the barracks to report the death of a Sikh trooper by murder in the bazaar. The man's name and regimental number proved him to have been one of D Squadron's men, and since its commander, Ranjoor Singh, was then in quarters, the news was brought to him at once.

"Killed where?" he demanded; so they told him.

"Exactly when?"

It became evident to Ranjoor Singh that there had been some truth after all in the babu's tale. The verbal precis of the only witness, given from memory, about a man who galloped away on horseback, threw no light at all on the case; so, because he could think of nothing better to do at the moment, the risaldar-major sent for a *tikka-gharri* and drove down to the morgue to identify the body.

On the way back from the morgue he looked in at the police station, but the babu had been gone some ten minutes when he arrived.

The police could tell him nothing. It was explained that the crowd directly after the murder had been too great to allow any but those nearest to see anything; and it was admitted that the crowd had been suddenly panic-stricken and had scattered before the police could secure witnesses. So he drove away, wondering, and ordered the driver to follow the road taken by the murdered trooper.

It was just on the edge of evening, when the lighted street-lamps were yet too pale to show distinctly, that he passed the disused boarded shop and saw, on the side of the street opposite, the babu who had brought him the story of riot that afternoon. He stopped his carriage and stepped out. On second thought he ordered the carriage away, for he was in plain clothes and not likely to attract notice; and he had a suspicion in his mind that he might care to investigate a little on his own account. He walked straight to the babu, and that gentleman eyed him with obvious distrust.

"Did you see my trooper murdered?" he demanded; for he had learned directness under Colonel Kirby, and applied it to every difficulty that confronted him.

Natives understand directness from an Englishman, and can parry it; but from another native it bewilders them, just as a left-handed swordsman is bewildered by another left-hander. The babu blinked.

"How much had you seen when you ran to warn me this afternoon?"

The babu looked pitiful. His fat defenseless body was an absolute contrast to the Sikh's tall manly figure. His eye was furtive, glancing ever sidewise; but the Sikh looked straight and spoke abruptly though with a note of kindness in his voice.

"There is no need to fear me," he said, since the babu would not answer. "Speak! How much do you know?"

So the babu took heart of grace, producing a voice from somewhere down in his enormous stomach and saying, of course, the very last thing expected of him.

"Grief chokes me!" he asserted.

"Take care that I choke thee not, *babuji!* I have asked a question. I am no lawyer to maneuver for my answer. Did you see that trooper killed?"

The babu nodded; but his nod was not much more than tentative. He could have denied it next minute without calling overly much on his imagination.

"Oh! Which way went the murderer?"

"Grief overwhelms me!" said the babu.

"Grief for what?"

"For my money—my good money—my emoluments!"

Direct as an arrow though he was in all his dealings, Ranjoor Singh had not forgotten how the Old East thinks. He recognized the preliminaries of a bargain, and searched his mind to recall how much money he had with him; to have searched his pocket would have been too puerile.

"What of them?"

"Lost!"

"Where? How?"

"While standing here, observing movements of him whom I suspected to be murderer, a person unknown—possibly a Sikh—perhaps not—removed money surreptitiously from my person."

"How much money?"

"Rupees twenty-five, annas eight," said the babu unwinking. He neither blushed nor hesitated.

"I will take compassion on your loss and replace five rupees of it," said Ranjoor Singh, "when you have told which way the murderer went."

"My eyes are too dim, my heart too full with grief," said the babu. "No man's memory works under such conditions. Now, that money—"

"I will give you ten rupees," said Ranjoor Singh.

This was too easy! The babu was prepared to bargain for an hour, fighting for rupee after rupee until his wit assured him he had reached the limit. Now he began to believe he had set the limit far too low.

"I do not remember," he said slowly but with great conviction, scratching at his stomach as if he kept his recollections stored there.

"You said twenty-five rupees, eight annas? Well, I will pay the half of it, and no more," said Ranjoor Singh in a new voice that seemed to suggest unutterable things. "Moreover, I will pay it when I have proved thy memory true. Now, scratch that belly of thine and let the thoughts come forth!"

"Nay, sahib, I forget."

Ranjoor Singh drew out his purse and counted twelve rupees and three quarters into the palm of his hand.

"Which way?" he demanded.

"Twenty-five rupees, eight annas of earned emolument—gone while I watched the movements of a murderer! It is not easy to keep brave heart and remember things!"

"See here, thou bellyful of memories! Remember and tell me, or I return this money to my purse and march thee by the nape of thy fat neck to the police station, where they will put thee in a cell for the night and jog thy memory in ways the police are said to understand! Speak! Here, take the money!"

The babu reached out a fat hand and the silver changed owners.

"There!" said the babu, jerking a thumb over his right shoulder. "Through that door!"

"That narrow teak door, down the passage?"

But the babu was gone, hurrying as if goaded by fear of hell and all its angels.

Ranjoor Singh strode across the street in a bee-line and entered the dark passage. He had seen the yellow light of a lamp-flame through a chink in an upper shutter, and he intended to try directness on the problem once again. It was ten full paces down the passage to the door; he counted them, finishing the last one with a kick against the panel that would have driven it in had it been less than teak. There came no answer, so he kicked again. Then he beat on the door with his clenched fists.

Presently he turned his back to the door and kept up a steady thunder on it with his heels. And then, after about five minutes, he heard movement within.

He congratulated himself then that the noise he had made had called the attention of passers-by and of all the neighbors, and though he had had no fear and no other intention than to enter the house at all costs, he certainly had that much less compunction now.

He heard three different bolts drawn back, and then there was a pause. He thought he heard whispering, so he resumed his thunder. Almost at once there followed the unmistakable squeak of a big beam turning on its pivot, and the door opened about an inch.

He pushed, but some one inside pushed harder, and the door closed again. So Ranjoor Singh leaned all his weight and strength against the door, drawing in his breath and shoving with all his might. Resistance ceased. The door flew inward, as it had done once before that day, and closed with a bang behind him.

CHAPTER V.

A regiment is more exacting of its colonel than ever was lady of her lord; the more truly he commands, the better it loves him, until at last the regiment swallows him and he becomes part of it, in thought and word and deed. Distractions such as polo, pig-sticking, tiger-shooting are tolerable insofar as they steady his nerve and train his hand and eye; to that extent they, too, subserve the regiment. But a woman is a rival. So it is counted no sin against a cavalry colonel should he be a bachelor.

There remained no virtue, then, in the eyes of Outram's Own for Colonel Kirby to acquire; he had all that they could imagine, besides at least a dozen they had not imagined before he came to them. There was not one black-bearded gentleman who couched a lance behind him but believed Colonel Kirby some sort of super-man; and, in return, Colonel Kirby found the regiment so satisfying that there was not even a lady on the sky-line who could look forward to encroaching on the regiment's preserves.

His heart, his honor, and his rare ability were all the regiment's, and the regiment knew it; so he was studied as is the lot of few. His servant knew which shoes he would wear on a Thursday morning, and would have them ready; the mess-cook spiced the curry so exactly to his taste that more than one cook-book claimed it to be a species apart and labeled it with his name. If he frowned, the troopers knew somebody had tried to flatter him; if he smiled, the regiment grinned; and when his face lacked all expression, though his eyes were more than usually quick, officer, non-commissioned officer and man alike would sit tight in the saddle, so to speak, and gather up their reins.

His mood was recognized that afternoon as he drove back from the club while he was yet four hundred yards away, although twilight was closing down. The waler mare—sixteen three and a half, with one white stocking and a blaze that could be seen from the sky-line—brought his big dog-cart through the street mud at a speed which would have insured the arrest of the driver of a motor; but that, if anything, was a sign of ordinary health.

Nor was the way he took the corner by the barrack gate, on one wheel, any criterion; he always did it, just as he never failed to acknowledge the sentry's salute by raising his whip. It needed the observant eyes of Outram's Own to detect the rather strained calmness and the almost inhumanly active eye.

"Beware!" called the sentry, while he was yet three hundred yards away. "Be awake!"

"Be awake! Be awake! Beware!"

The warning went from lip to lip, troop to troop, from squadron stables on to squadron stables, until six hundred men were ready for all contingencies. A civilian might not have recognized the difference, but Kirby's soldier servant awakened from his nap on the colonel's door-mat and straightened his turban in a hurry, perfectly well aware that there was something in the wind.

It was too early to dress for dinner yet; too late to dress for games of any kind. The servant was nonplussed. He stood in silence, awaiting orders that under ordinary circumstances, or at an ordinary hour, would have been unnecessary. But for a while no orders came. The only sound in those extremely unmarried quarters was the steady drip of water into a flat tin bath that the servant had put beneath a spot where the roof leaked; the rain had ceased but the ceiling cloth still drooped and drooled.

Suddenly Kirby threw himself backward into a long chair, and the servant made ready for swift action.

"Present my compliments to Risaldar-Major Ranjoor Singh sahib, and ask him to be good enough to see me here."

The servant saluted and was gone. Kirby relapsed again into the depth of the chair, staring at the wall in front of him, letting his eye travel from one to another of the accurately spaced-out pictures, pieces of furniture and trophies that proclaimed him unmarried. There was nothing whatever in his quarters to decoy him from his love. There were polo sticks in a corner where a woman would have placed a standard lamp, and where the flowers should have stood was a chest to hold horse-medicines. There was a vague smell about the place of varnish, polish and good leather.

The servant was back again, stiff at the salute, within five minutes. "*Ne hai.*"

"Not there? Not where? Not in his quarters? Then go and find him. Ask where he is. Hurry!"

So, since the regiment was keyed to watchfulness, it took about five minutes more before it was known that Ranjoor Singh was not in barracks. The servant returned to report that he had been seen driving toward the bazaar in a *tikka-gharri*.

Then entered Warrington, the adjutant, and the servant was dismissed at once.

"Bad business," said Warrington, looking thoroughly cheerful.

"What now?"

"One of Squadron D's men murdered in the bazaar this afternoon. Body's in the morgue in charge of the police. 'Nother man who was with him apparently missing. No explanation, and the p'lice say there aren't any clues."

He twisted at a little black mustache and began to hum.

"Know where Ranjoor Singh is by any chance?" asked Kirby.

"Give me three guesses—no, two. One—he's raising hell with all the police in Delhi. Two—he's at the scene of the murder, doing detective work on his own. I heard he'd driven away—and, anyhow, it's his squadron. Man's probably his second cousin, twenty or thirty times removed."

"Send somebody to find him!" ordered Kirby.

"Say you want to have a word with him?"

Kirby nodded, and Warrington swaggered out, humming to himself exactly as he hoped to be humming when his last grim call should come, the incarnation of efficiency, awake and very glad. A certain number of seconds after he had gone two mounted troopers clattered out toward the bazaar. Ten minutes later Warrington returned.

"D Squadron's squattin' on its hunkers in rings an' lookin' gloomy," he said, as if he were announcing some good news that had a touch of humor in it. "By the look of 'em you'd say they'd been passed over for active service and were meditatin' matrimony."

"By gad, Warrington! You don't know how near that guess is to the truth!"

Kirby's lips were smiling, but his voice was hard. Warrington glanced quickly at him once and then looked serious.

"You mean——"

"Yes," said Kirby.

"Has it broken yet?"

"No."

"Is it goin' to break?"

"Looks like it. Looks to me as if it's all been prearranged. Our crowd are sparring for time, and the Prussians are all in a hurry. Looks that way to me."

"And you mean—there's a chance—even a chance of us—of Outram's Own bein' out of it? Beg your pardon, sir, but are you serious?"

"Yes," said Kirby, and Warrington's jaw fell.

"Any details that are not too confidential for me to know?" asked Warrington.

"Tell you all about it after I've had a word with Ranjoor Singh."

"Hadn't I better go and help look for him?"

"Yes, if you like."

So, within another certain number of split seconds, Captain Charlie Warrington rode, as the French say, belly-to-the-earth, and the fact that the monsoon chose that instant to let pour another Noah's deluge seemed to make no difference at all to his ardor or the pace to which he spurred his horse.

An angry police officer grumbled that night at the club about the arrogance of all cavalrymen, but of one Warrington in particular.

"Wanted to know, by the Big Blue Bull of Bashan, whether I knew when a case was serious or not! Yes, he did! Seemed to think the murder of one sowar was the only criminal case in all Delhi, and had the nerve to invite me to set every constable in what he termed my parish on the one job. What did I say? Told him to call tomorrow, of course—said I'd see. Gad! You should have heard him swear then—thought his eyes 'ud burn holes in my tunic. Went careening out of the office as if war had been declared."

"Talking of war," said somebody, nursing a long drink under the swinging punkah, "do you suppose——"

So the manners of India's pet cavalry were forgotten at once in the vortex of the only topic that had interest for any one in clubdom, and it was not noticed whether Warrington or his colonel, or any other officer of native cavalry looked in at the club that night.

Warrington rode into the rain at the same speed at which he had galloped to the police station, overhauled one of the mounted troopers whom he himself had sent in search of Ranjoor Singh, rated him soundly in Punjabi for loafing on the way, and galloped on with the troop-horse laboring in his wake. He reined in abreast of the second trooper, who had halted by a cross-street and was trying to appear to enjoy the deluge.

"Any word?" asked Warrington.

"I spoke with two who said he entered by that door-that small door down the passage, sahib, where there is no light. It is a teak door, bolted and with no keyhole on the outside."

"Good for you," said Warrington, glancing quickly up and down the wet street, where the lamps gleamed deceptively in pools of running water. There seemed nobody in sight; but that is a bold guess in Delhi, where the shadows all have eyes.

He gave a quiet order, and trooper number one passed his reins to number two.

"Go and try that door. Kick it in if you can—but be quick, and try not to be noisy!"

The trooper swung out of the saddle and obeyed, while Warrington and the other man faced back to back, watching each way against surprise.

In India, as in lands less "civilized," the cavalry are not allowed to usurp the functions of police, and the officer or man who tries it does so at his own risk. There came a sound of sudden thundering on teak that ceased after two minutes.

"The door is stout. There is no answer from within," said the trooper.

"Then wait here on foot," commanded Warrington. "Get under cover and watch. Stay here until you're relieved, unless something particularly worth reporting happens; in that case, hurry and report. For instance"—he hesitated, trying to imagine something out of the unimaginable—"suppose the risaldar-major were to come out, then give him the message and come home with him. But—oh, suppose the place takes fire, or there's a riot, or you hear a fight going on inside—then hurry to barracks—understand?"

The wet trooper nodded and saluted.

"Get into a shadow, then, and keep as dry as you can," ordered Warrington. "Come on!" he called to the other man.

And a second later he was charging through the street as if he rode with dispatches through a zone of rifle fire. Behind him clattered a rain-soaked trooper and two horses.

Colonel Kirby stepped out of his bathroom just as Warrington arrived, and arranged his white dress-tie before the sitting-room mirror.

"Looks fishy to me, sir," said Warrington, hurrying in and standing where the rain from his wet clothes would do least harm.

There was a space on the floor between two tiger-skins where the matting was a little threadbare. Messengers, orderlies or servants always stood on that spot. After a moment, however, Kirby's servant brought Warrington a bathroom mat.

"How d'ye mean?"

Warrington explained.

"What did the police say?"

"Said they were busy."

"Now, I could go to the club," mused Kirby, "and see Hetherington, and have a talk with him, and get him to sign a search-warrant. Armed with that, we could——"

"Perhaps persuade a police officer to send two constables with it to-morrow morning!" said Warrington, with a grin.

"Yes," said Kirby.

"And if we do much on our own account we'll fall foul of the Indian Penal Code, which altereth every week," said Warrington.

"If it weren't for the fact that I particularly want a word with him," said Kirby, giving a last tweak to his tie and reaching out for his mess-jacket that the servant had laid on a chair, "there'd not be much ground that I can see for action of any kind. He has a right to go where he likes."

That point of view did not seem to have occurred to Warrington before; nor did he quite like it, for he frowned.

"On the other hand," said Kirby, diving into his mess-jacket and shrugging his neat shoulders until they fitted into it as a charger fits into his skin, "under the circumstances—and taking into consideration certain private information that has reached me—if I were supposed to be behind a bolted door in the bazaar, I'd rather appreciate it if Ranjoor Singh, for instance, were to—ah—take action of some kind."

"Exactly, sir."

"Hallo—what's that?"

A motor-car, driven at racing speed, thundered up the lane between the old stacked cannon and came to a panting standstill by the colonel's outer door. A gruff question was answered gruffly, and a man's step sounded on the veranda. Then the servant flung the door wide, and a British soldier stepped smartly into the room, saluted and held out a telegram.

Kirby tore it open. His eyes blazed, but his hands were steady. The soldier held out a receipt book and a pencil, and Kirby took time to scribble his initials in the proper place. Warrington, humming to himself, began to squeeze the rain out of his tunic to hide impatience. The soldier saluted, faced about and hurried to the waiting car. Then Kirby read the telegram. He nodded to Warrington. Warrington, his finger-ends pressed tight into his palms and his forearms quivering, raised one eyebrow.

"Yes," said Kirby.

"War, sir?"

"War."

"We're under orders?"

"Not yet. It says, 'War likely to be general. Be ready.' Here, read it for yourself."

"They wouldn't have sent us that if——"

"Addressed to O.C. troops. They had those ready written out and sent one to every O.C. on the list the second they knew."

"Well, sir?"

"Leave the room, Lal Singh!"

The servant, who was screwing up his courage to edge nearer, did as he was told.

Kirby stood still, facing the mirror, with both arms behind him.

"They're certain to send native Indian troops to Europe," he said.

"We're ready, sir! We're ready to a shoe-string! We'll go first!"

"We'll be last, Warrington, supposing we go at all, unless we find Ranjoor Singh! They'll send us to do police work in Bengal, or to guard the Bombay docks and watch the other fellows go. I'm going to the club. You'd better come with me. Hurry into dry clothes." He glanced at the clock. "We'll just have time to drive past the house where you say he's supposed to be, if you hurry."

The last three words were lost, for Captain Warrington had turned into a thunderbolt and disappeared; the noise of his going was as when a sudden windstorm slams all the doors at once. A moment later he could be heard shouting to his servant to be ready for him.

He certainly bathed, for the noise of the tub overturning when he was done with it was unmistakable. And eight minutes after his departure he was back again, dressed, cloaked and ready.

"Got your pistol, sir?"

"Yes," said Kirby.

"Thought I'd bring mine along. You never know, you know."

Together they climbed into the colonel's dog-cart, well smothered under waterproofs. Kirby touched up another of his road-devouring walers, the sais grabbed at the back seat and jumped for his life, and they shot out of the compound, down the line of useless cannon and out into the street, taking the corner as the honor of the regiment required. Then the two big side-lamps sent their shafts of light straight down the met-aled, muddy road, and the horse settled down between them to do his equine "demdest"; there was a touch on the reins he recognized.

They reached the edge of the bazaar to find the crowd stirring, although strangely mute.

"They'll have got the news in an hour from now," said Kirby. "They can smell it already."

"Wonder how much truth there is in all this talk about German merchants and propaganda."

"*H-rrrrr-ummm!*" said Kirby.

"Steady, sir! Lookout!"

The near wheel missed a native woman by a fraction of an inch, and her shrill scream followed them. But Kirby kept his eyes ahead, and the shadows continued to flash by them in a swift procession until Warrington leaned forward, and then Kirby leaned back against the reins.

"There he is, sir!"

They reined to a halt, and a drenched trooper jumped up behind to kneel on the back seat and speak in whispers.

"No sign of him at all?" asked Kirby.

"No, sahib. But there has been a light behind a shutter above there. It comes and goes. They light it and extinguish it."

"Has anybody come out of that door?"

"No, sahib."

"None gone in?"

"None."

"Any other door to the place?"

"There may be a dozen, sahib. That is an old house, and it backs up against six others."

"What we suffer from in this country is information," said Warrington, beginning to hum to himself.

But Kirby signed to the trooper, and the man began to scramble out of the cart.

"Between now and our return, report to the club if anything happens," called Warrington.

The whip swished, the horse shot forward, and they were off again as if they would catch up with the hurrying seconds. People scattered to the right and left in front of them; a constable at a street crossing blew his whistle frantically; once the horse slipped in a deep puddle, and all but came to earth; but they reached the club without mishap and drove up the winding drive at a speed more in keeping with convention.

"Oh, hallo, Kirby! Glad you've come!" said a voice.

"Evening, sir!"

Kirby descended, almost into the arms of a general in evening dress. They walked into the club together, leaving the adjutant wondering what to do. He decided to follow them at a decent distance, still humming and looking happy enough for six men.

"You'll be among the first," said the general. "Are you ready, Kirby—absolutely ready?"

"Yes."

"The wires are working to the limit. It isn't settled yet whether troops go from here via Canada or the Red Sea—probably won't be until the Navy's had a chance to clear the road. All that's known—yet—is that Belgium's invaded, and that every living man Jack who can be hurried to the front in time to keep the Germans out of Paris will be sent. Hold yourself ready to entrain any minute, Kirby."

"Is martial law proclaimed yet?" asked Kirby in a voice that the general seemed to think was strained, for he looked around sharply.

"Not yet. Why?"

"Information, sir. Anything else?"

"No. Good night."

"Good night, sir."

Kirby nearly ran into Warrington as he hurried toward the door.

"Find a police officer!" he ordered.

"They all passed you a minute ago, sir," answered Warrington. "They're headed for police headquarters. Heard one of 'em say so."

Kirby pulled himself together. A stranger would not have noticed that he needed it, but Warrington saw the effort and was glad.

"Go to police headquarters, then," he ordered. "Try to get them to bring a dozen men and search, that house; but don't say that Ranjoor Singh's in there."

"Where'll I find you, sir?"

"Barracks. Oh, by the way, we're a sure thing for the front."

"I knew there was some reason why I was feelin' cheerful!" said Warrington. "The risaldar-major looks like gettin' left."

"Unless," said Kirby, "you can get the police to act tonight—or unless martial law's proclaimed at once, and I can think of an excuse to search the house with a hundred men myself. Find somebody to give you a lift."

Kirby swung into his dog-cart, the sais did an acrobatic turn behind, and again the horse proceeded to lower records. Zigzag-wise, through streets that were growing more and yet more thronged instead of silent, they tore barrackward, missing men by a miracle every twelve yards. Kirby's eyes were on a red blotch, now, that danced and glowed above the bazaar a mile ahead. It reminded him of pain.

Presently the horse sniffed smoke, and notified as much before settling down into his stride again. The din of hoarse excitement reached Kirby's ears, and in a moment more a khaki figure leaped out of a shadow and a panting trooper snatched at the back seat, was grabbed by the sais, and swung up in the rear.

"Sahib——"

"All right. I know," said Kirby, though he did not know how he knew.

They raced through another dozen streets until the glare grew blinding and the smoke nearly choked him. Then they were stopped entirely by the crowd, and Colonel Kirby sat motionless; for he had a nearly perfect view of a holocaust. The house in which Ranjoor Singh was supposed to be was so far burned that little more than the walls was standing.

CHAPTER VI.

There were police and to spare now, nor any doubt of it. Even the breath of war's beginning could not keep them elsewhere when a fire had charge in the densest quarters of the danger zone. The din of ancient Delhi roared skyward, and the Delhi crowd surged and fought to be nearer to the flame; but the police already had a cordon around the building, and another detachment was forcing the swarms of men and women into eddying movement in which something like a system developed presently, for there began to be a clear space in which the fire brigade could work.

"Any bodies recovered?" asked Colonel Kirby, leaning from the seat of his high dogcart to speak to the English fireman who stood sentry over the water-plug.

"No, sir. The fire had too much headway before the alarm went in. When we got here the whole lower part was red-hot."

"Any means of escape from the building from the rear?"

"As many as from a rat-run, sir. That house is as old as Delhi—about; and there are as any galleries up above connecting with houses at the rear as there are run-holes from cellar to cellar."

"Any chance for anybody down in the cellar?"

"Doubt it, sir. The fire started there; the water'll do what the fire left undone. Pretty bad trap, sir, I should say, if you asked me."

"No reports of escape or rescue?"

"None that I've heard tell of."

"And the house seems doomed, eh? Be some days before they can sort the debris over?"

"Lucky if we save the houses nearest it! Look, sir! There she goes!"

The roof fell in, sending five separate volumes of red sparks up into the cloudy night as floor after floor collapsed beneath the weight. The thunder of it was almost drowned in a roar of delight, for the crowd, sensing the new spirit of its masters, was in a mood for the terrible. Then silence fell, as if that had been an overture.

Out of the silence and through the sea of hot humanity, the white of his dress-shirt showing through the unbuttoned front of a military cloak, Warrington rode a borrowed Arab pony, the pony's owner's sais running beside him to help clear a passage. Warrington was still humming to himself as he dismissed both sais and pony and climbed up beside Kirby in the dog-cart.

"If Ranjoor Singh's in that house, he's in a predicament," he said cheerfully. "I went to police headquarters, and the first officer I spoke to told me to go to hell. So I went into the next office, where all the big panjandrums hide—and some of the little ones—and they told me what you know, sir, that the house is in flames and every policeman who can be spared is on the job, so I came to see. If Ranjoor Singh's in there—but I don't believe he is!"

"Why don't you?"

"I don't believe the Lord 'ud send us active service—not a real red war against a real enemy—and play a low-down trick on Ranjoor Singh. Ranjoor Singh's a gentleman. It wouldn't be sportsmanlike to let him die before the game begins."

For a minute or two they watched the sparks go up and the crowd striking at the rats that still seemed to find some place of exit.

"There's a place below there that isn't red—hot yet," said Kirby. "Those rats are not cooked through. Did you tell the police that you wanted a search warrant?"

"Yes. Might as well argue with an ant-heap. All of 'em too busy tryin' for commissions in the Volunteers to listen. They've got it all cut an' dried—somebody in the basement upset a lamp—nobody upstairs—nobody to turn in the alarm until the fire had complete charge! They offer to prove it when the fire's out and they can sort the ashes."

"Um-m-m! Tell 'em a trooper of ours saw a light there?"

"Yes."

"What did they say?"

"'Doubtless the lamp that was kicked over!'"

Colonel Kirby clucked to his horse and worked a way out to the edge of the crowd with the skill of one whose business is to handle men in quantity. Then he shot like a dart up side streets and made for barracks by a detour.

"Gad!" said Warrington suddenly.

"Who's told 'em d'you suppose?"

"Dunno, sir. News leaks in Delhi like water from a lump of ice."

In the darkness of the barrack wall there were more than a thousand men, women and children, many of them Sikhs, who clamored to be told things, and by the gate was a guard of twenty men drawn up to keep the crowd at bay. The shrill voices of the women drowned the answers of the native officer as well as the noise of the approaching wheels, and the guard had to advance into the road to clear a way for its colonel.

The native officer saluted and grinned.

"Is it true, sahib?" he shouted, and Kirby raised his whip in the affirmative. From that instant the guard began to make more noise than the crowd beyond the wall.

Kirby whipped his horse and took the drive that led to his quarters at a speed there was no overhauling. He wanted to be alone. But his senior major had forestalled him and was waiting by his outer door.

"Oh, hallo, Brammle. Yes, come in."

"Is it peace, Jehu?" asked Brammle.

"War. We'll be the first to go. No, no route yet—likely to get it any minute."

"I'll bet, then. Bet you it's Bombay—a P. and O.—Red Sea and Marseilles! Oh, who wouldn't be light cavalry? First-class all the way, first aboard, and first crack at 'em! Any orders, sir?"

"Yes. Take charge. I'm going out, and Warrington's going with me. Don't know how long we'll be gone. If anybody asks for me, tell him I'll be back soon. Tell the men."

"Somebody's told 'em—listen!"

"Tell 'em that whoever misbehaves from now forward will be left behind. Give 'em my definite promise on that point!"

"Anything else, sir?"

"No."

"Then see you later."

"See you later."

The major went away, and Kirby turned to his adjutant.

"Go and order the closed shay, Warrington. Pick a driver who won't talk. Have some grub sent in here to me, and join me at it in half an hour; say fifteen minutes later. I've some things to see to."

Kirby wanted very much to be alone. The less actual contact a colonel has with his men, and the more he has with his officers, the better—as a rule; but it does not pay to think in the presence of either. Officers and men alike should know him as a man-who-has-thought, a man in whose voice is neither doubt nor hesitation.

Thirty minutes later Warrington found him just emerging from a brown study.

"India's all roots-in-the-air an' dancin'!" he remarked cheerfully. "There was a babu sittin' by the barrack gate who offers to eat a German a day, as long as we'll catch 'em for him. He's the same man that was tryin' for a job as clerk the other day."

"Fat man?"

"Very."

"Uh-h-h! No credentials—bad hat! Send him packing?"

"The guard did."

Food was laid on a small table by a silent servant who had eyes in the back of his head and ears that would have caught and analyzed the lightest whisper; but the colonel and his adjutant ate hurriedly in silence, and the only thing remarkable that the servant was able to report to the regiment afterward was that both drank only water. Since all Sikhs are supposed to be abstainers from strong drink, that was accepted as a favorable omen.

The shay arrived on time to the second. It was the only closed carriage the regiment owned—a heavy C-springed landau thing, taken over from the previous mess. The colonel peered through outer darkness at the box seat, but the driver did not look toward him; all he could see was that there was only one man on the box.

"Where to?" asked Warrington.

"The club."

Warrington jumped in after him, and the driver sent his pair straining at the traces as if they had a gun behind them. Three hundred yards beyond the barrack wall Colonel Kirby knelt on the front seat and poked the driver from behind.

"Oh! You?" he remarked, as he recognized a native risaldar of D Squadron. Until the novelty wears off it would disconcert any man to discover suddenly that his coachman is a troop commander.

"D'you know a person named Yasmini?" he asked.

"Who does not, sahib?"

"Drive us to her house—in a hurry!"

The immediate answer was a plunge as the whip descended on both horses and the heavy carriage began to sway like a boat in a beam-sea swell. They tore through streets that were living streams of human beings—streams that split apart to let them through and closed like water again behind them. With his spurred heels on the front seat, Warrington hummed softly to himself as ever, happy, so long as there was plenty of action.

"I've heard India spoken of as dead," he remarked after a while. "Gad! Look at that color against the darkness!"

"If Ranjoor Singh is dead, I'm going to know it!" said Colonel Kirby. "And if he isn't dead, I'm going to dig him out or know the reason why. There's been foul play, Warrington. I happen to know that Ranjoor Singh has been suspected in a certain quarter. Incidentally, I staked my own reputation on his honesty this afternoon. And besides, we can't afford to lose a wing commander such as he is on the eve of the real thing. We've got to find him!"

Once or twice as they flashed by a street-lamp they were recognized as British officers, and then natives, who would have gone to some trouble to seem insolent a few hours before, stopped to half-turn and salaam.

"Wonder how they'd like German rule for a change?" mused Warrington wryly.

"India doesn't often wear her heart on her sleeve," said Kirby.

"It's there tonight!" said Warrington. "India's awake, if this is Delhi and not a nightmare! India's makin' love to the British soldier-man!"

They tore through a city that is polychromatic in the daytime and by night a dream of phantom silhouettes. But, that night, day and night were blended in one uproar, and the Chandni Chowk was at floodtide, wave on wave of excited human beings pouring into it from a hundred by-streets and none pouring out again.

So the risaldar drove across the Chandni Chowk, fighting his way with the aid of whip and voice, and made a wide circuit through dark lanes where groups of people argued at the corners, and sometimes a would-be holy man preached that the end of the world had come.

They reached Yasmini's from the corner farthest from the Chandni Chowk, and sprang out of the carriage the instant that the risaldar drew rein. "Wait within call!" commanded Kirby, and the risaldar raised his whip. Then, with his adjutant at his heels, he dived through the gloomy opening in a wall that Yasmini devised to look as little like an approach to her—or heaven—as possible.

"Wonder if he's brought us to the right place?" he whispered, sniffing into the moldy darkness.

"Dunno, sir. There're stairs to your left."

They caught the sound of faint flute music on an upper floor, and as Kirby felt cautiously for his footing on the lower step Warrington began to whistle softly to himself. Next to war, an adventure of this kind was the nearest he could imagine to sheer bliss, and it was all he could do to contrive to keep from singing. The heavy teak stairs creaked under their joint weight, and though their eyes could not penetrate the upper blackness, yet they both suspected rather than sensed some one waiting for them at the top.

Kirby's right hand instinctively sought a pocket in his cloak. Warrington felt for his pistol, too.

For thirty or more seconds—say, three steps—they went up like conspirators, trying to move silently and holding to the rail; then the absurdity of the situation appealed to both, and without a word said each stepped forward like a man, so that the staircase resounded.

They stumbled on a little landing after twenty steps, and wasted about a minute knocking on what felt like the panels of a door; but then Warrington peered into the gloom higher up and saw dim light.

So they essayed a second flight of stairs, in single file as before, and presently—when they had climbed some ten steps and had turned to negotiate ten more that ascended at an angle—a curtain moved a little, and the dim light changed to a sudden shaft that nearly blinded them.

Then a heavy black curtain was drawn back on rings, and a hundred lights, reflected in a dozen mirrors, twinkled and flashed before them so that they could not tell which way to turn. Somewhere there was a glass-bead curtain, but there were so many mirrors that they could not tell which was the curtain and which were its reflections.

The curtains all parted, and from the midst of each there stepped a little nutbrown maid, who seemed too lovely to be Indian. Even then they could not tell which was maid and which reflections until she spoke.

"Will the sahibs give their names?" she asked in Hindustani; and her voice suggested flutes.

She smiled, and her teeth were whiter than a pipe-clayed sword-belt; there is nothing on earth whiter than her teeth were.

"Colonel Kirby and Captain Warrington" said Kirby.

"Will the sahibs state their business?"

"No!"

"Then whom do the sahibs seek to see?"

"Does a lady live here named Yasmini?"

"Surely, sahib."

"I wish to talk with her."

A dozen little maids seemed to step back through a dozen swaying curtains, and a second later for the life of them they could neither of them tell through which it was that the music came and the smell of musk and sandal-smoke. But she came back and beckoned to them, laughing over her shoulder and holding the middle curtain apart for them to follow.

So, one after the other, they followed her, Kirby—as became a seriously-minded colonel on the eve of war—feeling out of place and foolish, but Warrington, possessed by such a feeling of curiosity as he had never before tasted.

The heat inside the room they entered was oppressive, in spite of a great open window at which sat a dozen maids, and of the punkahs swinging overhead, so Kirby undid his cloak and walked revealed, a soldier in mess dress.

"Look at innocence aware of itself!" whispered Warrington.

"Shut up!" commanded Kirby, striding forward.

A dozen—perhaps more—hillmen, of three or four different tribes, had sat back against one wall and looked suspicious when they entered, but at sight of Kirby's military clothes they had looked alarmed and moved as if a whip had been cracked not far away. The Northern adventurer does not care to be seen at his amusements, nor does he love to be looked in on by men in uniform.

But the little maid beckoned them on, still showing her teeth and tripping in front of them as if a gust of wind were blowing her. Her motion was that of a dance reduced to a walk for the sake of decorum.

Through another glass-bead curtain at the farther end of the long room she led them to a second room, all hung about with silks and furnished with deep-cushioned divans. There were mirrors in this room, too, so that Kirby laughed aloud to see how incongruous and completely out of place he and his adjutant locked. His gruff laugh came so suddenly that the maid nearly jumped out of her skin.

"Will the sahibs be seated?" she asked almost in a whisper, as if they had half-frightened the life out of her, and then she ran out of the room so quickly that they were only aware of the jingling curtain.

So they sat down, Kirby trying the cushions with his foot until he found some firm enough to allow him to retain his dignity. Cavalry dress-trousers are not built to sprawl on cushions in; a man should sit reasonably upright or else stand.

"I'll say this for myself," he grunted, as he settled into place, "it's the first time in my life I was ever inside a native woman's premises."

Warrington did not commit himself to speech.

They sat for five minutes looking about them, Warrington beginning to be bored, but Kirby honestly interested by the splendor of the hangings and the general atmosphere of Eastern luxury. It was Warrington who grew uneasy first.

"Feel as if any one was lookin' at you, sir?" he asked out of one side of his mouth. And then Kirby noticed it, and felt his collar awkwardly.

In all the world there is nothing so well calculated to sap a man's prepossession as the feeling that he is secretly observed. There was no sound, no movement, no sign of any one, and Warrington looked in the mirrors keenly while he pretended to be interested in his little mustache. Yet the sweat began to run down Colonel Kirby's temples, and he felt at his collar again to make sure that it stood upright.

"Yes," he said, "I do. I'm going to get up and walk about."

He paced the length of the long room twice, turning quickly at each end, but detecting no movement and no eyes. Then he sat down again beside Warrington; but the feeling still persisted.

Suddenly a low laugh startled them, a delicious laugh, full of camaraderie, that would have disarmed the suspicion of a wolf. Just as unexpectedly a curtain less than a yard away from Kirby moved, and she stood before them—Yasmini. She could only be Yasmini. Besides, she had jasmine flowers worked into her hair.

Like a pair of bull buffaloes startled from their sleep, the colonel and his adjutant shot to their feet and faced her, and to their credit let it be recorded that they dropped their eyes, both of them. They felt like bounders. They hated themselves for breaking in on such loveliness.

"Will the sahibs not be seated again?" she asked them in a velvet voice; and, sweating in the neck, they each sat down.

Now that the first feeling of impropriety had given way to curiosity, neither had eyes for anything but her. Neither had ever seen anything so beautiful, so fascinating, so impudently lovely. She was laughing at them; each knew it, yet neither felt resentful. "Well?" she asked in Hindustani, arching her eyebrows questioningly.

And Colonel Kirby stammered because she had made him think of his mother, and the tender prelude to a curtain lecture. Yet this woman was not old enough to have been his wife!

"I-I-I came to ask about a friend of mine—by name Risaldar— Major Ranjoor Singh. I understand you know him?"

She nodded, and Kirby fought with a desire to let his mind wander.

The subtle hypnotism that the East knows how to stage and use was creeping over him. She stood so close! She seemed so like the warm soft spirit of all womanhood that only the measured rising and falling of her bosom, under the gauzy drapery, made her seem human and not a spirit. Subtly, ever so cunningly, she had contrived to touch a chord in Colonel Kirby's heart that he did not know lived any more. Warrington was speechless; he could not have trusted himself to speak. She had touched another chord in him.

"He came here more than once, or so I've been given to understand," said Kirby, and his own voice startled him, for it seemed harsh. "He is said to have listened to a lecture here—I was told the lecture was delivered by a German—and there was some sort of a fracas outside in the street afterward. I'm told some of his squadron were near, and they thrashed a man. Now, Ranjoor Singh is missing."

"So?" said Yasmini, arching her whole lithe body into a setting for the prettiest yawn that Kirby had ever seen. "So the Jat is missing! Yes, he came here, sahib. He was never invited, but he came. He sat here saying nothing until it suited him to sit where another man was; then he struck the other man—so, with the sole of his foot—and took the man's place, and heard what he came to hear. Later, outside in the street, he and his men set on the Afridi whom he had struck with his foot and beat him."

"I have heard a variation of that," said Kirby.

"Have you ever heard, sahib, he who strikes the wearer of a Northern knife is like to feel that knife? So Ranjoor Singh, the Jat, is missing?"

"Yes," said Kirby, frowning, for he was not pleased to hear Ranjoor Singh spoken of slightingly. A Jat may be a good enough man, and usually is, but a Sikh is a Jat who is better.

"And if he is missing, what has that to do with me?" asked Yasmini.

"I have heard—men say——"

"Yes?" she said, laughing, for it amused her almost more than any other thing to see dignity disarmed.

"Men say that you know most of what goes on in Delhi——"

"And——?" She was Impudence arrayed in gossamer.

Colonel Kirby pulled himself together; after all, it was not for long that anything less than an army corps could make him feel unequal to a situation. This woman was the loveliest thing he had ever seen, but....

"I've come to find out whether Ranjoor Singh's alive or dead," he said sternly, "and, if he's alive, to take him away with me."

She smiled as graciously as evening smiles on the seeded plains, and sank on to a divan with the grace it needs a life of dancing to bestow.

"Sahib," she said, with a suddenly assumed air of candidness, "they have told the truth. There is little that goes on in Delhi—in the world—that I can not hear of if I will. The winds of the world flow in and out of these four walls."

"Then where is Ranjoor Singh?" asked Colonel Kirby.

She did not hesitate an instant. He was watching her amazing eyes that surely would have betrayed her had she been at a moment's loss; they did not change nor darken for a second.

"How much, does the sahib know already?" she asked calmly, as if she wished to spare him an unnecessary repetition of mere beginnings.

"A trooper of D Squadron—that's Ranjoor Singh's squadron—was murdered in the bazaar this afternoon. The risaldar-major went to the morgue to identify the body—drove through the bazaar, and possibly discovered some clue to the murderer. At all events, he is known to have entered a house in the bazaar, and that house is now in flames."

"The sahib knows that much? And am I to quell the flames?" asked Yasmini. She neither sat nor lay on the divan. She was curled on it, leaning on an elbow, like an imp from another world.

"Who owns that house?" asked Kirby, since he could think of nothing else to ask.

"That is the House-of-the-Eight-Half-brothers," said Yasmini. "He who built it had eight wives, and a son by each. That was ages ago, and the descendants of the eight half-brothers are all at law about the ownership. There are many stories told about that house."

Suddenly she broke into laughter, leaning on her hand and mocking them as Puck mocked mortals. A man could not doubt her. Colonel and adjutant, both men who had seen grim service and both self-possessed as a rule, knew that she could read clean through them, and that from the bottom of her deep, wise soul she was amused.

"I am from the North," she said, "and the North is cold; there is little mercy in the hills, and I was weaned amid them. Yet—would the sahib not better beg of me?"

"How d'ye mean?" asked Kirby, surprised into speaking English.

"*Three days* ago there came a wind that told *me* of war—of a world-war, surely not this time stillborn. Two years ago the same wind brought me news of its conception, though the talk of the world was then of universal peace and of horror at a war that was. Now, tonight, this greatest war is loose, born and grown big within three days, but conceived two years ago—Russia, Germany, Austria, France are fighting—is it not so? Am I wrong?"

"I came to ask about Ranjoor Singh," said Colonel Kirby, twisting at his closely cropped mustache.

There was a hint of iron in his voice, and he was obviously not the man to threaten and not fulfill. But she laughed in his face.

"All in good time!" she answered him. "You shall beg for your Ranjoor Singh, and then perhaps he shall step forth from the burning house! But first you shall know why you *must* beg."

She clapped her hands, and a maid appeared. She gave an order, and the maid brought sherbet that Kirby sniffed suspiciously before tasting. Again she laughed deliciously.

"Does the sahib think that he could escape alive from this room did I will otherwise?" she asked. "Would I need to drug—I who have so many other means?"

Now, it is a maxim of light cavalry that the best means of defense lies in attack; a threat of force should be met by a show of force, and force by something quicker. Kirby's eyes and his adjutant's met. Each felt for his hidden pistol. But she laughed at them with mirth that was so evidently unassumed that they blushed to their ears.

"Look!" she said; and they looked.

Two great gray cobras, male and female, swayed behind them less than a yard away, balanced for the strike, hoods raised. The awful, ugly black eyes gleamed with malice. And a swaying cobra's head is not an easy thing to hit with an automatic-pistol bullet, supposing, for wild imagination's sake, that the hooded devil does not strike first.

"It is not wise to move!" purred Yasmini.

They did not see her make any sign, though she must have made one, for their eyes were fixed on the swaying snakes, and their brains were active with the problem of whether to try to shoot or not. It seemed to them that the snakes reached a resolution first, and struck. And in the same instant as each drew his pistol the hooded messengers of death were jerked out of sight by hands that snatched at horsehair from behind the hangings.

"I have many such!" smiled Yasmini, and they turned to meet her eyes again, hoping she could not read the fear in theirs. "But that is not why the sahib shall beg of me." Kirby was not too overcome to notice the future tense. "That is only a reason why the sahibs should forget their Western manners. But—if the pistols please the sahibs———"

They stowed their pistols away again and sat as if the very cushions might be stuffed with snakes, both of them aware that she had produced a mental effect which was more to her advantage than the pistols would have been had they made her a present of them. She gave a sudden shrill cry that startled them and made them look wildly for the door; but she had done no more than command a punkah-wallah, and the heavy-beamed punkah began to swing rhythmically overhead, adding, if that were possible, to the mesmeric spell.

"Now," she said, "I will tell a little of the why of things." And Colonel Kirby hoped it was the punkah, and not funk, that made the sweat stream down his neck until his collar was a mere uncomfortable mess. "For more than a year there has been much talk in India. The winds have brought it all to me. There was talk—and the government has known it, for I am one of those who told the government—of a ripe time for a blow for independence.

"There have been agents of another Power, pretending to be merchants, who have sown their seed carefully in the bazaars. And then there went natives in the pay of the merchants who had word with native sowars, saying that it is not well to be carried over sea to fight another's quarrels. All this the government knew, though, of course, thou art not the government, but only a soldier with a ready pistol and a dull wit."

"What bearing has this on Ranjoor Singh?" asked Kirby. It was so long since he had been spoken to so bluntly that he could not sit still under it.

"I am explaining why the colonel sahib shall beg for his Ranjoor Singh," she smiled. "Does the fire burn yet, I wonder?"

She struck a gong, and a maid appeared like an instant echo.

"Does the fire still burn?" she asked.

The maid disappeared, and was gone five minutes, during which Kirby and Warrington sat in silent wonder. They wondered chiefly what the regiment would say if it knew—and whether the regiment would ever know. Then the maid came back.

"It burns," she said. "I can see flame from the roof, though not so much flame."

"So," said Yasmini. "Listen, sahibs."

It is doubtful if a trumpet could have summoned them away, for she had them bound in her spells, and each in a different spell, as her way is. She had little need to order them to listen.

"The talk in the bazaars did little harm, for the fat *bunnias* know well whose rule has given them their pickings. They talk for the love of words, but they trade for the love of money, and the government protects their money. Nay, it was not the *bunnias* who mattered.

"But there came a day when the rings of talk had reached the hills, and hillmen came to Delhi to hear more, as they ever have come since India was India. And it was clear then to the government that proof of disloyalty among the native regiments would set the hillmen screaming for a holy war-for the hills are cold, sahibs, and the hillmen have cold hearts and are quick to take advantage, even as I am, of others' embarrassment. Hillmen have no mercy, Colonel sahib. And I was weaned amid the hills."

It seemed to Kirby and Warrington both—for not all their wits were stupefied—that she was sparring for time. And then Warrington saw a face reflected in one of the mirrors and nudged Kirby, and Kirby saw it too. They both saw that she was watching it. It was a fat face, and it looked terrified, but the lips did not move and only the eyes had expression. In a moment a curtain seemed to be drawn in front of it, and Yasmini took up her tale.

"And then, sahibs, as I have told already, there came a wind that whistled about war; and it pleased the government to know which, if any, of the native regiments had been affected by the talk. So a closer watch was set, then a net was drawn, and Ranjoor Singh ran into the net."

"An antelope might blunder into a net set for a tiger," said Kirby. "I am here to cut him out again."

Yasmini laughed.

"With pistols to shoot the cobras and sweat to put out flame? Nay, what is there to cut but the dark that closes up again? Sahib, thou shalt *beg* for Ranjoor Singh, who struck a hillman in my house, he was so eager to hear treason!"

"Ranjoor Singh's honor and mine are one!" said Colonel Kirby, using a native phrase that admits no double meaning, and for a second Yasmini stared at him in doubt.

She had heard that phrase used often to express native regard for a native, or for an Englishman, but never before by an Englishman for a native.

"Then beg for him!" she grinned mischievously. "Aye, I know the tale! It is the eve of war, and he commands a squadron, and there is need of him. Is it not so? Yet the house that he entered burns. And the hillman's knife is long and keen, sahib! Beg for him!"

Kirby had risen to his feet, and Warrington followed suit. Kirby's self-possession was returning and she must have known it; perhaps she even intended that it should. But she lay curled on the divan, laughing up at him, and perfectly unimpressed by his recovered dignity.

"If he's alive, and you know where he is," said Kirby, "I will pay you your price. Name it!"

"Beg for him! There is no other price. The House-of-the-Eight-Half-brothers burns! Beg for him!"

Now, the colonel of a regiment of light cavalry is so little given to beg for things that the word beg has almost lapsed out of his vocabulary from desuetude.

"I beg you to tell me where he is," he said stiffly, and she clapped her hands and laughed with such delight that he blushed to his ears again.

"I have had a prince on his knees to me, and many a priest," she chuckled, "aye, and many a soldier—but never yet a British colonel sahib. Kneel and beg!"

"Why—what—what d'ye mean?" demanded Kirby.

"Is his honor not your honor? I have heard it said. Then beg, Colonel sahib, on your knees—on those stiff British knees—beg for the honor of Ranjoor Singh!"

"D'you mean—d'you mean——?"

"Beg for his honor, beg for his life, on your knees, Colonel sahib!"

"I could look the other way, sir," whispered Warrington, for the regiment's need was very real.

"Nay, both of you! Ye shall both beg!" said Yasmini, "or Ranjoor Singh shall taste a hillman's mercy. He shall die so dishonored that the regiment shall hang its head in shame."

"Impossible!" said Kirby. "His honor is as good as mine!"

"Then beg for his *and* thine—on your knees, Colonel sahib!"

Then it seemed to Colonel Kirby that the room began to swim, for what with the heat and what with an unconquerable dread of snakes, he was not in shape to play his will against this woman's.

"What if I kneel?" he asked.

"I will promise you Ranjoor Singh, alive and clean!"

"When?"

"In time!"

"In time for what?"

"Against the regiment's need!"

"No use. I want him at once!" said Colonel Kirby.

"Then go, sahib! Put out the fire with the sweat that streams from thee! Nay, go, both of you—ye have my leave to go! And what is a Sikh risaldar more or less? Nay, go, and let the Jat die!"

It is not to be written lightly that the British colonel of Outram's Own and his adjutant both knelt to a native woman—if she is a native—in a top back-room of a Delhi bazaar. But it has to be recorded that for the sake of Ranjoor Singh they did.

They knelt and placed their foreheads where she bade them, against the divan at her feet, and she poured enough musk in their hair, for the love of mischief, to remind them of what they had done until in the course of slowly moving nature the smell should die away. And then in a second the lights went out, blown by a fan from behind the silken hangings.

They heard her silvery laugh, and they heard her spring to the floor. In cold, creeping sweat they listened to footsteps, and a little voice whispered in Hindustani:

"This way, sahibs!"

They followed, since there was nothing else to do and their pride was all gone, to be pushed and pulled by unseen hands and chuckling girls down stairs that were cut out of sheer blackness. And at the foot of the dark a voice that Warrington recognized shed new interest but no light on the mystery.

"Salaam, sahibs," said a fat babu, backing through a door in front of them and showing himself silhouetted against the lesser outer darkness. "Seeing regimental risaldar on the box seat, I took liberty. The risaldar-major is sending this by as yet unrewarded messenger, and word to the effect that back way out of burning house was easier than front way in. He sends salaam. I am unrewarded messenger."

He slipped something into Colonel Kirby's hands, and Kirby struck a match to examine it. It was Ranjoor Singh's ring that had the regimental crest engraved on it.

"Not yet rewarded!" said the babu.

CHAPTER VII.

That's the man whose face was in the mirror!" said Warrington suddenly, reaching out to seize the babu's collar. "He's the man who wanted to be regimental clerk! He's the man who was offering to eat a German a day! ... No—stand still, and I won't hurt you!"

"Bring him out into the fresh air!" ordered Kirby.

The illimitable sky did not seem big enough just then; four walls could not hold him. Kirby, colonel of light cavalry, and considered by many the soundest man in his profession, was in revolt against himself; and his collar was a beastly mess.

"Hurry out of this hole, for heaven's sake!" he exclaimed.

So Warrington applied a little science to the babu, and that gentleman went out through a narrow door backward at a speed and at an angle that were new to him—so new that he could not express his sensations in the form of speech. The door shut behind them with a slam, and when they looked for it they could see no more than a mark in the wall about fifty yards from the bigger door by which they had originally entered.

"There's the carriage waiting, sir!" said Warrington, and with a glance toward it to reassure himself, Kirby opened his mouth wide and filled his lungs three times with the fresh, rain-sweetened air.

There were splashes of rain falling, and he stood with bared head, face upward, as if the rain would wash Yasmini's musk from him. It was nearly pitch-dark, but Warrington could just see that the risaldar on the box seat raised his whip to them in token of recognition.

"Now then! Speak, my friend! What were you doing in there?" demanded Warrington.

"No, not here!" said Kirby. "We might be recognized. Bring him into the shay."

The babu uttered no complaint, but allowed himself to be pushed along at a trot ahead of the adjutant, and bundled head-foremost through the carriage door.

"Drive slowly!" ordered Kirby, clambering in last; and the risaldar sent the horses forward at a steady trot.

"Now!" said Warrington.

"H-r-r-ump!" said Kirby.

"My God, gentlemen!" said the babu. "Sahibs, I am innocent of all complicitee in this or any other eventualitee. I am married man, having family responsibilitee and other handicaps. Therefore——"

"Where did you get this ring?" demanded Kirby.

"That? Oh, that!" said the babu. "That is veree simplee told. That is simple little matter. There is nothing untoward in that connection. Risaldar-Major Ranjoor Singh, who is legal owner of ring, same being his property, gave it into my hand."

"When?"

Both men demanded to know that in one voice.

"Sahibs, having no means of telling time, how can I guess?"

"How long ago? About how long ago?"

"Being elderly person of advancing years and much, adipose tissue, I am not able to observe more than one thing at a time. And yet many things have been forced on my attention. I do not know how long ago."

"Since I saw you outside the barrack gate?" demanded Warrington.

"Oh, yes. Oh, certainly. By all means!"

"Less than two hours ago, sir!" said Warrington, looking at his watch.

"Then he isn't burned to death!" said Kirby, with more satisfaction than he had expressed all the evening.

"Oh, no, sir! Positivelee not, sahib! The risaldar-major is vitalitee!"

"Where did he give you the ring?"

"Into the palm of my hand, sahib."

"Where—in what place—in what street—at whose house?"

"At nobody's house, sahib. It was in the dark, and the dark is big."

"Did he give it you at Yasmini's?"

"Oh, no, sahib! Positivelee not!"

"Where is he now?"

"Sahib, how should I know, who am but elderly person of no meta-physical attainments, only failed B.A.?"

"What did he say when he gave it to you?"

"Sahib, he threatened me!"

"Confound you, what did he say?"

"He said, '*Babuji*, present this ring to Colonel Kirby sahib. You will find him, *babuji*, where you will find him, but in any case you will lose no time at all in finding him. When you have given the ring to him he will ask you questions, and you will say Ranjoor Singh said, "All will presently be made clear"; and should you forget the message, *babuji*, or should you fail to find him soon, there are those who will make it their urgent business, *babuji*, to open that belly of thine and see what is in it!' So, my God, gentlemen! I am veree timid man! I have given the ring and the message, but how will they know that I have given it? I did not think of that! More-over, I am unrewarded—I have no emolument—as yet!"

"How will *who* know?" demanded Warrington.

"They, sahib."

"Who are they?" asked Kirby.

"The men who will investigate the inside of my belly, sahib. Oh, a belly is so sensitive! I am afraid!"

"Did he tell you who 'they' were?"

"No, sahib. Had he done so, I would at once have sought police pro-tection. Not knowing names of individuals, what was use of going to po-lice, who would laugh at me? I went to Yasmini, who understands all things. She laughed, too; but she told me where is Colonel Kirby sahib."

Colonel Kirby became possessed of a bright idea, his first since Yasmini had thrown her spell over him. "Could you find the way," he asked, "to wherever it was that the Risaldar-Major gave you that ring?"

The babu thrust his head out of the carriage window and gazed into the dark for several minutes.

"Conceivablee yes, sahib."

"Then tell the driver where to turn!"

"I could direct with more discernment from box-seat," said the babu, with a hand on the door.

"No, you don't!" commanded Warrington.

"Let go that handle! What I want to know is why were you so afraid at Yasmini's?"

"I, sahib?"

"Yes, you! I saw your face in a mirror, and you were scared nearly to death. Of what?"

"Who is not afraid of Yasmini? Were the sahibs not also afraid?"

"Of what besides Yasmini were you afraid? Of what in particular?"

"Of her cobras, sahib!"

"What of them?" asked Warrington, with a reminiscent shudder.

"Certain of her women showed them to me."

"Why?"

"To further convince me, sahib, had that been necessary. Oh, but I was already quite convinced. Bravery is not my *vade mecum!*"

"Confound the man! To convince you of what?"

"That if I tell too much one of those snakes will shortlee be my bed-mate. Ah! To think of it causes me to perspirate. Sahibs, that is a——"

"You shall go to jail if you don't tell me what I want to know!" said Colonel Kirby.

"Ah, sahib, I was jail clerk once—dismissed for minor offenses but cumulative in effect. Being familiar with inside of jail, am able to make choice."

"Get on the box-seat with him!" commanded Kirby. "Let him show the driver where to turn. But watch him! Keep hold of him!"

So again the babu was propelled on an involuntary course, and Warrington proceeded to pinch certain of his fat parts to encourage him to mount the box with greater speed; but his helplessness became so obvious that Warrington turned friend and shoved him up at last, keeping hold of his loin-cloth when he wedged his own muscular anatomy into the small space left.

"To the right," said the babu, pointing. And so the risaldar drove to the right.

"To the left," said the babu, and Warrington made note of the fact that they were not so very far away from the House-of-the-Eight-Half-brothers.

Soon the babu began to scratch his stomach.

"What's the matter?" demanded Warrington.

"They said they would cut my belly open, sahib! Belly so sensitive!"

Warrington laughed sympathetically; for the fear was genuine and candidly expressed. The babu continued scratching.

"To the right," he said after a while, and the risaldar drove to the right, toward where a Hindu temple cast deep shadows, and a row of trees stood sentry in spasmodic moonlight. In front of the temple, seated on a mat, was a wandering fakir of the none-too-holy type. By his side was a flat covered basket.

"Look, sahib!" said the babu; and Warrington looked.

"My belly crawls!"

"What's the matter, man?"

"He is a fakir. There are snakes in that basket—cobras, sahib! Ow-ow-ow!"

Warrington, swaying precariously over the edge, held tight by the loin-cloth, depending on it as a yacht in a tideway would to three hundred pounds of iron.

"Oh, cobras are so veree dreadful creatures!" wailed the babu, caressing his waist again. "Look, sahib! Look! Oh, look! Between devil and over-sea what should a man do? Ow!"

The carriage lurched at a mud-puddle. The babu's weight lurched with it, and Warrington's center of gravity shifted. The babu seemed to shrug away from the snakes, but the effect was to shove Warrington the odd half-inch it needed to put him overside. He clung to the loin-cloth and pulled hard to haul himself back again, and the loin-cloth came away.

"Halt!" yelled Warrington; and the risaldar reined in.

But the horses took fright and plunged forward, though the risaldar swore afterward that the babu did nothing to them; he supposed it must have been the fakir squatting in the shadows that scared them.

And whatever it may have been—snakes or not—that had scared the babu, it had scared all his helplessness away. Naked from shirt to socks, he rolled like a big ball backward over the carriage top, fell to earth behind the carriage, bumped into Warrington, who was struggling to his feet, knocking him down again, and departed for the temple shadows, screaming. The temple door slammed just as Warrington started after him.

By that time the risaldar had got the horses stopped, and Colonel Kirby realized what had happened.

"Come back, Warrington!" he ordered peremptorily.

Warrington obeyed, but without enthusiasm.

"I can run faster than that fat brute, sir!" he said. "I saw him go into the temple. We won't find Ranjoor Singh now in a month of Sundays!"

He was trying to wipe the mud from himself with the aid of the loin-cloth.

"Anyhow, I've got the most important part of his costume," he said vindictively. "Gad, I'd like to get him on the run now through the public street!"

"Come along in!" commanded Kirby, opening the door. "There has been trouble enough already without a charge of temple breaking. Tell the risaldar to drive back to quarters. I'm going to get this musk out of my hair before dawn!"

Warrington sniffed as he climbed in. The outer night had given him at least a standard by which to judge things.

"I'd give something to listen to the first man who smells the inside of this shay!" he said cheerily. "D 'you suppose we can blame it on the babu, sir?"

"We can try!" said Kirby. "Is that his loin-cloth you've got still?"

"Didn't propose to leave it in the road for him to come and find, sir! His present shame is about the only consolation prize we get out of the evening's sport. I wish it smelt of musk—but it doesn't; it smells of babu—straight babu, undiluted. Hallo—what's this?"

He began to untwist a corner of the cloth, holding it up to get a better view of it in the dim light that entered through the window. He produced a piece of paper that had to be untwisted, too.

"Got a match, sir?"

Kirby struck one.

"It's addressed to 'Colonel Kirby sahib!' Bet you it's from Ranjoor Singh! Now—d'you suppose that heathen meant to hold on to that until he could get his price for it?"

"Dunno," said Kirby with indifference, opening the note as fast as trembling fingers could unfold it. He would not have admitted to himself what his fingers testified so plainly—the extent of his regard for Ranjoor Singh.

The note was short, and Kirby read it aloud, since it was not marked private, and there was nothing in it even the babu might not have read:

"To Colonel Kirby sahib, from his obedient servant, Risaldar-Major Ranjoor Singh—Leave of absence being out of question after declaration of war, will Colonel Kirby sahib please put in Order of the Day that Risaldar-Major Ranjoor Singh is assigned to special duty, or words to same effect?"

"Is that all?" asked Warrington.

"That's all," said Kirby.

"Suppose it's a forgery?"

"The ring rather proves it isn't, and I've another way of knowing."

"Oh!"

"Yes," said Kirby.

They sat in silence in the swaying shay until the smell of musk and the sense of being mystified became too much for Warrington, and he began to hum to himself. Humming brought about a return to his usual wide-awakefulness, and he began to notice things.

"Shay rides like a gun," he said suddenly.

Kirby grunted.

"All the weight's behind and—" He put his head out of the window to investigate, but Kirby ordered him to sit still.

"Want to be recognized?" he demanded. "Keep your head inside, you young ass!"

So Warrington sat back against the cushions until the guard at the barrack gate turned out to present arms to the risaldar's raised whip. As if he understood the requirements of the occasion without being told, the risaldar sent the horses up the drive at a hard gallop. It was rather more than half-way up the drive that Warrington spoke again.

"Feel that, sir?" he asked.

"I ordered that place to be seen to yesterday!" growled Kirby. "Why wasn't it done?"

"It was, sir."

"Why did we bump there, then?"

"Why aren't we running like a gun any longer?" wondered Warrington. "Felt to me as if we'd dropped a load."

"Well, here we are, thank God! What do you mean to do?"

"Rounds," said Warrington.

"Very well."

Kirby dived through his door, while Warrington went behind the shay to have a good look for causes. He could find none, although a black leather apron, usually rolled up behind in order to be strapped over baggage when required, was missing.

"Didn't see who took that apron, did you?" he asked the risaldar; but the risaldar had not known that it was gone.

"All right, then, and thank you!" said Warrington, walking off into the darkness bareheaded, to help the smell evaporate from his hair; and the shay rumbled away to its appointed place, with the babu's loin-cloth inside it on the front seat.

It need surprise nobody that Colonel Kirby found time first to go to his bathroom. His regiment was as ready for active service at any minute as a fire-engine should be—in that particular, India's speed is as three to Prussia's one. The moment orders to march should come, he would parade it in full marching order and lead it away. But there were no orders yet; he had merely had warning.

So he sent for dog-soap and a brush, and proceeded to scour his head. After twenty minutes of it, and ten changes of water, when he felt that he dared face his own servant without blushing, he made that wondering Sikh take turns at shampooing him until he could endure the friction no longer.

"What does my head smell of now?" he demanded.

"Musk, sahib!"

"Not of dog-soap?"

"No, sahib!"

"Bring that carbolic disinfectant here!"

The servant obeyed, and Kirby mixed a lotion that would outsmell most things. He laved his head in it and washed it off sparingly.

"Bring me brown paper?" he ordered then; and again the wide-eyed Sikh obeyed.

Kirby rolled the paper into torches, and giving the servant one, proceeded to fumigate the room and his own person until not even a bloodhound could have tracked him back to Yasmini's, and the reek of musk had been temporarily, at least, subdued into quiescence.

"Go and ask Major Brammle to come and see me," said Kirby then.

Brammle came in sniffing, and Kirby cursed him through tight lips with words that were no less fervent for lack of being heard.

"Hallo! Burning love-letters? The whole mess is doin' the same thing. Haven't had time to burn mine yet—was busy sorting things over when you called. Look here!"

He opened the front of his mess-jacket and produced a little lace handkerchief, a glove and a powder-puff.

"Smell 'em!" he said. "Patchouli! Shame to burn 'em, what? S'pose I must, though."

"Any thing happen while I was gone?" asked Kirby.

"Yes. Most extraordinary thing. You know that a few hours ago D Squadron were all sitting about in groups looking miserable? We set it down to their trooper being murdered and another man being missing. Well, just about the time you and Warrington drove off in the mess shay, they all bucked up and began grinning! Wouldn't say a word. Just grinned, and became the perkiest squadron of the lot!

"Now they're all sleeping like two-year-olds. Reason? Not a word of reason! I saw young Warrington just now on his way to their quarters with a lantern, and if he can find any of 'em awake perhaps he can get the truth out of 'em, for they'll talk to him when they won't to anybody else. By the way, Warrington can't have come in with you, did he?"

Kirby ignored the question.

"Did you tell Warrington to go and ask them?" he demanded.

"Yes. Passed him in the dark, but did not recognize him by the smell. No—no! Got as near him as I could, and then leaned up against the scent to have a word with him! Musk! Never smelt anything like it in my life! Talk about girls! He must be in love with half India, and native at that! Brazen-faced young monkey! I asked him where he got the disinfectant, and he told me he fell into a mud-puddle!"

"Perhaps he did," said Kirby. "Was there mud on him?"

"Couldn't see. Didn't dare get so near him! Don't you think he ought to be spoken to? I mean, the eve of war's the eve of war and all that kind of thing, but——"

"I wish you'd let me see the Orders of the Day," Kirby interrupted. "I want to make an addition to them."

"I'll send an orderly."

"Wish you would."

Five minutes later Kirby sat at his private desk, while Brammle puffed at a cigar. After a lot of thinking, he wrote: "Risaldar-Major Ranjoor Singh (D Squadron) assigned to special duty."

He handed the orders back to Brammle, and the major eyed the addition with subdued amazement.

"What'll D Squadron say?" he asked.

"Remains to be seen," said Kirby.

Outside in the muggy blackness that shuts down on India in the rains, Warrington walked alone, swinging a lantern and chuckling as he reflected what D Squadron would invent as a reason for the smell that walked with him. For he meant to wake D Squadron and learn things.

But all at once it occurred to him that he had left the babu's loincloth on the inside front seat of the shay; and, because if that were seen it would have given excuse for a thousand tales too many and too imaginative, he hurried in search of it, taking a short cut to where by that time the shay should be. On his way, close to his destination, he stumbled over something soft that tripped him. He stooped, swung the lantern forward, and picked up—the missing leather apron from behind the shay.

The footpath on which he stood was about a yard wide; the shay could not possibly have come along it. And it certainly had been behind the shay when they left barracks. Moreover, close examination proved it to be the identical apron beyond a shadow of a doubt.

Warrington began to hum. And then he ceased humming. Then he set the lantern down and stepped away from it sidewise until its light no longer shone on him. He listened, as a dog does, with intelligence and skill. Then, suddenly, he sprang and lit on a bulky mass that yielded—gasped—spluttered—did anything but yell.

"So you rode on the luggage-rack behind the carriage, did you, *babuji?*" he smiled. "And curled under the apron to look like luggage when we passed the guard, eh?"

"But, my God, sahib!" said a plaintive voice. "Should I walk through Delhi naked? You, who wear pants, you laugh at me, but I assure you, sahib——"

"Hush!" ordered Warrington; and the babu seemed glad to hush.

"There was a note in a corner of that cloth of yours!"

"And the sahib found it? Oh, then I am relieved. I am preserved from pangs of mutual regret!"

"Why didn't you give that note to Colonel Kirby sahib when you had the chance? Eh?" asked Warrington, keeping firm hold of him.

"Sahib! Your honor! Not being yet remunerated on account of ring and verbal message duly delivered, commercial precedent was all on my side that I should retain further article of value pending settlement. Now, I ask you——"

"Where was Ranjoor Singh when he gave you that ring and message?" demanded Warrington, increasing his grip on the babu's fat arm.

"Sahib, when I have received payment for first service rendered, my disposition may be changed. I am as yet in condition of *forma pauperis.*"

Still holding him tight, Warrington produced twenty rupees in paper money. "Can you see those, *babuji*? See them? Then earn them!"

"Oh, my God, sahib, I have positivelee earned a lakh of rupees this night already!"

"Where was Risaldar-Major Ranjoor Singh when he——"

Footsteps were approaching—undoubtedly a guard on his way to investigate. The babu seemed to sense Warrington's impatience.

"Sahib," he said, "I am very meek person, having family of wife and children all dependent. Is that rupees twenty? I would graciously accept same, and positivelee hold my tongue!"

The steps came nearer.

"I was on my way to D Squadron quarters, sahib, to narrate story and pass begging bowl. Total price of story rupees twenty. Or else the sahib may deliver me to guard, and guard shall be regaled free gratis with full account of evening's amusement? Yes?"

The steps came nearer yet. Recognizing an officer, the men halted a few paces away.

"Sahib, for sum of rupees twenty I could hold tongue for twenty years, unless in meantime deceased, in which case——"

"Take 'em!" ordered Warrington; and the babu's fingers shut tight on the money.

"Guard!" ordered Warrington. "Put this babu out into the street!"

"Good night, sahib!" said the babu. "Kindlee present my serious respects to the colonel sahib. Salaam, sahib!"

But Warrington had gone into the darkness.

CHAPTER VIII.

So in a darkness that grew blacker every minute, Warrington swung his lantern and found his way toward D Squadron's quarters. He felt rather pleased with himself. From his own point of view he would have rather enjoyed to have a story anent himself and Yasmini go the round of barracks—with modifications, of course, and the kneeling part left out—but he realized that it would not do at all to have Colonel Kirby's name involved in anything of the sort, and he rather flattered himself on his tact in bribing the babu or being blackmailed by him.

"Got to admit that babu's quite a huntsman!" he told himself, beginning to hum. "One day, if the war doesn't account for me, I'll come back and take a fall out of that babu. Hallo—what's that? Who in thunder—who's waking up the horses at this unearthly hour? Sick horse, I suppose. Why don't they get him out and let the others sleep?"

He began to hurry. A light in stables close to midnight was not to be accounted for on any other supposition than an accident or serious emergency, and if there were either it was his affair as adjutant to know all the facts at once.

"What's going on in there?" he shouted in a voice of authority while he was yet twenty yards away. There was no answer. He could hear a horse plunge, but nothing more.

"Um-m-m! Horse cast himself!" he straightway decided.

But there was no cast horse, as he was aware the moment he had looked down both long lines of sleepy brutes that whickered their protest against interrupted sleep. At the far end he could see that two men labored, and a big horse fiercely resented their unseasonable attentions to himself. He walked down the length of the stable, and presently recognized Bagh, Ranjoor Singh's charger.

"What are you grooming him for at this hour?" he demanded.

"It is an order, sahib."

"Whose order?"

"Ranjoor Singh sahib's order."

"The deuce it is! When did the order come?"

"But now."

"Who brought it?"

"A babu, with a leather apron."

Warrington walked away ten paces in order to get command of himself, and pinch himself, and make quite sure he was awake.

"A fat babu?" he asked, walking back again.

"Very fat," said one of the troopers, continuing to brush the resentful charger.

"So he delivered his message first, and then went to hunt for his loin-cloth!" mused Warrington. "And he had enough intuition, and guts enough, to look for it first in the shay! I'm beginning to admire that man!" Aloud he asked the trooper: "What was the wording of the risaldar-major sahib's message?"

"'Let Bagh be well groomed and held ready against all contingencies!'" said the trooper.

"Then take him outside!" ordered Warrington. "Groom him where you won't disturb the other horses! How often have you got to be told that a horse needs sleep as much as a man? The squadron won't be fit to march a mile if you keep 'em awake all night! Lead him out quietly, now! Whoa, you brute! Now—take him out and keep him out—put him in the end stall in my stable when you've finished him—d'you hear?"

He flattered himself again. With all these mysterious messages and orders coming in from nowhere, he told himself it would be good to know at all times where Ranjoor Singh's charger was, as well as a service to Ranjoor Singh to stable the brute comfortably. He told himself that was a very smart move, and one for which Ranjoor Singh would some day thank him, provided, of course, that—

"Provided what?" he wondered half aloud. "Seems to me as if Ranjoor Singh has got himself into some kind of a scrape, and hopes to get out of it by the back-door route and no questions asked! Well, let's hope he gets out! Let's hope there'll be no court-martial nastiness! Let's hope—

oh, damn just hoping! Ranjoor Singh's a better man than I am. Here's believing in him! Here's to him, thick and thin! Forward—walk—march!"

He turned out the guard, and the particular troop sergeant with whom he wished to speak not being on duty, he ordered him sent for. Ten minutes later the sergeant came, still yawning, from his cot.

"Come over here, Arjan Singh," he called, thinking fast and furiously as he led the way.

If he made one false move or aroused one suspicion in the man's mind, he was likely to learn less than nothing; but if he did not appear to know at least something, he would probably learn nothing either.

As he turned, at a distance from the guard-room light, to face the sergeant, though not to meet his eyes too keenly, the fact that would not keep out of his brain was that the fat babu had been out in the road, offering to eat Germans, a little while before he and the colonel had started out that evening. And, according to what Brammle had told him when they met near the colonel's quarters, it was very shortly after that that the squadron came out of its gloom.

"What was the first message that the babu brought this evening?" he asked, still being very careful not to look into the sergeant's eyes. He spoke as comrade to comrade—a servant of the "Salt" to another servant of the "Salt."

"Which babu, sahib?" asked Arjan Singh, unblinking.

Now, in all probability, this man—since he had been asleep—knew nothing about the message to groom Bagh. To have answered, "The babu who spoke about the charger," might have been a serious mistake.

"Arjan Singh, look me in the eyes!" he ordered, and the Sikh obeyed. He was taller than Warrington, and looked down on him.

"Are you a true friend of the risaldar-major?"

"May I die, sahib, if I am not!"

"And I? What of me? Am I his friend or his enemy?"

The sergeant hesitated.

"Can I read men's hearts?" he asked.

"Yes!" said Warrington. "And so can I. That is why I had you called from your sleep. I sent for you to learn the truth. What was the message given by the fat babu to one of the guard by the outer gate this evening, and delivered by him or by some other man to D Squadron?"

"Sahib, it was not a written message."

"Repeat it to me."

"Sahib, it was verbal. I can not remember it."

"Arjan Singh, you lie! Did I ever lie to you? Did I ever threaten you and not carry out my threats—promise you and not keep my promise? I am a soldier! Are you a cur?"

"God forbid, sahib! I——"

"Arjan Singh! Repeat that message to me word for word, please, not as a favor, nor as obeying an order, but as a friend of Ranjoor Singh to a friend of Ranjoor Singh!"

"The message was to the squadron, not to me, sahib."

"Are you not of the squadron?"

"Make it an order, sahib!"

"Certainly not—nor a favor either!"

"Sahib, I——"

"Nor will I threaten you! I guarantee you absolute immunity if you refuse to repeat it. My word on it! I am Ranjoor Singh's friend, and I ask of his friend!"

"The babu said: 'Says Ranjoor Singh, "Let the squadron be on its best behavior! Let the squadron know that surely before the blood runs he will be there to lead it, wherever it is! Meanwhile, let the squadron be worthy of its salt and of its officers!"'"

"Was that all?" asked Warrington.

"All, sahib. May my tongue rot if I lie!"

"Thank you, Arjan Singh. That's all. You needn't mention our conversation. Good night."

"Fooled," chuckled Warrington. "She's fooled us to the limit of our special bent, and I take it that's stiff-neckedness!"

He hurried away toward Colonel Kirby's quarters, swinging his lantern and humming to himself.

"And this isn't the Arabian Nights!" he told himself. "It's Delhi—Twentieth Century A.D.! Gad! Wouldn't the whole confounded army rock with laughter!"

Then he stopped chuckling, to hurry faster, for a giant horn had rooted chunks out of the blackness by the barrack gate, and now what sounded like a racing car was tearing up the drive. The headlights dazzled him, but he ran and reached the colonel's porch breathless. He was admitted at once, and found the colonel with Brammle, facing an aide-de-camp. In the colonel's hand was a medium-sized, sealed envelope.

"Shall I repeat it, sir?" asked the aide-de-camp.

"Yes, if you think it necessary" answered Kirby.

"The sealed orders are not to be opened until out at sea. You are expected to parade at dawn the day after tomorrow, and there will be somebody from headquarters to act as guide for the occasion. In fact, you will be guided at each point until it is time to open your orders. No explanations will be given about anything until later on. That's all. Good night, sir—and good luck!"

The aide-de-camp held out his hand, and Colonel Kirby shook it a trifle perfunctorily; he was not much given to display of sentiment. The aide-de-camp saluted, and a minute later the giant car spurned the gravel out from under its rear wheels as it started off to warn another regiment.

"So we've got our route!" said Kirby.

"And, thank God, we take our own horses!" said Brammle fervently.

"Bet you a thousand the other end's Marseilles!" said Warrington. "We're in luck. They'd have mounted us on bus-horses if we hadn't brought our own; we'd have had to ring a bell to start and stop a squadron. Who wouldn't be light cavalry?"

Kirby put the sealed letter in an inside pocket.

"I'm going to sleep," said Brammle, yawning. "Night, sir!"

"Night!" said Kirby; but Warrington stayed on. He went and stood near the window, and when Kirby had seen Brammle to the door, he joined him there.

"What now, Warrington?"

"Caught 'em grooming Ranjoor Singh's charger in the dark!"

"Why?"

"Said it was an order from Ranjoor Singh!"

"I'm getting tired of this. I don't know what to make of it."

"That isn't nearly the worst, sir. Listen to this! Long before Yasmini promised us—before we knelt to save his life and honor—Ranjoor Singh had sent a message to his squadron guaranteein' to be with 'em before the blood runs! Specific guarantee, and no conditions!"

"Then——"

"Exactly, sir!"

"She fooled us, eh?"

"D'you suppose she's for or against the government, sir?"

"I don't know. Thank God we've got our marching orders! Go and wash your head! And, Warrington—hold your tongue!"

Warrington held up his right hand.

"So help me, sir!" he grinned, "But will she hold hers?"

CHAPTER IX.

Now, India is unlike every other country in the world in all particulars, and Delhi is in some respects the very heart through which India's unusualness flows. Delhi has five railway stations with which to cope with latter-day floods of paradoxical necessity; and nobody knew from which railway station troops might be expected to entrain or whither, although Delhi knew that there was war.

There did not seem to be anything very much out of the ordinary at any of the stations. In India one or two sidings are nearly always full of empty trains; there did not seem to be more of them than usual.

At the British barracks there was more or less commotion, because Thomas Atkins likes to voice his joy when the long peace breaks at last and he may justify himself; but in the native lines, where dignity is differently understood, the only men who really seemed unusually busy were the farriers, and the armorers who sharpened swords.

The government offices appeared to be undisturbed, and certainly no more messengers ran about than usual, the only difference was that one or two of them were open at a very early hour. But even in them—and Englishmen were busy in them—there seemed no excitement. Delhi had found time in a night to catch her breath and continue listening; for, unlike most big cities that brag with or without good reason, Delhi is listening nearly all the time.

A man was listening in the dingiest of all the offices on the ground floor of a big building on the side away from the street—a man in a drab silk suit, who twisted a leather watch-guard around his thumb and untwisted it incessantly. There was a telephone beside him, and a fair-sized pile of telegraph forms, but beyond that not much to show what his particular business might be. He did not look aggressive, but he seemed nervous, for he jumped perceptibly when the telephone-bell rang; and being a government telephone, with no commercial aims, it did not ring loud.

"Yes," he said, with the receiver at his ear. "Yes, yes. Who else? Oh, I forgot for the moment. Four, three, two, nine, two. Give yours! Very well, I'm listening."

Whoever was speaking at the other end had a lot to say, and none of it can have been expected, for the man in the drab silk suit twisted his wrinkled face and worked his eyes in expressions that began with displeasure and passed through different stages of surprise to acquiescence.

"I want you to know," he said, "that I got my information at first hand. I got it from Yasmini herself, from three of the hill-men who were present, and from the Afridi who was kicked and beaten. All except the Afridi, who wasn't there by that time, agreed that Ranjoor Singh had words with the German afterward. Eh? What's that?"

He listened again for about five minutes, and then hung up the receiver with an expression of mixed irritation and amusement.

"Caught me hopping on the wrong leg this time!" he muttered, beginning to twist at his watch-guard again.

Presently he sat up and looked bored, for he heard the fast trot of a big, long-striding horse. A minute later a dogcart drew up in the street, and he heard a man's long-striding footsteps coming round the corner.

"Like horse, like man, like regiment!" he muttered. "Pick his stride or his horse's out of a hundred, and"—he pulled out his nickel watch—"he's ten minutes earlier than I expected him! Morning, Colonel Kirby!" he said pleasantly, as Kirby strode in, helmet in hand. "Take a seat."

He noticed Kirby's scalp was red and that he smelt more than faintly of carbolic.

"Morning!" said Kirby.

"I'm wondering what's brought you," said the man in drab.

"I've come about Ranjoor Singh," said Kirby; and the man in drab tried to look surprised.

"What about him? Reconsidered yesterday's decision?"

"No," said Kirby. "I've come to ask what news you have of him." And Kirby's eye, that some men seemed to think so like a bird's, transfixed the man in drab, so that he squirmed as if he had been impaled.

"You must understand, Colonel Kirby—in fact, I'm sure you do un-derstand—that my business doesn't admit of confidences. Even if I wanted to divulge information, I'm not allowed to. I stretched a point yes-terday when I confided in you my suspicions regarding Ranjoor Singh, but that doesn't imply that I'm going to tell you all I know. I asked you what *you* knew, you may remember."

"I told you!" snapped Kirby. "Is Ranjoor Singh still under suspicion?"

That was a straight question of the true Kirby type that admitted of no evasion, and the man in drab pulled his watch out, knocking it on the desk absent-mindedly, as if it were an egg that he wished to crack. He must either answer or not, it seemed, so he did neither.

"Why do you ask?" he parried.

"I've a right to know! Ranjoor Singh's my wing commander, and a better officer or a more loyal gentleman doesn't exist. I want him! I want to know where he is! And if he's under a cloud, I want to know why! Where is he?"

"I don't know where he is," said the man in drab. "Is he—ah—absent without leave?"

"Certainly not!" said Kirby. "I've seen to that!"

"Then you've communicated with him?"

"No."

"Then if his regiment were to march without him——"

"It won't if I can help it!" said Kirby.

"And if you can't help it, Colonel Kirby?"

"In that case he has got what he asked for, and there can be no charge against him until he shows up."

"I understand you have your marching orders?"

"I have sealed orders!" snapped Kirby.

"To be opened at sea?"

"To be opened when I see fit!"

"Oh!"

"Yes," said Kirby. "Now, I asked you if Ranjoor Singh was still under suspicion!"

"My good sir, I am not the arbiter of Ranjoor Singh's destiny! How should I know?"

"I intend to know!" vowed Kirby, rising.

"I'm prepared to state that Ranjoor Singh is not in danger of arrest. I don't see that you have any right to ask more than that, Colonel Kirby. Martial law has been declared this morning, and things don't take their ordinary course any longer, you know."

Kirby paced once across the office floor, and once back again. Then he faced the man in drab as a duelist faces his antagonist.

"I don't like to go over men's heads," he said, "as you threatened to do to me, for instance, yesterday. If you will give me satisfactory assurance that Ranjoor Singh is being treated as a loyal officer should be, I will ask no more. If not, I shall go now to the general commanding. As you say, there's martial law now, he's the man to see."

"Colonel Kirby," said the man in drab, twisting at his watch-guard furiously, "if you'll tell me what's in your sealed orders—open them and see—I'll tell you what little I know about Ranjoor Singh, and we'll call it a bargain!"

"I wasn't joking," said Kirby, turning red as his scalp from the roots of his hair to his collar.

"I'm in deadly earnest!" said the man in drab.

So, without a word more, Colonel Kirby hurried out again, carrying his saber in his left hand at an angle that was peculiar to him, and that illustrated determination better than words could have done.

His huge horse plunged away almost before he had gained the seat, and, saber and all, he gained the seat at a step-and-a-jump. But the sais was not up behind, and Kirby had scarcely settled down to drive before the man in drab had the telephone mouthpiece to his lips and had given his mysterious number again—4-3-2-9-2.

"He's coming, sir!" he said curtly.

Somebody at the other end apparently asked, "Who is coming?" for the man in drab answered:

"Kirby."

Five minutes later Kirby caught a general at breakfast, and was received with courtesy and feigned surprise.

"D'you happen to know anything about my risaldar-major, Ranjoor Singh?" asked Kirby, after a hasty apology for bursting in.

"Why?"

"He was under suspicion yesterday—I was told so. Next he disap-

peared. Then I received a message from him asking me to assign him to
special duty; that was after I'd more than half believed him burned to
death in a place called the 'House-of-the-Eight-Half-brothers.' He has
sent some most extraordinary messages to his squadron by the hand of a
mysterious babu, but not a word of explanation of any kind. Can you tell
me anything about him, sir?"

"Wasn't a trooper of yours murdered yesterday?" the general asked.

"Yes," said Kirby.

"And another missing?"

"Yes, sir."

"Did Ranjoor Singh go off to search for the missing man?"

"I was told so."

"H-rrrr-ump! Well, I'm glad you came; you've saved me trouble! Did
you put Ranjoor Singh in Orders as assigned to special duty?"

"Yes."

"What is the missing trooper's name?"

"Jagut Singh."

"Well, please enter him in Orders, too."

"Special service?"

"Special service," said the general. "How about Ranjoor Singh's
charger?"

"I understand he's been kept well groomed by Ranjoor Singh's orders, and my adjutant tells me he has the horse in care in his own stable."

The general made a note.

"Whose stable?" he asked.

"Warrington's."

"Warrington, of Outram's Own, eh? Captain Warrington?"

The general wrote that down, while Kirby watched him bewildered.

"Well now, Kirby, that'll be all right Have the horse left there, will
you? I hope You've been able to dispose of your own horses to advantage.
Two chargers don't seem a large allowance for a commanding officer of a
cavalry regiment, but that's all you can take with you. You'll have to leave
the rest behind."

"Haven't given it a thought, sir! Too busy thinking about Ranjoor
Singh. Worried about him."

"Shouldn't worry!" said the general. "Ranjoor Singh's all right."

"That's the first assurance I've had of it, except by way of a mysterious note," said Kirby.

"By all right, I mean that he isn't in disgrace. But now about your horses and private effects. You've done nothing about them?"

"I'll have time to attend to that this afternoon, sir."

"Oh, no, you won't. That's why I'm glad you came! These"—he gave him a sealed envelope—"are supplementary orders, to be opened when you get back to barracks. I want you out of the way by noon if possible. We'll send a man down this morning to take charge of whatever any of you want kept, and you'd better tell him to sell the rest and pay the money to your bankers; he'll be a responsible officer. That's all. Goodbye, Kirby, and good luck!"

The general held out his hand.

"One more minute, sir," said Kirby. "About Ranjoor Singh!"

"What about him?"

"Well, sir—what about him?"

"What have you heard?"

"That—I've heard a sort of promise that he'll be with his squadron, to lead it, before the blood runs."

"Won't that be time enough?" asked the general, smiling. He was looking at Kirby very closely. "Not sick, are you?" he asked. "No? I thought your scalp looked rather redder than usual."

Kirby flushed to the top of his collar instantly, and the general pretended to arrange a sheaf of papers on the table.

"One reason why you're being sent first, my boy," said the general, holding out his hand again, "is that you and your regiment are fittest to be sent. But I've taken into consideration, too, that I don't want you or your adjutant killed by a cobra in any event. And—*snf*—*snf*—the salt sea air gets rid of the smell of musk quicker than anything. Goodbye, Kirby, my boy, and God bless you!"

"Goodbye, sir!"

Kirby stammered the words, and almost ran down the steps to his waiting dog-cart. As all good men do, when undeserved ridicule or blame falls on them, he wondered what in the world he could have done wrong.

He had no blame for anybody, only a fierce resentment of injustice—an almost savage sense of shame that any one should know about the adventure of the night before, and a rising sense of joy in his soldier's heart because he had orders in his pocket to be up and doing. So, and only so, could he forget it all.

He whipped up his horse and went down the general's drive at a pace that made the British sentry at the gate grin from ear to ear with whole-souled approval. He did not see a fat babu approach the general's bungalow from the direction of the bazaar. The babu salaamed profoundly, but Kirby's eyes were fixed on the road ahead, and his thoughts were deep in the future. He saw nothing except the road, until he took the last corner into barracks on one wheel, and drew up a minute later in front of the bachelor quarters that had sheltered him for the past four years.

"Pack! Campaign kit! One trunk!" he ordered his servant. "Orderly!"

An orderly ran in from outside.

"Tell Major Brammle and Captain Warrington to come to me!"

It took ten minutes to find Warrington, since every job was his, and nearly every responsibility, until his colonel should take charge of a paraded, perfect regiment, and lead it away to its fate. He came at last, however, and on the run, and Brammle with him.

"Orders changed!" said Kirby. "March at noon! Man'll be here this morning to take charge of officers' effects. Better have things ready for him and full instructions. One trunk allowed each officer. Two chargers."

"Destination, sir?" asked Brammle.

"Not disclosed!"

"Where do we entrain?" asked Warrington.

"We march out of Delhi," replied Kirby. "Entrain later, at a place appointed on the road."

Warrington began to hum to himself and to be utterly, consciously happy. "Then I'll get a move on!" he said, starting to hurry out. "Everything's ready, but——"

"Wait a minute!" commanded Kirby; and Warrington remained in the room after Brammle had left it.

"You haven't said anything to anybody, of course, about that incident last night?"

"No, sir."

"Then *she* has!"

Warrington whistled.

"Are you sure she has?"

"Quite. I've just had proof of it!"

"Makes a fellow reverence the sex!" swore Warrington.

"It'll be forgotten by the time we're back in India," said Kirby solemnly. "Remember to keep absolutely silent about it. The best way to help others forget it is to forget it yourself. Not one word now to anybody, even under provocation!"

"Not a word, sir!"

"All right. Go and attend to business!"

What "attending to business" meant nobody can guess who has not been in at the breaking up of quarters at short notice. Everything was ready, as Warrington had boasted, but even an automobile may "stall" for a time in the hands of the best chauffeur, and a regiment contains as many separate human equations as it has men in its ranks.

The amount of personal possessions that had to be jettisoned, or left to the tender mercies of a perfunctory agent, would have wrung groans from any one but soldiers. The last minute details that seemed to be no-body's job, and that, therefore, all fell to Warrington because somebody had to see to them, were beyond the imagination of any but an adjutant, and not even Warrington's imagination proved quite equal to the task.

"We're ready, sir!" he reported at last to Kirby. "We're paraded and waiting. Brammle's inspected 'em, and I've done ditto. There are only thir-teen thousand details left undone that I can't think of, and not one of 'em's important enough to keep us waitin'!"

So Kirby rode out on parade and took the regiment's salute. There was nobody to see them off. There were not even women to wail by the barrack gate, for they marched away at dinner-time and official lies had been distributed where they would do most good.

Englishman and Sikh alike rode untormented by the wails or waving farewells of their kindred; and there was only a civilian on a white pony, somewhere along ahead, who seemed to know that they were more than just parading. He led them toward the Ajmere Gate, and by the time that the regiment's luggage came along in wagons, with the little rear-guard last of all, it was too late to run and warn people. Outram's Own had gone at high noon, and nobody the wiser!

There was no music as they marched and no talking. Only the jingling bits and rattling hoofs proclaimed that India's best were riding on a sudden summons to fight for the "Salt." They marched in the direction least expected of them, three-quarters of a day before their scheduled time, and even "Guppy," the mess bull-terrier, who ran under the wagon with the officers' luggage, behaved as if all ends of the world were one to him. He waved his tail with dignity and trotted in content.

Hard by the Ajmere Gate they halted, for some bullock carts had claimed their centuries-long prerogative of getting in the way. While the bullocks, to much tail-twisting and objurgation, labored in the mud in every direction but the right one, Colonel Kirby sat his charger almost underneath the gate, waiting patiently. Then the advance-guard clattered off and he led along.

He never knew where it came from and he never tried to guess. He caught it instinctively, and kept it for the sake of chivalry, or perhaps because she had made him think for a moment of his mother. At all events, the bunch of jasmine flowers that fell into his lap found a warm berth under his buttoned tunic, and he rode on through the great gate with a kinder thought for Yasmini than probably she would guess.

With that resentment gone, he could ride now as suited him, with all his thoughts ahead, and there lacked then only one thing to complete his pleasure—he missed Ranjoor Singh.

It was not that the squadron would lack good leading. An English officer had taken Ranjoor Singh's place. It was the man he missed—the decent loyal gentleman who had worked untiringly to sweat a squadron into shape to Kirby's liking and never once presumed, nor had taken offense at criticism—the man who had been good enough to understand the ethics of an alien colonel, and to translate them for the benefit of his command. It is not easy for a Sikh to rise to the rank of major and lead a squadron for the Raj.

He counted Ranjoor Singh his friend, and he knew that Ranjoor Singh would have given all the rest of his life to ride away now for only one encounter on a foreign battle-field. Nothing, nothing less than the word of Ranjoor Singh himself, would ever convince him of the man's disloyalty. And he would have felt better if he could have shaken hands with Ranjoor Singh before going, since it seemed to be the order of the day that the Sikh should stay behind.

It did not seem quite the thing to be riding away to war with the best native officer in all India somewhere in Delhi on "special service"—whatever that might be.

He was given, as a rule, to smiling at any man who did his best. On any other day he would have very likely exchanged a joke with the bullock-man who labored so unavailingly to get the road cleared in a hurry. But today, since his thoughts were of Ranjoor Singh, he paid the man no attention; he had not even formed a mental picture of him by the time he passed the gate.

It was Warrington, cantering up from behind a minute or so later, who changed the color of the earth and sky.

"Did you recognize him, sir?"

"Whom?"

"Ranjoor Singh!"

"No! Where?"

"Not the bullock-man who blocked the road, but the man who ran out from behind the gate and straightened things out again. That man was Ranjoor Singh in mufti!"

"What makes you think so?"

"I recognized him. So did his squadron—look at them! They're riding like new men!"

Kirby looked, and there was no doubt about D Squadron.

"Is he there still?" he asked.

"I can see a man standing there—see him? Fellow in white between two bullock carts?"

Kirby pulled out to the roadside and let the regiment pass him. Then he cantered back. The man between the bullock carts had his back turned, and was gazing toward Delhi under his hand.

"Ranjoor Singh!" said Kirby, reining suddenly. "Is that you?"

"Uh?" The man faced about. He was no more Ranjoor Singh than he was Colonel Kirby.

"Where's the man who came from behind the gate to clear the road?"

The man pointed toward the gate. Inside, within the gloom of the gate itself, Kirby was certain he saw a Sikh who stood at the salute. He cantered to the gate, for he would have given a year's pay for word with Ranjoor Singh. But when he reached the gate the man was gone.

"And he promised he'd be there to lead his squadron when the blood runs," wondered Kirby.

CHAPTER X.

Ranjoor Singh; on the trail of a murderer, shoved with his whole strength against a little door of the House-of-the-Eight-Half-brothers. It yielded suddenly. He shot in headlong, and the door slammed behind him. As he fell forward into pitch blackness he was conscious of shooting bolts behind and of the squeaking of a beam swung into place.

But, having served the Raj for more years than he wanted to remember, through three campaigns in the Himalayas, once against the Masudis, and once in China, he was in full possession of trained soldier senses. Darkness, he calculated instantly, was a shield to him who can use it, and a danger only to the unwary; and there are grades of wariness, just as there are grades of sloth.

Two men who thought themselves so wide awake as to be beyond the reach of government, each threw a noosed rope, and caught each other. Ranjoor Singh could not see the ropes, but he could hear the stifled swearing and the ensuing struggle; and an ear is as good as an eye in the dark.

Something—he never knew what—warned him to duck and step forward. He felt the whistle of a club that missed him by so little as to make the skin twitch on the back of his neck. His right leg shot sidewise, and he tripped a man. In another second he had the club, and there was no measurable interval of time then before the darkness was a living miracle of blows that came from everywhere and missed nothing.

Three men went down, and Ranjoor Singh was in command of a situation whose wherefore and possibilities he could not guess until an electric torch declared itself some twenty feet away, at more than twice his height, and he stood vignetted in a circle of white light.

"The sahib proves a gentle guest!" purred a voice he thought he recognized. It was a woman's. "Has the sahib a pistol with him?"

Ranjoor Singh, cursing his own neglect of soldierly precaution, saw fit not to answer. A human arm reached like a snake into the ring of light. He struck at it with the club, and a groan announced that he had struck hard enough.

"Does the sahib think that the noise of a pistol would cause his friends to come? Is Ranjoor Singh ashamed? Speak, sahib! Is it well to break into a house and be surly with the hostess?"

Ranjoor Singh stepped backward, and the ring of light followed him, until he stood pressed against the teak door and could feel the heavy beam that ran up and down it, locked firmly above and below. He prodded over his head behind him with the club, trying to find what held the beam, and the ring of light lifted a foot or two, then five feet, until its center was on the center of the club's handle.

A pistol cracked and flashed then, from behind the light, and the club splintered. He dropped it, and the torch-light ceased, leaving him dazed, but not so dazed that he did not hear a man sneak up and carry the splintered club away. He followed after the man, for he knew now that he was in a narrow passage and no man could get by him to attack from behind.

But again the torch-light sought him out. Half-way to the foot of steep stairs that he could dimly outline he halted, for advance against hidden pistol-fire and dazzling light was futile.

"Look!" said the same soft, woman's voice. "Look, sahib! See, Ranjoor Singh! The hooded death! See the hooded death behind you!"

It was not her command that made him look. He knew better than to turn his head at an unseen woman's bidding in the dark. But he heard them hiss, and he turned to see four cobras come toward him, with the front third of their bodies raised from the floor and their hoods extended. He saw that a panel in the wooden wall had slid, and the last snake's tail was yet inside the gap. There was no need of a man to slip between him and the door!

"There are more in the wall, Ranjoor Singh! Will they follow thee upstairs? See, they come! Step swiftly, for the hooded death is swift!"

The light went out again, and his ears were all he had to warn him of the snakes' approach—ears and imagination. Swift as a well launched charge of light cavalry, he leaped for the stairs and took them four at a time. He reached the top one sooner than he knew it. The torch flashed in his eyes, and he saw a pistol-mouth just beyond arm-reach.

"Stand, Ranjoor Singh!" said a voice that he felt sure he recognized. His eyes began to search beyond the light for glimpses of dim outline.

"Back, Ranjoor Singh! Back to the right—toward that door! In, through that door—so!"

He obeyed, since he knew now with whom he had to deal. There was no sense at all in taking liberties with Yasmini. He stepped into a bare, dark, teak-walled room, and she followed him, and she had scarcely closed the door at her back before another door opened at the farther end, and two of her maids appeared, carrying candle-lamps.

"What do you want with me?" demanded Ranjoor Singh.

"Nay! Did I invite the sahib?"

"I came about a murderer who entered by that door through which I came."

"To pay him the reward, perhaps?" she asked impudently.

"Is this thy house?" asked Ranjoor Singh.

"This is the House-of-the-Eight-Half-brothers, sahib."

"This is a hole where murderers hide! A man of mine was slain in the street below, and the murderer came in here. Where is he now?"

"He and the fool who followed him," said Yasmini, poising herself like a nodding blossom and smiling like the promise of new love, as she paused to be insolent and let the insolence sink home, "are at my mercy!"

Ranjoor Singh did not answer, but she could draw no amusement from his silence, for his eye was unafraid.

"I am from the North, where the quality of mercy is thought weakness," she smiled sweetly.

"Who asks mercy? I was seen and heard to enter. There will be a hundred seeking me within an hour!"

"Sahib, within two hours there will be five thousand around this house, yet none will seek to enter! And they will find no murderer, though thou shalt see thy murderer. Come this way, sahib."

A whiff of warm wind might have blown her, so swiftly, lissomely she ran toward the other door, laughing back at him across her shoulder and leaving a trail of aromatic scent. The two maids held their candle-lanterns high, and, striding like a soldier, Ranjoor Singh followed Yasmini, not caring that the maids shut the heavy door behind him and bolted it. He argued to himself that he was as safe in one room as in another, and she as dangerous; also, that it made no difference in which room he might be when the squadron or his colonel missed him.

"Look, Ranjoor Singh! Look through that hole!"

There was plenty of light in this room, for there was a lantern in every corner. He could see that she was gazing through a hole in the wall at something that amused her, and she motioned to another hole eight feet away from it. He crossed a floor that was solid and age-old; no two planks of it were of even width or length, but none creaked.

At her invitation he looked through the little square hole she pointed out. And then, for the first time, he confessed surprise.

"Thou, Jagut Singh!" he exclaimed.

He stepped back, blinked to reassure himself, and stepped to the hole again. Back to back, tied right hand to right, left hand to left, so that their arms were crossed behind them, and lashed waist to waist, a trooper of D Squadron and the Afridi whom lie had kicked at Yasmini's sat on the floor facing opposite walls. Dumb misery was stamped on the Sikh's face, the despair of evaporated savagery on the Afridi's.

"Jagut Singh!" said the risaldar-major, louder this time; and the trooper looked up, almost as if hope had been that instant born in him. Then he grinned. A white row of ivory showed between his black beard and mustache. He tried to look sidewise, but the rope that held him tight to the Afridi hurt his neck.

"I knew it, sahib!" he shouted. "I knew that one would come for me! This hill wildcat has fought until the ropes cut both of us; but take time, sahib! I can wait. Attend to the duty first. Only let him who comes bring water with him, for this is a thirsty place!"

Ranjoor Singh looked sidewise. He could see that Yasmini was absorbed in contemplation of her prisoners. Her little lithe form was pressed tightly against the wall, less than two yards away. He could guess, and he had heard a dozen times, that dancing had made her stronger than a panther and more swift. Yet he thought that if he had her in his arms he could crush those light ribs until she would yield and order her prisoner released. The trooper's confidence deserved immediate, not postponed, reward.

He watched for a minute. He could see that her bosom rose and fell regularly against the woodwork; she was all unconscious of her danger, he was sure of it. He changed his position, and she neither looked nor moved. He changed it again, so that his weight was all on his left foot; he was sure she had not noticed. Then he sprang.

He sprang sidewise, as a horse does that sees a snake by the roadside, every nerve and sinew keyed to the tightest pitch—eye, ear and instinct working together. And she, in the same second, turned to meet him smiling, with outstretched arms, as if she would meet him half-way and hug him to her bosom, only she stepped a pace backward, instead of forward as she had seemed to intend.

He landed where he had meant to, on the spot where she had stood. His left hand clutched at the wall, and a second too late he made a wild grab at the hole she had peered through, trying to get his fingers into it. What she had done he never knew, but the floor she had stood on yielded, and he heard her laugh as he slipped through the opening like a tiger into a pit-trap, and fell downward into blackness.

With a last tremendous effort he caught at the floor and held himself suspended by his finger-ends. But she came and trod on them, and though her weight was light, malice made her skillful, and she hurt him until he had to set his teeth and drop.

"Forget not thy trooper in his need!" she called, as he fell away through the opening. And then the trap shut.

To his surprise he did not fall very far, and though he landed on an elbow and a hip, he struck so softly that for a moment he believed he must be mad, or dead, or dreaming. Then his fingers, numb from Yasmini's pressure, began to recognize the feel of gunny-bags, and of cotton-wool, and of paper. Also, he smelled kerosene or something very like it.

"Forget not the water for thy trooper, Ranjoor Singh!"

He looked up to see Yasmini's face framed in the opening, and he thought there was more devilment expressed in it, for all her loveliness, than in her voice that never quite lost its hint of laughter. He did not answer, and the trap-door closed again.

He knelt and began to grope through the dark on hands and knees, but gave that up presently because the dust from old sacks and piles of rubbish began to choke him. Then rats came to investigate him. He heard several of them scamper close, and one bit his leg; so he made ready to fight for his life against the worst enemy a man may have, praying a little in the Sikh way, that does not reckon God to be far off at any time.

Suddenly the trap-door opened, and the rats scampered away from the light and noise.

"Thus is a soldier answered!" muttered Ranjoor Singh.

"Is the risaldar-major sahib thirsty?" wondered Yasmini.

He could hear her pouring water out of a brass ewer into a dish, and pouring it back again. The metal rang and the water splashed deliriously, but Ranjoor Singh was not very thirsty yet; he had been thirstier on parade a hundred times.

When her head and shoulders darkened the aperture, he did not trouble this time to look at her.

"Is it dark down there?" she asked him; but he did not answer.

So she struck a match and lit a newspaper. In a moment a ball of fire was floating downward to him, and it was then that the smell of dust and kerosene entered his consciousness as pincers enter the flesh of men in torment. He stood up with hands upstretched to catch the fire—caught it—bore it downward—and smothered it in gunny-bags.

"Still dark?" she said, looking through the aperture once more. "I will send another one!"

So Ranjoor Singh found his tongue and cursed her with a force and comprehensiveness that only Asia can command; he gave her to understand that the next fire she dropped on him should be allowed to work God's will and burn her—her, her rats, her cobras, and her cutthroats. Two honest Sikhs, he swore, would die well to such an end.

"Drop thy fire and I will fan the flame!" he vowed.

"I will send my cobras down to keep the sahib company!" she mocked.

But Ranjoor Singh proposed to take one danger at a time, and he was quite sure that she wanted him alive, not dead, for otherwise he would have been dead already. He held his tongue and listened while she splashed the water.

"Thy trooper is very thirsty, sahib!"

She was on a warmer scent now, for that squadron of his and the men of his squadron were the one love of his warrior life. Some spirit of malice whispered her as much.

"The trooper shall have water when Ranjoor Singh sahib has promised on his Sikh honor."

"Promised what?" His voice betrayed interest at last; it suggested future possibilities instead of a grim present.

"That he will do what is required of him!"

"Is that the price of a drink for Jagut Singh?"

"Aye! Will the sahib pay, or will he let the trooper parch?"

"Ask Jagut Singh! Go, ask him! Let it be as he answers!"

He could hear her hurry away, although she slammed the trap-door shut. Evidently she was not satisfied to speak through the little hole, and he suspected that she was showing the man water, perhaps giving some to the Afridi for sweet suggestion's sake. She was back within five minutes, and by the way she opened the trap and grinned at him he knew what her answer would be.

"He begs that you promise! He begs, sahib! He says he is thy trooper, thy dog, thy menial, and very thirsty!"

"Bring some one who knows better how to lie!" said Ranjoor Singh. "I *know* what his answer was! He said, 'Say to the risaldar-major sahib that I have eaten salt, but I am not thirsty!' Go, tell him his answer was a good one, and that I know he said it! I know that man, as men know each other. Thou art a woman, and thy knowledge is but emptiness. Thou hast heard now twice what the answer is, once from him and once from me!"

"I will leave thee to the rats!" she said, slamming the trap-door tight.

The rats came, and he began to grope about for a weapon to use against them. He caught one rat in his fingers, squeezed the squealing brute to death and flung it away, and he heard a hundred of its messmates race to devour the carcass.

He began to see little active eyes around him in the blackness, that watched his every movement, and he kept moving since that seemed to puzzle them. Also he wondered, as a drowning man might wonder about things, how long it would be before Colonel Kirby would send for him to ask about the murdered trooper. Something would happen then, he felt quite sure.

The rats by this time had grown very daring, and he had been bitten again twice; he found time to wonder what lies Yasmini would tell to account for her share in things. Ranjoor Singh did not doubt she would lie herself out of it, but he wondered just how, along what unexpected line. It began to seem to him that the colonel and his squadron were a very long time coming.

"But they will come!" he assured himself.

He was nearer to the mark when he expected unexpectedness from Yasmini, for she did not disappoint him. A door opened at one end of the black dark cellar, and again the rats scampered for cover as Yasmini herself stood framed in it, with a lantern above her head. She was alone, and he could not see that she had any weapon.

"This way, sahib!" she called sweetly to him.

Never—North, South, East or West, in olden days or modern—did a siren call half so seductively. Every move she ever made was poetry expressed, but framed in a golden aura shed by the lamp, and swaying in the velvet blackness of the pit's mouth, she was, it seemed to Ranjoor Singh, as no man had ever yet seen woman.

"Come, sahib!" she called again; and he moved toward her.

"Food and water wait! Thy trooper has drunk his fill. Come, sahib!"

She made no move at all to protect herself from him. She did not lead into the cavern beyond the door. She waited, leaning against the door-post, smiling as if they were old friends who understood each other.

"I but tried thee, Ranjoor Singh!" she smiled, looking up into his face and holding the lantern closer to his eyes, as if she would read behind them. "Thou art a soldier, and not a buffalo at all! I am sorry that I called thee buffalo. My heart goes out ever to a brave man, Ranjoor Singh!"

He was actually at her side, her clothes touched his, and he could have flung his arms around her. But it was the move next after that which seemed obscure. He wondered what her reply would be; and, moving the lantern a little, she read the hesitation in his eyes—the wavering between desire for vengeance, a soldierly regard for sex, and mistrust of her apparent helplessness. And, being Yasmini, she dared him.

"Like swords I have seen!" she laughed. "Two cutting edges and a point! Not to be held save by the hilt, eh, Ranjoor Singh? Search me for weapons first, and then use that dagger in thy hair—I am unarmed!"

"Lead on!" he commanded in a voice that grated harshly, for it needed all his willpower to prevent his self-command from giving out. He knew that behind temptation of any kind there lie the iron teeth of unexpected consequences.

She let the lantern swing below her knees and leaned back to laugh at him, until the cavern behind her echoed as if all the underworld had seen and was amused.

"I called thee a buffalo!" she panted. "Nay, I was very wrong! I laugh at my mistake! Come, Ranjoor Singh!"

With a swing of the lantern and a swerve of her lithe body, she slipped out of his reach and danced down an age-old hewn-stone passage, out of which doors seemed to lead at every six or seven yards; only the doors were all made fast with iron bolts so huge that it would take two men to manage them.

He hurried after her. But the faster he followed the faster she ran, until it needed little imagination to conceive her a will-o'-the-wisp and himself a crazy man.

"Come!" she kept calling to him. "Come!"

And then she commenced to sing, as if dark passages beneath the Delhi streets were a fit setting for her skill and loveliness. Ranjoor Singh had never heard the song before. It was about a tiger who boasted and fell into a trap. It made him more cautious than he might have been, and when the darkness began to grow less opaque he slowed into a walk. Then he stood still, for he could not see her any longer.

It occurred to him to turn back. But that thought had not more than crossed his mind when a noose was pulled tight around his legs and a big sheet, thrown out of the darkness, was wrapped and wrapped about him until he could neither shout nor move. He knew that they were women who managed the sheet, because he bit one's finger through it and she screamed. Then he heard Yasmini's voice close to his ear.

"Thy colonel sahib and another are outside!" she whispered. "It is not well to wait here, Ranjoor Singh!"

Next he felt a great rush of air, and after that the roar of flame was so unmistakable—although he could feel no heat yet—that he wondered whether he was to be burned alive.

"Is it well alight?" asked Yasmini.

"Yes!" said a maid whose teeth chattered.

"Good! Presently the fools will come and pour water enough to fill this passage. Thus none may follow us! Come!"

Ranjoor Singh was gathered up and carried by frightened women— he could feel them tremble. For a moment he felt the outer air, and he caught the shout of a crowd that had seen flames. Then he was thrown face downward on the floor of some sort of carriage and driven away.

He lost all sense of direction after a moment, though he did not forget to count, and by his rough reckoning he was driven through the streets for about nine minutes at a fast trot. Then the carriage stopped, and he was carried out again, up almost endless stairs, across a floor that seemed yet more endless, and thrown into a corner.

He heard a door slam shut, and almost at the same moment his fingers, that had never once ceased working, tore a corner of the sheet loose.

In another minute he was free.

He threw the sheet from him and looked about, accustoming his eyes to darkness. Presently, not far from him, he made out the sheeted figure of another man, who lay exactly as he had done and worked with tired fingers. He drew the dagger out of his hair and cut the man loose.

"Jagut Singh!" he exclaimed.

The trooper stood up and saluted.

"Who brought thee here?"

"Women, sahib, in a carriage!"

"When?"

"Even now!"

"Where is that Afridi?"

"Dead, sahib!"

"How?"

"She brought us water in a brass vessel, saying it was by thy orders, sahib. She cut us loose and gave him water first. Then, while she gave me to drink the Afridi attacked her, and I slew him with my hands, tearing his throat out—thus! While the life yet fluttered in him they threw a sheet over me—and here I am! Salaam, sahib!"

The trooper saluted again.

"Who made thee prisoner in the first place?"

"Hillmen, sahib, at the orders of the Afridi who is now dead. They made ready to torture me, showing me the knives they would use. But she came, and they obeyed her, binding the Afridi fast to me. After that I heard the sahib's voice, and then this happened. That is all, sahib."

"Well!" said Ranjoor Singh. And for the third time his trooper saw fit to salute him.

CHAPTER XI.

Men say Yasmini does not sleep. Of course, that is absurd. None the less, it is certain she must do much of her plotting in the daytime, for by night, until after midnight, she is always the Yasmini whom the Northern gentry know, at home to all comers in her wonderful apartment.

It is ever a mystery to them how she knows all that is going on in Delhi, and in India, and in the greater outer world, although they themselves bring her information that no government could ever suck out of the silent hills. They know where she keeps her cobras—where the strong-box is, in which her jewels lie crowded—who run her errands—and some of her past history, for not even a mongoose is more inquisitive than a man born in the hills, and Yasmini has many maids. But none—not even her favorite, most confidential maids—know what is in the little room that she reaches down a private flight of stairs that have a steel door at the top.

She keeps the key to that steel door, and it has, besides, a combina-tion lock that only she understands.

Once a very clever hillman, who had been south for an education and had learned skepticism in addition to the rule of three, undertook to discover wires leading over roof-tops to that room; but he searched for a week and did not find them. When his search was over, and all had done laughing at him, he was found one night with a knife-wound between his shoulder-blades, and, later still, Yasmini sang a song about him. None searched for wires after that, and the consensus of opinion still is that she makes magic in the room below-stairs.

She sought that room the minute Ranjoor Singh was safely locked in with his trooper, although her maids reported more than one Northern gentleman waiting impatiently in the larger of her two reception-rooms for official information of the war. Government bulletins are regarded as pure fiction always, unless confirmed by Yasmini.

And, within five minutes of Ranjoor Singh's release of his trooper from the sheet, no less a personage than a general officer had thrown aside other business and had drawn on a cloak of secrecy that not even his own secretary could penetrate.

"Closed carriage!" he ordered; and, as though the fire brigade were doing double duty, a carriage came, and the horses, rump-down, halted from the gallop outside his door.

"Pathan turban!" he ordered; and his servant brought him one.

"Sheepskin cloak!"

In a moment the upper half of him would have passed in the dark for that of a rather portly Northern trader. He decided that a rug would do the rest, and snatched one as he ran for the carriage with the turban under his arm. He gave no order to the driver other than "Cheloh!" and that means "Go ahead"; so the driver, who was a Sikh, went ahead as the guns go into action, asway and aswing, regardless of everything but speed.

"Yasmini's!" said the general, at the end of a hundred yards; and the Sikh took a square, right-angle turn at full gallop with a neatness the Horse Artillery could not have bettered. There seemed to be no need of further instructions, for the Sikh pulled up unbidden at the private door that is to all appearance only a mark on the dirty-looking wall.

With a rug around his middle, there shot out then what a watching small boy described afterward as "a fat hill-rajah on his way to be fleeced." The carriage drove on, for coachmen who wait outside Yasmini's door are likely to be butts for questions. The door opened without any audible signal, and the man with the rug around his middle disappeared.

He had ceased to bear any resemblance to any one but a stout English general in mess-dress by the time he reached the dark stairhead; and Yasmini took the precaution of being there alone to meet him. She held, a candle-lantern.

"Whom have you?" he demanded.

They seemed to understand each other—these two. He paid her no compliments, and she expected none; she made no attempt at all to flatter him or deceive him. But, being Yasmini, it did not lie in her to answer straightly.

"I set a trap and a buffalo blundered into it! He will do better than any other!"

"Whom have you?"

"Risaldar-Major Ranjoor Singh!"

The general whistled softly.

"Of the Sikh Light Cavalry?" he asked.

"One of Kirby sahib's officers, and a trooper into the bargain!"

The general whistled again.

"There were two troopers whom I meant to catch," she said hurriedly, for it was evident that the general did not at all approve of the turn affairs had taken. "I had a trap for them at the House-of-the-Eight-Half-brothers, and some hillmen in there ready to rush out and seize them as they passed. But a fool Afridi murdered one, and I only got there in the nick of time to save the other's life. I meant that Ranjoor Singh, who is a buffalo, should be troubled about his troopers and suspected on his own account, for he and I have a private quarrel. I did not mean to catch him, or make use of him. But he walked into the trap. What shall be done with him? Let the sahib say the word and——"

Her gesture was inimitable. Not so the gurgle that she gave, for a man's breath bubbling through the blood of a slit throat makes the same shuddersome sound exactly. The general took no notice whatever of that, for wise men of the West understand the East's attempts to scandalize them. It is the everlasting amusement of Yasmini, and a thousand others, to pretend that the English are even more blood careless than themselves, just as it is their practice to build confidently on the opposite fact.

"Did *you* fire the House-of-the-Eight-Half-brothers?" asked the general suddenly. "Am I a sweeper?" she retorted.

"Did you order it done?"

"Did Jumna rise when the rain came? There were six good cobras of mine burned alive, to say nothing of the bones of a dead Afridi! Nay, sahib, I ordered a clear trail left from there to here, connecting me and thee and Ranjoor Singh to the Germans and a dog of an Afridi murderer. I left a trail that even the police could follow!"

"Whose property is that house?"

"Whose? Ask the lawyers! They have fought about it in the courts until lawyers own every stick and stone of it, and now the lawyers fight one another! The government will spend a year now," she laughed, "seeking whom to fine for the fire. It will be good to see the lawyers run to cover!"

"This is a bad business!" said the general sternly; and he used two words in the native tongue that are thirty times more expressive of badness as applied to machinations than are the English for them. "The plan was to kidnap a trooper, or two troopers—to tempt him, or them—and, should they prove incorruptible, to give them certain work to do. And what have you done?"

Yasmini laughed at him—merry, mocking laughter that stung him because it was so surely genuine. She did not need to tell him in words that she was not afraid of him; she could laugh in his face and make the truth sink deeper.

"And now what will the *burra* sahib do?" she mocked. "There is war—a great war—a war of all the world—but Yasmini fired a rat-run and avenged a murdered Sikh. First let us punish Yasmini! Shall I send for police to arrest me, *burra* sahib? Or shall I send a maid in search of babu Sita Ram that the game may continue?"

"What do you want Sita Ram for?"

"Sita Ram is nearly always useful, sahib. He is on a message now. He is a fool who likes to meddle where he *thinks* none notice him. Such are the sort who cost least and work the longest hours. Who, for instance, sahib, is to balk Kirby sahib when he grows suspicious and begins to search in earnest for his Ranjoor Singh? He knew that Ranjoor Singh was at the House-of-the-Eight-Half-brothers; there was a man on watch outside. He will come here next, for Ranjoor Singh has been reported to him as having talked with Germans in my house."

"Reported by whom?"

"By the Afridi who is now dead."

"Who killed the Afridi?"

"Does the *burra* sahib think I killed him?"

"I asked a question!" snapped the general.

"In the first place, then, Ranjoor Singh, the buffalo, struck the Afridi with his foot. The Afridi, who was a dog with yellow teeth, went outside to sing sweet compliments to Ranjoor Singh. Certain Sikhs heard him— of whom one was the trooper who waits in another room with Ranjoor Singh—and they beat him nearly to death because, being buffaloes themselves, they love Ranjoor Singh, who is the greatest buffalo of all.

"For revenge, the Afridi told tales of Ranjoor Singh, and later knifed one Sikh trooper who had beaten him. The other trooper followed him into the House-of-the-Eight-Half-brothers, where he soon had opportunity for vengeance. Now the *burra* sahib knows all. Is it not a sweet love-story! Now the *burra* sahib may arrest everybody, and all will be well!"

"Where did Ranjoor Singh kick the Afridi?"

"Here—in my house!"

"Then he was here?"

"How else would he kick the man here? Could he send his foot by messenger?"

"Was the German here? Did he have word with the German?"

"Surely. He spoke with him alone. So the Afridi reported him to the 'Rat sahib.'"

The general frowned. However deeply the military may intrigue, they neither like nor profess to like civilians who play the same game.

"If Ranjoor Singh is under suspicion, what is the use of——"

"Oh, all men are alike!" jeered Yasmini, holding up the light and looking more impudent than the general had ever seen her—and he had seen her often, for most of his private information about the regions north of the Himalayas had come through her in one way or another, and often enough from her lips direct. "I have said that Ranjoor Singh is a buffalo! He was born a buffalo—he has been trained to be one by the British— he likes to be one—and he will die one, with a German bullet in his belly, unless this business prove too much for him and he dies of fretting before he can get away to fight!

"I—look at me, sahib! I have tempted Ranjoor Singh, and he did not yield a hair! I stood closer to him than I am to you, and his pulse beat no faster! All he thought of was whether he could crush me and make me give up my prisoner.

"Ranjoor Singh is a buffalo of buffaloes—a Jat buffalo of no imag- ination and no sense. He is buffalo enough to love the British Raj and his squadron of Jat farmers with all his stupid Sikh heart! There *could* not be a better for the purpose than this Ranjoor Singh! He is stupid enough, and nearly blunt enough, to be an Englishman. He is just of the very cal- iber to fool a German! Trust me, sahib—I, who picked the man who——"

"That'll do!" said the general; and Yasmini laughed again like the tinkling of a silver bell.

There came then a soft rap on the door. It opened about six inches, and a maid whispered.

"Wait!" ordered Yasmini. "Come through! Wait here!" She pulled the maid through the door to the little back stair-head landing. "Did you hear?" she hissed excitedly. "She says Kirby sahib has come, and another with him!"

She was twitching with excitement. Her fingers clutched the general's sleeve, and he found himself thinking of his youth. He released her fingers gently and she spared a giggle for him.

"Bad business!" said the general again. "Kirby will ask questions and go away; but the troopers of Ranjoor Singh's squadron will come later, and they will not go away in such a hurry. You can fool Colonel Kirby sahib, but you can not fool a hundred troopers!"

"No?" she purred. She had done thinking and was herself again, impudent and artful. "I can fool anybody, and any thousand men! I have sent Sita Ram already with a message to the troopers of Ranjoor Singh's squadron. The message was supposed to be from him, and it was worded just as he would have worded it. Presently Sita Ram will come back, when he has helped himself to payment. Then I can send him with yet another message.

"Go and put thoughts into the buffalo's head, General sahib, and be quick! There must be a message—a written message from Ranjoor Singh to Kirby sahib—and a token—forget not the token, in proof that the writing is not forged! Forget not the token. There must surely be a token!"

She pushed the general forward down a passage, through a series of doors, and down another passage—halted him while she fitted a strange native key into a lock—opened another door, and pushed him through. Then she ran back to her maid.

"Send somebody to find Sita Ram! Bid him hurry! When he comes, put him in the small room next the cobras, and let him be shown the cobras until fear of too much talking has grown greater in him than the love of being heard! Then let me see him in a mirror, so that I may know when it is time. Have cobras in a hair-noose ready, close behind where the sahibs sit, and watch through the hangings for my signal! Both sahibs will kneel to me. Then watch for another signal, and let all lights be blown out instantly! Or, if the sahibs do not kneel (though they *shall!*), then watch yet more closely for a signal which I will give to extinguish lights.

"So—now, go! Am I beautiful? Are my eyes bright? Twist me that jasmine in my hair—so. Very good. Now run—I will surprise them through the hangings!"

So Yasmini surprised Kirby and his adjutant, as has been told, and it need not be repeated how she humbled the pride of India's army on their knees. She would have to forego the delight of being Yasmini before she could handle any situation or plan any coup along ordinary lines, and Kirby and his adjutant were not the first Englishmen, nor likely to be the last, to feed her merriment.

The general, for his part, had—even although pushed without ceremony through a door—behaved with perfect confidence, for he knew that, whatever her whim or her sense of humor, or her impudence, Yasmini would not fail him in the pinch. Even she, whose jest it is to see men writhe under her hand, has to own somebody her master, and though she would giggle at the notion of fearing any one man, or any dozen, she does fear the representative of what she and perhaps a hundred others call "The Game." For the night, and for the place, the general was that representative, and however much he might disapprove, he had no doubt of her.

Ranjoor Singh stood aghast at sight of him, and the trooper saluted like an automaton, since nothing save obedience was any affair of his.

"Evening, Risaldar-Major!" smiled the general.

"Salaam, General sahib!"

"To save time, I will tell you that I know stage by stage just how you got here."

Ranjoor Singh looked suspicious. For five-and-twenty years he had watched British justice work, and British justice gives both sides a hearing; he had not told his own version yet.

"I know that you have had word in another part of this house with a German, who pretends to be a merchant but who is really a spy."

Ranjoor Singh looked even more suspicious. The charge was true, though, so he did not answer.

"Your being brought to this house was part of a plan—part of the same plan that leaves the German still at liberty. You are wanted to take further part in it."

"General sahib, am I an officer of the Raj or am I dreaming?"

Ranjoor Singh had found his tongue at last, and the general noted with keen pleasure that eye, voice and manner were angry and unafraid.

"I command a squadron, sahib, unless I have been stricken mad! Since when is a squadron commander brought face-downward in a carriage out of rat-traps by a woman to do a general's bidding? That has been my fate tonight. Now I am wanted to take further part! Is my honor not yet dirtied enough, General sahib? I will take no further part. I refuse to obey! I order this trooper not to obey. I demand court martial!"

"I see I'd better begin with an apology," smiled the general! He was not trying to pretend he felt comfortable.

"Nay, sahib! I would accept no apology. It must first be proved to me that he, who tells me I am wanted to take further part in this rat-hole treachery, is not a traitor to the Raj! I have read of generals turning traitors! I have read about Napoleon; I know how his generals behaved when the sand in his glass seemed run. I am for the Raj in this and in any other hour! I refuse to obey or to accept apology! Let the explanation be made me at court martial, with Colonel Kirby sahib present to bear witness to my character!"

"As you were!"

The general's eyes met those of the Sikh officer, and neither could have told then, or at any other time, what exactly it was that each man recognized.

"Ranjoor Singh, when I entered this house ten minutes ago I had no notion I should find you here. I have served the same 'Salt' with you, on the same campaigns. I even wear the same medals. In the same house I am entitled to the same credit.

"I am here on urgent business for the Raj, and you are here owing to a grave mistake, which I admit and for which I tender you the most sincere apology on behalf of the government, but which I can not alter. I expected to find a trooper here, not necessarily of your regiment, who should have been waylaid and tempted beyond any doubt as to his trustworthiness.

"I received a message that Yasmini had two absolutely honest men ready, and I came at once to give them their instructions. I ask you to sacrifice your pride, as we all of us must on occasion, and your rights, as is a soldier's privilege, and see this business through to a finish. It is too late to make other arrangements, Ranjoor Singh."

"Sahib, squadron-leading is my trade! I am not cut out for rat-run soldiering! I am willing to leave this house and hold my tongue, and to take this trooper with me and see that he holds his tongue. By nine tomorrow morning I will have satisfied myself that you are for and not against the Raj. And having satisfied myself, I and this trooper here will hold our tongues for ever. *Bass!*"

The general stood as still on his square foot of floor as did Ranjoor Singh on his. It was the fact that he did not flinch and did not strut about, but stood in one spot with his arms behind him that confirmed Ranjoor Singh in his reading of the general's eye.

"You may leave the house, then, and take your trooper. I accept your promise. Before you go, though, I'll tell you something. The ordering of troops for the front—for France—is in my hands. Your regiment is slated for tomorrow. But it can't go unless you'll see this through. The whole regiment will be needed, instead, to mount guard over Delhi."

"The regiment is to go, sahib, and my squadron, and—and I not? I am not to go?"

"That is the sacrifice you are asked to make!"

"Have I made no sacrifices for the Raj? How has my life been spent? Sahib——"

The Sikh's voice broke and he ceased speaking, but the general, too, seemed at a loss for words.

"Sahib—do I understand? If I do this—this rat-business, whatever it is—Colonel Kirby and the regiment go, and another leads my squadron? And unless I do this, whatever it is, the regiment will not go?"

The general nodded. He felt and looked ashamed.

"Has war been declared, sahib?"

"Yes. Germany has invaded Belgium."

For a second the Sikh's eyes blazed, but the fire died down again. He clasped his hands in front of him and hung his head. "I will do this thing that I am asked to do," he said; but his words were scarcely audible. His trooper came a step closer, to be nearer to Ranjoor Singh in his minute of acutest agony.

"Thou and I, Jagut Singh! We both stay behind!"

"Now, Risaldar-Major, I want you to listen! You've promised like a man," said the general. "I'll make you the best promise I can in return. Mine's conditional, but it's none the less emphatic. If possible, you shall catch your regiment before it puts to sea. If that's impossible, you shall take passage on another ship and try to overtake it. If that again is impossible, you shall follow your regiment and be in France in time to lead your squadron. I think I may say you are sure to be there before the regiment goes into action. But, understand—I said, 'If possible!'"

Ranjoor Singh's eye brightened and he straightened perceptibly.

"This trooper, sahib——"

"My promise is for him as well."

"We accept, sahib! What is the duty?"

"First, write a note to Colonel Kirby—I'll see that it's delivered—asking him to put your name in Orders as assigned to special duty. Here's paper and a fountain pen."

"Why should all this be secret from Colonel Kirby?" asked Ranjoor Singh. "There is no wiser and no more loyal officer!"

"Nor any officer more pugnacious on his juniors' account, I assure you! I can't imagine his agreeing to the use I'm making of you. I've no time to listen to his protests. Write, man, write!"

"Give me the paper and the pen, sahib!"

Ranjoor Singh wrote by the light of a flickering oil lamp, using his trooper's shoulder for support. Finally he passed the finished note back to the general.

"Now some token, please, Risaldar-Major, that Colonel Kirby will be sure to recognize—something to prove that the note is not forged."

Ranjoor Singh pulled a ring from his finger and held it out.

"Colonel Kirby sahib gave me this," he said simply.

"Thanks. Shake hands, will you? I've been talking to a man tonight—to two men—if I ever did in my life! I shall go now and give this letter to somebody to deliver to Colonel Kirby, and I shall not see you again probably until all this is over. Please do what Yasmini directs until you hear from me or can see for yourself that your task is finished. Depend on me to remember my promise!"

Ranjoor Singh saluted, military-wise, although he was not in uniform. The general answered his salute and left the room, to be met by a maid, who took the note and the ring from him. Five minutes later, with his rough disguise resumed, the general hunted about among the shadows of the neighboring streets until he had found his carriage. He recognized, but was not recognized by, the risaldar perched on the box-seat of Colonel Kirby's shay.

CHAPTER XII.

B lack smoke still billowed upward from the gutted House-of-the-Eight-Half-brothers, and although there were very few stars visible, a watery moon looked out from between dark cloudracks and showed up the smoke above the Delhi roofs. Yasmini picked the right simile as usual. It looked as if the biggest genie ever dreamed of must be hurrying out of a fisherman's vase.

"And who is the fisherman?" she laughed, for she is fond of that sort of question that sets those near her thinking and disguises the trend of her own thoughts as utterly as if she had not any.

"The genie might be the spirit of war!" ventured a Baluchi, forgetting the one God of his Koran in a sententious effort to please Yasmini.

She flashed a glance at him.

"Or it might be the god of the Rekis," she suggested; and everybody chuckled, because Baluchis do not relish reference to their lax religious practice any more than they like to be called "desert people." This man was a Rind Baluch of the Marri Hills, and proud of it; but pride is not always an asset at Yasmini's.

They—and the police would have dearly loved to know exactly who "they" were—stood clustered in Yasmini's great, deep window that overlooks her garden—the garden that can not be guessed at from the street. There was not one of them who could have explained how they came to assemble all on that side of the room; the movement had seemed to evolve out of the infinite calculation that everybody takes for granted, and Moslems particularly, since there seems nothing else to do about it.

It did not occur to anybody to credit Yasmini with the arrangement, or with the suddenly aroused interest in smoke against the after-midnight sky. Yet, when another man entered whose disguise was a joke to any practiced eye—and all in the room were practiced—it looked to the newcomer almost as if his reception had been ready staged.

He was dressed as a Mohammedan gentleman. But his feet, when he stood still, made nearly a right angle to each other, and his shoulders had none of the grace that goes with good native breeding; they were proud enough, but the pride had been drilled in and cultivated. It sat square. And if a native gentleman had walked through the streets as this man walked, all the small boys of the bazaars would have followed him to learn what nation his might be.

Yasmini seemed delighted with him. She ran toward him, curtsied to him, and called him *bahadur*. She made two maids bring a chair for him, and made them set it near the middle of the window whence he could see the smoke, pushing the men away on either side until he had a clear view.

But he knew enough of the native mind, at all events, to look at the smoke and not remark on it. It was so obvious that he was meant to talk about the smoke, or to ask about it, that even a German Orientalist understanding the East through German eyes had tact enough to look in silence, and so to speak, "force trumps."

And that again, of course, was exactly what Yasmini wanted. Moreover, she surprised him by not leading trumps.

"They are here," she said, with a side-wise glance at the more than thirty men who crowded near the window.

The German—and he made no pretense any longer of being anything but German—sat sidewise with both hands on his knees to get a better view of them. He scanned each face carefully, and each man entertained a feeling that he had been analyzed and ticketed and stood aside.

"I have seen all these before," he said. "They are men of the North, and good enough fighters, I have no doubt. But they are not what I asked for. How many of these are trained soldiers? Which of these could swing the allegiance of a single native regiment. It is time now for proofs and deeds. The hour of talk is gone. Bring me a soldier!"

"These also say it is all talk, sahib—words, words, words! They say they will wait until the fleet that has been spoken of comes to bombard the coast. For the present there are none to rally round."

"Yet you hinted at soldiers!" said the German. "You hinted at a regiment ready to revolt!"

"Aye, sahib! I have repeated what *these* say. When the soldier comes there shall be other talk! See yonder smoke, *bahadur?*"

Now, then, it was time to notice things, and the German gazed over the garden and Delhi walls and roofs at what looked very much more important than it really was. It looked as if at least a street must be on fire.

"He made that holocaust, did the soldier!"

Yasmini's manner was of blended awe and admiration.

"He was suspected of disloyalty. He entered that house to make arrangements for the mutiny of a whole regiment of Sikhs, who are not willing to be sent to fight across the sea. He was followed to the house, and so, since he would not be taken, he burned all the houses. Such, a man is he who comes presently. Did the sahib hear the mob roar when the flames burst out at evening? No? A pity! There were many soldiers in the mob, and many thousand discontented people!"

She went close to the window, to be between the German and the light, and let him see her silhouetted in an attitude of hope awakening. She gazed at the billowing smoke as if the hope of India were embodied in it. "It was thus in '57," she said darkly. "Men began with burnings!"

Brown eyes, behind the German, exchanged glances, for the East is chary of words when it does not understand. The German nodded, for he had studied history and was sure he understood.

"Sahib *hai!*" said a sudden woman's voice, and Yasmini started as if taken by surprise. There were those in the room who knew that when taken by surprise she never started; but they were not German. "He is here!" she whispered; and the German showed that he felt a crisis had arrived. He settled down to meet it like a soldier and a man.

"Salaam!" purred Yasmini in her silveriest voice, as Ranjoor Singh strode down the middle of the room with the dignity the West may some day learn.

"See!" whispered Yasmini. "He trusts nobody. He brings his own guard with him!"

By the door at which he had entered stood a trooper of D Squadron, Outram's Own, no longer in uniform, but dressed as a Sikh servant. The man's arms were folded on his breast. The rigidity, straight stature, and attitude appealed to the German as the sight of sea must have to the ancient Greeks.

"Salaam!" said Ranjoor Singh.

The German noticed that his eyes glowed, but the rest of him was all calm dignity.

"We have met before," said the German, rising. "You are the Sikh with whom I spoke the other night—the Sikh officer—the squadron leader!"

"*Ja!*" said Ranjoor Singh; and the one word startled the German so that he caught his breath.

"*Sie sprechen Deutsch?*"

"*Ja wohl!*"

The German muttered something half under his breath that may have been meant for a compliment to Ranjoor Singh, but the risaldar-major missed it, for he had stepped up to the nearest of the Northern gentlemen and confronted him. There was a great show of looking in each other's eyes and muttering under the breath some word and counter-word. Each made a sign with his right hand, then with his left, that the German could not see, and then Ranjoor Singh stepped sidewise to the next man.

Man by man, slowly and with care, the Sikh looked each man present in the eyes and tested him for the password, while Yasmini watched admiringly.

"Any who do not know the word will die tonight!" she whispered; and the German nodded, because it was evident that the Northerners were quite afraid. He approved of that kind of discipline.

"These are all true men—patriots," said Ranjoor Singh, walking back to him. "Now say what you have to say."

"*Jetzt——*" began the German.

"Speak Hindustani that they all may understand," said Ranjoor Singh; and the others gathered closer.

"My friend, I am told——"

But Yasmini broke in, bursting between Ranjoor Singh and the German. "Nay, let the sahibs go alone into the other room. Neither will speak his mind freely before company—is it not so? Into the other room, sahibs, while we wait here!"

Ranjoor Singh bowed, and the German clicked his heels together. Ranjoor Singh made a sign, but the German yielded precedence; so Ranjoor Singh strode ahead, and the German followed him, wishing to high Heaven he could learn to walk with such consummate grace. As they disappeared through the jingling bead-curtain, the Sikh trooper followed them, and took his stand again with folded arms by the door-post. The German saw him, and smiled; he approved of that.

Then Yasmini gathered her thirty curious Northerners together around her and proceeded to entertain them while the plot grew nearer to its climax in another room. She led them back to the divans by the inner wall. She set them to smoking while she sang a song to them. She parried their questions with dark hints and innuendoes that left them more mystified than ever; yet no man would admit he could not understand what she was saying.

And then she danced to them. She danced for an hour, to the wild minor music that her women made, and she seemed to gather strength and lightness as the night wore on. Near dawn the German and Ranjoor Singh came out together, to find her yet dancing, and she ceased only to pull the German aside and speak to him.

"Does he *really* speak German?" she whispered.

"He? He has read Nietzsche and von Bernhardi in the German!"

"Who are they?"

"They are difficult to read—philosophers."

"Has he satisfied you?"

"He has promised that he will."

"Then go before I send the rest away!"

So the German tried to look like a Mohammedan again, and went below to a waiting landau. Before he was half-way down the stairs Yasmini's hands gripped tight on Ranjoor Singh's forearms and she had him backed into a corner.

"Ranjoor Singh, thou art no buffalo! I was wrong! Thou are a great man, Ranjoor Singh!"

She received no answer.

"What hast thou promised him?"

"To show him a mutinous regiment of Sikhs."

"And what has he promised?"

"To show me what we seek."

She nodded.

"Good!" she said.

"So now I promise thee something," said Ranjoor Singh sternly. "Tomorrow—perhaps today—I shall eat black shame on thy account, for this is thy doing. Later I will go to France. But later again, I will come back and——"

"And love me as they all do!" laughed Yasmini, pushing him away.

CHAPTER XIII.

Beyond question Yasmini is a craftsman of amazing skill, and her genius—as does all true genius—extends to the almost infinite consideration of small details. The medium in which she works—human weakness—affords her unlimited opportunity; and she owns the trick, that most great artists win, of not letting her general plan be known before the climax. Neither friend nor enemy is ever quite sure which is which until she solves the problem to the enemy's confusion.

But Yasmini could have failed in this case through overmuch finesse. She was not used to Germans, and could not realize until too late that her compliance with this man's every demand only served to make him more peremptory and more one-sided in his point of view. From a mere agent, offering the almost unimaginable in return for mere promises, he had grown already into a dictator, demanding action as a prelude to reward. He had even threatened to cause her, Yasmini, to be reported to the police unless she served his purpose better!

If she had obeyed the general and had picked a trooper for the business in hand, it is likely that Yasmini would have had to write a failure to her account. She had come perilously near to obedience on this occasion, and it had been nothing less than luck that put Ranjoor Singh into her hands, luck being the pet name of India's kindest god. He was needed in the instant when he came to bring the German back to earth.

The Sikh had a rage in his heart that the German mistook for zeal and native ferocity; his manners became so brusk under the stress of it that they might almost have been Prussian, and, met with its own reflection, that kind of insolence grows limp.

Having agreed to lie, Ranjoor Singh lied with such audacity and so much skill that it would have needed Yasmini to dare disbelieve him.

The German sat in state near Yasmini's great window and received, one after another, liars by the dozen from the hills where lies are current coin. Some of them had listened to his lectures, and some had learned of them at second hand; every man of them had received his cue from Yasmini. There was too much unanimity among them; they wanted too little and agreed too readily to what the German had to say; he was growing almost suspicious toward half-past ten, when Ranjoor Singh came in.

There was no trooper behind him this time, for the man had been sent to watch for the regiment's departure, and to pounce then on Bagh, the charger, and take him away to safety. After the charger had been groomed and fed and hidden, the trooper was to do what might be done toward securing the risaldar-major's kit; but under no condition was the kit to have precedence.

"Groom him until he shines! Guard him until I call for him! Keep him exercised!" was the three-fold order that sang through the trooper's head and overcame astonishment in the hurry to obey.

Now it was the German's turn to be astonished. Ranjoor Singh strode in, dressed as a Sikh farmer, and frowned down Yasmini's desire to poke fun at him. The German rose to salute him, and the Sikh acknowledged the salute with a nod such as royalty might spare for a menial.

"Come!" he said curtly, and the German followed him out through the door to the stair-head where so many mirrors were. There Ranjoor Singh made quite a little play of making sure they were not overheard, while the German studied his own Mohammedan disguise from twenty different angles.

"Too much finery!" growled Ranjoor Singh. "I will attend to that. First, listen! Other than your talk, I have had no proof at all of you! You are a spy!"

"I am a——"

"You are a spy! All the spies I ever met were liars from the ground up! I am a patriot. I am working to save my country from a yoke that is unbearable, and I *must* deal in subterfuge and treachery if I would win. But you are merely one who sows trouble. You are like the little jackal—the dirty little jackal—who starts a fight between two tigers so that he may fill his mean belly! Don't speak—listen!"

The German's jaw had dropped, but not because words rushed to his lips. He seemed at a loss for them.

"You made me an offer, and I accepted it," continued Ranjoor Singh. "I accepted it on behalf of India. I shall show you in about an hour from now a native regiment—one of the very best native regiments, so mutinous that its officers must lead it out of Delhi to a camp where it will be less dangerous and less likely to corrupt others."

The German nodded. He had asked no more.

"Then, if you fail to fulfill your part," said Ranjoor Singh grimly, "I shall lock you in the cellar of this house, where Yasmini keeps her cobras!"

"*Vorwarts!*" laughed the German, for there was firm conviction in every word the Sikh had said. "I will show you how a German keeps his bargain!"

"A German?" growled Ranjoor Singh. "A German—Germany is nothing to me! If Germany can pick the bones I leave, what do I care? One does not bargain with a spy, either; one pays his price, and throws him to the cobras if he fail! Come!"

The question of precedence no longer seemed to trouble Ranjoor Singh; he turned his back without apology, and as the German followed him downstairs there came a giggle from behind the curtains.

"Were we overheard?" he asked.

But Ranjoor Singh did not seem to care any more, and did not trouble to answer him.

Outside the door was a bullock-cart, of the kind in which women make long journeys, with a painted, covered super-structure. The German followed Ranjoor Singh into it, and without any need for orders the Sikh driver began to twist the bullocks' tails and send them along at the pace all India loves. Then Ranjoor Singh began to pay attention to the German's dress, pulling off his expensive turban and replacing that and his clothes with cheaper, dirtier ones.

"Why?" asked the German.

"I will show you why," said Ranjoor Singh.

Then the two men sat back, each against a side of the cart, squatting native style.

"This regiment that I will show you is mine," said Ranjoor Singh. "I command a squadron of it—or, rather, did, until I became suspected. Every man in the regiment is mine, and will follow me at a word. When I give the word they will kill their English officers."

He leaned his head out of the opening to spit; there seemed something in his mouth that tasted nasty.

"Why did they mutiny?" asked the German.

"Ordered to France!" said Ranjoor Singh, with lowered eyes.

For a while there was silence as the cart bumped through the muddy rutty streets; the only sound that interfered with thought was the driver's voice, apostrophizing the bullocks; and the abuse he poured on them was so time-honored as to be unnoticeable, like the cawing of the city crows.

"It is strange," said the German, after a while. "For years I have tried to get in touch with native officers. Here and there I have found a Sepoy who would talk with me, but you are the first officer." He was brown-studying, talking almost to himself. He did not see the curse in the risal-dar-major's eyes.

"I have found plenty of merchants who would promise to finance revolt, and plenty of hillmen who would promise anything. But all said, 'We will do what the army does!' And I could not find in all this time, among all those people, anybody to whom I dared show what we—Germany—can do to help. I have seen from the first it was only with the aid of the army that we could accomplish anything, yet the army has been unapproachable. How is it that you have seemed so loyal, all of you, until the minute of war?"

Ranjoor Singh spat again through the opening with thoroughness and great deliberation. Then he proceeded to give proof that, as Yasmini had said, he was really not a buffalo at all. A fool would have taken chances with any one of a dozen other explanations. Ranjoor Singh, with an expression that faintly suggested Colonel Kirby, picked the right, convincing one.

"The English are not bad people," he said simply. "They have left India better than they found it. They have been unselfish. They have treated us soldiers fairly and honorably. We would not have revolted had the opportunity not come, but we have long been waiting for the opportunity.

"We are not madmen—we are soldiers. We know the value of mere words. We have kept our plans secret from the merchants and the hillmen, knowing well that they would all follow our lead. If you think that you, or Germany, have persuaded us, you are mistaken. You could not persuade me, or any other true soldier, if you tried for fifty years!

"It is because we had decided on revolt already that I was willing to listen to your offer of material assistance. We understand that Germany expects to gain advantage from our revolt, but we can not help that; that is incidental. As soldiers, we accept what aid we can get from anywhere!"

"So?" said the German.

"*Ja!*" said Ranjoor Singh. "And that is why, if you fail me, I shall give you to Yasmini's cobras!"

"You will admit," said the German, "when I have shown you, that Germany's foresight has been long and shrewd. Your great chance of success, my friend, like Germany's in this war, depends on a sudden, swift, tremendous success at first; the rest will follow as a logical corollary. It is the means of securing that first success that we have been making ready for you for two years and more."

"You should have credit for great secrecy," admitted Ranjoor Singh. "Until a little while ago I had heard nothing of any German plans."

"Russia got the blame for what little was guessed at!"

"Oh!" said Ranjoor Singh.

A little before midday they reached the Ajmere Gate, and the lumbering cart passed under it. At the farther side the driver stopped his oxen without orders, and Ranjoor Singh stepped out, looking quickly up and down the road. There were people about, but none whom he chose to favor with a second glance.

Close by the gate, almost under the shadow of it, and so drab and dirty as to be almost unnoticeable, there was a little cotton-tented booth, with a stock of lemonade and sweetmeats, that did interest him. He looked three times at it, and at the third look a Mohammedan wriggled out of it and walked away without a word.

"Come!" commanded Ranjoor Singh, and the German got out of the cart, looking not so very much unlike the poor Mohammedan who had gone away.

"Get in there!" The German slipped into the real owner's place. So far as appearances went, he was a very passable sweetmeat and lemonade seller, and Ranjoor Singh proved totally competent to guard against all contingencies.

He picked a long stick out of the gutter and took his stand near by, frowning as he saw a carriage he suspected to be Yasmini's drive under the gate and come to a stand at the roadside, fifty or sixty yards away.

"If the officers should recognize me," he growled to the German, though seeming not to talk to him at all, "I should be arrested at once, and shot later. But the men *will* recognize me, and you shall see what you shall see!"

Three small boys came with a coin to spend, but Ranjoor Singh drove them away with his long stick; they argued shrilly from a distance, and one threw a stone at him, but finally they decided he was some new sort of plain-clothes "constabeel," and went away.

One after another, several natives came to make small purchases, but, not being boys any longer, a gruff word was enough to send them running. And then came the clatter of hoofs of the advance-guard, and the German looked up to see a fire in Ranjoor Singh's eyes that a caged tiger could not have outdone.

All this while the bullock-cart in which they had come remained in the middle of the road, its driver dozing dreamily on his seat and the bullocks perfectly content to chew the cud. At the sound of the hoofs behind him, the driver suddenly awoke and began to belabor and kick his animals; he seemed oblivious of another cart that came toward him, and of a third that hurried after him from underneath the gate. In less than sixty seconds all three carts were neatly interlocked, and their respective drivers were engaged in a war of words that beggared Babel.

The advance-guard halted and added words to the torrent. Colonel Kirby caught up the advance-guard and halted, too.

"Does he look like a man who commands a loyal regiment?" asked Ranjoor Singh; and the German studied the bowed head of a man who at that minute was regretting his good friend the risaldar-major.

"You will note that he looks chastened!"

The German nodded.

In his own good time Ranjoor Singh ran out and helped with that long stick of his to straighten out the mess; then in thirty seconds the wheels were unlocked again and the carts moving in a hurry to the roadside. The advance-guard moved on, and Kirby followed. Then, troop by troop, the whole of Outram's Own rode by, and the German began to wonder. It seemed to him that the rest of the officers were not demure enough, although he admitted to himself that the enigmatic Eastern faces in the ranks might mean anything at all. He noted that there was almost no talking, and he took that for a good sign for Germany.

D Squadron came last of all, and convinced him. They rode regretfully, as men who missed their squadron leader, and who, in spite of a message from him, would have better loved to see him riding on their flank.

But Ranjoor Singh stepped out into the road, and the right-end man of the front four recognized him. Not a word was said that the German could hear, but he could see the recognition run from rank to rank and troop to troop, until the squadron knew to a man; he saw them glance at Ranjoor Singh, and from him to one another, and ride on with a new stiffening and a new air of "now we'll see what comes of it!"

It was as evident, to his practiced eye, that they were glad to have seen Ranjoor Singh, and looked forward to seeing him again very shortly, as that they were in a mood for trouble, and he decided to believe the whole of what the Sikh had said on the strength of the obvious truth of part of it.

"Watch now the supply train!" growled Ranjoor Singh, as the wagons began to rumble by.

The German had no means of knowing that the greater part of the regiment's war provisions had gone away by train from a Delhi station. The wagons that followed the regiment on the march were a generous allowance for a regiment going into camp, but not more than that. The spies whose duty it was to watch the railway sidings reported to somebody else and not to him.

Ranjoor Singh beckoned him after a while, and they came out into the road, to stand between two of the bullock-wagons and gaze after the regiment. The shuttered carriage that Ranjoor Singh had suspected to be Yasmini's passed them again, and the man beside the driver said something to Ranjoor Singh in an undertone, but the German did not hear it; he was watching the colonel and another officer talking together beside the road in the distance. The shuttered carriage passed on, but stopped in the shadow of the gate.

"Look!" said the German. "I thought that officer—the adjutant, isn't he—recognized you. Now he is pointing you out to the colonel! Look!"

Ranjoor Singh did look, and he saw that Colonel Kirby was waiting to let the regiment go by. He knew what was passing through Kirby's mind, since it is given to some men, native and English, to have faith in each other. And he knew that there was danger ahead of him through which he might not come with his life, perhaps even with his honor. He would have given, like Kirby, a full year's pay for a hand-shake then, and have thought the pay well spent.

Kirby began to canter back.

"He has recognized you!" said the German.

"And he is coming to cut me down!" swore Ranjoor Singh.

He dragged the German back behind the nearest cart, and together they ran for the gloom of the big gate, leaving the driver of the bullock-cart standing at gaze where Ranjoor Singh had stood. The door of the shuttered carriage flew open as they reached it, and Ranjoor Singh pushed the German in. He stood a moment longer, with his foot on the carriage step, watching Colonel Kirby; he watched him question the bullock-cart driver.

Then a voice that he recognized said, "Buffalo!" and he followed into the carriage, shutting the door behind him.

The carriage was off almost before the door slammed.

"Am I to be kept waiting for a week, while a Jat farmer gazes at cattle on the road?" demanded Yasmini, sitting forward out of the darkest corner of the carriage and throwing aside a veil. "He cares nothing for thee!" she whispered. "Didst thou see the jasmine drop into his lap from the gate? That was mine! Didst thou see him button it into his tunic? So, Ranjoor Singh! That for thy colonel sahib! And his head will smell of *my* musk for a week to come! What—what fools men are! *Jaldee, jaldee!*" she called to the driver through the shutters, and the man whipped up his pair.

It was more than scandalous to be driven through Delhi streets in a shuttered carriage with a native lady, and even the German's presence scarcely modified the sensation; the German did not appreciate the rarity of his privilege, for he was too busy staring through the shutters at a world which tried its best to hide excitement; but Ranjoor Singh was aware all the time of Yasmini's mischievous eyes and of mirth that held her all but speechless. He knew that she would make up tales about that ride, and would have told them to half of India to his enduring shame before a year was out.

"Are you satisfied?" she asked the German, after a long silence.

"Of what?" asked the German.

"That Ranjoor Singh sahib can do what he has promised."

The German laughed.

"I have an excuse for doing what I promised," he said, "if that is what you mean."

"That regiment," said Ranjoor Singh, since he had made up his mind to lie thoroughly, "will camp a day's march out of Delhi. The men will wait to hear from me for a day or two, but after that they will mutiny and be done with it; the men are almost out of hand with excitement."

"You mean——"

The German's eyebrows rose, and his eyes sought Ranjoor Singh's.

"I mean that now is the time to do your part, that I may continue doing mine!" he answered.

"What I have to offer would be of no use without the regiment to use it," said the German. "Let the regiment mutiny, and I will lead you and it at once to what I spoke of."

"No," said Ranjoor Singh.

"What then?"

"It does not suit my plan, or my convenience, that there should be any outbreak until I myself have knowledge of all my resources. When everything is in my hand, I will strike hard and fast in my own good time."

"You seem to forget," said the German, "that the material aid I offer is from Germany, and that therefore Germany has a right to state the terms. Of course, I know there are the cobras, but I am not afraid of them. Our stipulation is that there shall be at least a show of fight before aid is given. If the cobras deal with me, and my secret dies with me, there will be one German less and that is all. That regiment I have seen looks ripe for mutiny."

Ranjoor Singh drew breath slowly through set teeth.

"Let it mutiny," said the German, "and I am ready with such material assistance as will place Delhi at its mercy. Delhi is the key to India!"

"It shall mutiny tonight!" said Ranjoor Singh abruptly.

The German stared hard at him, though not so hard as Yasmini; the chief difference was that nobody could have told she was staring, whereas the German gaped.

"It shall mutiny tonight, and you shall be there! You shall lead us then to this material aid you promise, and after that, if it all turns out to be a lie, as I suspect, we will talk about cobras."

For a minute, two minutes, three minutes, while the rubber tires bumped along the road toward Yasmini's, the German sat in silence, looking straight in front of him.

"Order horses for him and me!" commanded Ranjoor Singh; and Yasmini bowed obedience.

"When will you start?" the German asked.

"Now! In twenty minutes! We will follow the regiment and reach camp soon after it."

"I must speak first with my colleagues," said the German.

"No!" growled the Sikh.

"My secret information is that several regiments are ordered oversea. Some of them will consent to go, my friend. We will do well to wait until as many regiments as possible are on the water, and then strike hard with the aid of such as have refused to go."

The carriage drew up at Yasmini's front door, and a man jumped off the box seat to open the carriage.

"Say the rest inside!" she ordered. "Go into the house! Quickly!"

So the German stepped out first, moving toward the door much too spryly for the type of street merchant he was supposed to be.

"Do you mean that?" whispered Yasmini, as she pushed past Ranjoor Singh. "Do you mean to ride away with him and stage a mutiny? How can you?"

"She-buffalo!" he answered, with the first low laugh she had heard from him since the game began.

She ran into the house and all the way up the two steep flights of stairs, laughing like a dozen peals of fairy bells.

At the head of the stairs she began to sing, for she looked back and saw babu Sita Ram waddling wheezily upstairs after Ranjoor Singh and the German.

"The gods surely love Yasmini!" she told her maids. "Catch me that babu and bottle him! Drive him into a room where I can speak with him alone!"

"Oh, my God, my God!" wailed the babu at the stair-head from amid a maze of women who hustled and shoved him all one way, and that the way he did not want to go. "I must speak with that German gentleman who was giving lecture here—must positivelee give him warning, or all his hopes will be blasted everlastinglee! No—that is room where are cobras—I will not go there!"

In three native languages, one after the other, he pleaded and wailed to no good end; the women were too many for him. He was shoved into a small room as a fat beast is driven into a slaughter-stall, and a door was slammed shut on him. He screamed at an unexpected voice from behind a curtain, and a moment later burst into a sweat from reaction at the sight of Yasmini.

"Listen, *babuji*," she purred to him.

"Who was that man asking for me?" demanded the German.

"How should I know?" snorted Ranjoor Singh. "Are we to turn aside for every fat babu that asks to speak to us? I have sent for horses."

"I will speak with that man!" said the German.

He began to walk up and down the length of the long room, pushing aside the cushions irritably, and at one end knocking over a great bowl of flowers. He did not appear conscious of his clumsiness, and did not seem to see the maids who ran to mop up the water. At the next turn down the room he pushed between them as if they had not been there. Ranjoor Singh stood watching him, stroking a black beard reflectively; he was sure that Yasmini would make the next move, and was willing to wait for it.

"The horses should be here in a few minutes," he said hopefully, after a while, for he heard a door open.

Then babu Sita Ram burst in, half running, and holding his great stomach as he always did when in a hurry.

"Oh, my God!" he wailed. "Quick! Where is German gentleman? And not knowing German, how shall I make meaning clear? German should be reckoned among dead languages and—Ah! My God, sir, you astonish me! Resemblance to Mohammedan of no particular standing in community is first class! How shall I——"

"Say it in English!" said the German, blocking his way.

"My God, sahib, it is bad news! How shall I avoid customaree stigma attaching to bearer of ill tidings?"

"Speak!" said the German. "I won't hurt you!"

"Sahib, in pursuit unavailingly of chance emolument in neighborhood of Chandni Chowk just recently——"

"How recently?" the German asked.

"Oh, my God! So recently that there are yet erections of cuticle all down my back! Sahib, not more than twenty minutes have elapsed, and I saw this with my own eyes!"

"Saw what—where?"

"Where? Have I not said where? My God, I am so upset as to be losing sense of all proportion! Where? At German place of business—Sigelman and Meyer—in small street leading out of Chandni Chowk. In search of chance emolument, and finding none yet—finding none yet, sahib—sahib, I am poor man, having wife and familee dependent and also many other disabilitees, including wife's relatives."

The German gave him some paper money impatiently. The babu unfolded it, eyed the denomination with a spasm of relief, folded it again, and appeared to stow it into his capacious stomach.

"Sahib, while I was watching, police came up at double-quick march and arrested everybodee, including all Germans in building. There was much annoyance manifested when search did not reveal presence of one other sahib. So I ran to give warning, being veree poor man and without salaried employment."

"What happened to the Germans?"

"Jail, sahib! All have gone to jail! By this time they are all excommunication, supplied with food and water by authorities. Having once been jail official myself, I can testify——"

"What happened to the office?"

"Locked up, sahib! Big red seal—much sealing wax, and stamp of police department, with notice regarding penalty for breaking same, and also police sentry at door!"

Looking more unlike a Mohammedan street vender than ever, the German began to pace the room again with truly martial strides, frowning as he sought through the recesses of his mind for the correct solution of the problem.

"Listen!" he said, coming to a stand in front of Ranjoor Singh. "I have changed my mind!"

"The horses are ready," answered Ranjoor Singh.

"The German government has been to huge expense to provide aid of the right kind, to be ready at the right minute. My sole business is to see that the utmost use is made of it."

"That also is my sole business!" vowed Ranjoor Singh.

"You have heard that the police are after me?"

Ranjoor Singh nodded.

"Can you get away from here unseen—unknown to the police?"

Ranjoor Singh nodded again, sure of Yasmini's resource.

Again the German began to pace the room, now with his hands behind him, now with folded arms, now with his chin down to his breast, and now with a high chin as he seemed on the verge of reaching some determination. And then Yasmini began to loose the flood of her resources, that Ranjoor Singh might make use of what he chose; she was satisfied to leave the German in the Sikh's hands and to squander aid at random.

Men began to come in, one at a time. They would whisper to Ranjoor Singh, and hurry out again. Some of them would whisper to Yasmini over in the window, and she would give them mock messages to carry, very seriously. Babu Sita Ram was stirred out of a meditative coma and sent hurrying away, to come back after a little while and wring his hands. He ran over to Yasmini.

"It is awful!" he wailed. "Soon there will be no troops left with which to quell Mohammedan uprising. All loyal troops are leaving, and none but disloyal men are left behind. The government is mad, and I am veree much afraid!"

Yasmini quieted him, and Ranjoor Singh, pretending to be busy with other messengers, noted the effect of the babu's wail on the German. He judged the "change of mind" had gone far enough.

"We should lose time by following my regiment," he said at last. "There are now five more regiments ready to mutiny, and they will come to me to wherever I send for them."

The German's blue eyes gazed into the Sikh's brown ones very shrewdly and very long. His hand sought the neighborhood of his hip, and dwelt there a moment longer than the Sikh thought necessary.

"I have decided we must hurry," he said. "I will show you what I have to show. I will not be taking chances. You must bring a messenger, and he must go for your mutineers while you stay there with me. When we are there, you will be in my power until the regiments come; and when they come I will surrender to you. Do you agree?"

"Yes," said Ranjoor Singh.

"Then choose your messenger. Choose a man who will not try to play tricks—a man who will not warn the authorities, because if there is any slip, any trickery, I will undo in one second all that has been done!"

So Ranjoor Singh conferred with Yasmini over the two great bowls of flowers that always stand in her big window; and she suppressed a squeal of excitement while she watched the German resume his pacing up and down.

"Take Sita Ram!" she advised.

Ranjoor Singh scowled at the babu.

"That fat bellyful of fear!" he growled. "I would rather take a pig!"

"All the same, take Sita Ram!" she advised.

So the babu was roused again out of a comfortable snooze, and Yasmini whispered to him something that frightened him so much that he trembled like a man with palsy.

"I am married man with children!" he expostulated.

"I will be kind to your widow!" purred Yasmini.

"I will not go!" vowed the babu.

"Put him in the cobra room!" she commanded, and some maids came closer to obey.

"I will go!" said Sita Ram. "But, oh, my God, a man should receive pecuniary recompense far greater than legendary ransom! I shall not come back alive! I know I shall not come back alive!"

"Who cares, *babuji?*" asked Yasmini.

"True!" said Sita Ram. "This is land of devil-take-hindmost, and with my big stomach I am often last. I am veree full of fear!"

"We shall need food," interposed the German. "Water will be there, but we had better have sufficient food with us for two nights."

Yasmini gave a sharp order, and several of her maids ran out of the room. Ten minutes later they returned with three baskets, and gave one each to the German, to Ranjoor Singh, and to Sita Ram. Sita Ham opened his and peered in. The German opened his, looked pleased, and closed the lid again. Ranjoor Singh accepted his at its face value, and did not open it.

"May the memsahib never lack plenty from which to give!" he said, for there is no word for "Thank you" in all India.

"I will bless the memsahib at each mouthful!" said Sita Ram.

"Truly a bellyful of blessings!" laughed Yasmini.

Then they all went to the stair-head and watched and listened through the open door while a closed carriage was driven away in a great hurry. Three maids and six men came upstairs one after another, at intervals, to report the road all clear; the first carriage had not been followed, and there was nobody watching; another carriage waited. Babu Sita Ram was sent downstairs to get into the waiting carriage and stay there on the lookout.

"Now bring him better clothes!" said Ranjoor Singh.

But Yasmini had anticipated that order.

"They are in the carriage, on the seat," she said.

So the German went downstairs and climbed in beside the babu, changing his turban at once for the better one he found waiting in there.

"This performance is worth a rajah's ransom!" grumbled Sita Ram. "Will sahib not put elbow in my belly, seeing same is highly sensitive?"

But the German laughed at him.

"Love is rare, non-contagious sickness!" asserted Sita Ram with sober conviction.

At the head of the stairs Ranjoor Singh and Yasmini stood looking into each other's eyes. He looked into pools of laughter and mystery that told him nothing at all; she saw a man's heart glowing in his brown ones.

"It will be for you now," said Ranjoor Singh, "to act with speed and all discretion. I don't know what we are going to see, although I know it is artillery of some sort. I am sure he has a plan for destroying every trace of whatever it is, and of himself and me, if he suspects treachery. I know no more. I can only go ahead."

"And trust me!" said Yasmini.

The Sikh did not answer.

"And trust me!" repeated Yasmini. "I will save you out of this, Ranjoor Singh sahib, that we may fight our quarrel to a finish later on. What would the world be without enemies? You will not find artillery!"

"How do you know?"

"I have known for nearly two years what you will find there, my friend! Only I have not known exactly where to find it. And yet sometimes I have thought that I have known that, too! Go, Ranjoor Singh. You will be in danger. Above all, do not try to force that German's hand too far until I come with aid. It is better to talk than fight, so long as the enemy is strongest!"

"Woman!" swore Ranjoor Singh so savagely that Yasmini laughed straight into his face. "If you suspect—if you can guess where we are going—send men to surround the place and watch!"

"Will a tiger walk into a watched lair?" she answered. "Go, talker! Go and do things!"

So, swearing and dissatisfied, Ranjoor Singh went down and climbed on to the box seat of a two-horse carriage.

"Which way?" he asked; and the German growled an answer through the shutters.

"Now straight on!" said the German, after fifteen minutes. "Straight on out of Delhi!"

They were headed south, and driving very slowly, for to have driven fast would have been to draw attention to themselves. Ranjoor Singh scarcely troubled to look about him, and Sita Ram fell into a doze, in spite of his protestations of fear. The German was the only one of the party who was at pains to keep a lookout, and he was most exercised to know whether they were being followed; over and over again he called on Ranjoor Singh to stop until a following carriage should overtake them and pass on.

So they were a very long time driving to Old Delhi, where the ruins of old cities stand piled against one another in a tangled mass of verdure that is hardly penetrable except where the tracks wind in and out. The shadow of the Kutb Minar was long when they drove past it, and it was dusk when the German shouted and Ranjoor Singh turned the horses in between two age-old trees and drew rein at a shattered temple door.

Some monkeys loped away, chattering, and about a thousand parakeets flew off, shrilling for another roost. But there was no other sign of life to be seen about.

"Stable the horses in here!" said the German; and they did so, Ranjoor Singh dipping water out of a rain-pool and filling a stone trough that had once done duty as receptacle for gifts for a long-forgotten god. Then they pushed the carriage under a tangle of hanging branches.

"Look about you!" advised the German, as he emptied food for the horses on the temple floor; and babu Sita Ram made very careful note of the temple bearings, while Ranjoor Singh and the German blocked the old doorway with whatever they could find to keep night-prowlers outside and the horses in.

Then the German led the way into the dark, swinging a lantern that he had unearthed from some recess. Babu Sita Ram walked second, complaining audibly and shuddering at every shadow. Last came Ranjoor Singh, grim, silent. And the rain beat down on all three of them until they were drenched and numb, and their feet squelched in mud at every step.

For all the darkness, Ranjoor Singh made note of the fact that they were following a wagon track, into which the wheels of a native cart had sunk deep times without number. He knew only native ox-carts leave a track like that.

It must have been nine o'clock, and the babu was giving signs of nearly complete exhaustion, when they passed beyond a ring of trees into a clearing. They stood at the edge of the clearing in a shadow for about ten minutes, while the German watched catwise for signs of life.

"It is now," he said, tapping Ranjoor Singh's chest, "that you begin to be at my mercy. I assure you that the least disobedience on your part will mean your instant death!"

"Lead on!" growled Ranjoor Singh.

"Do you recognize the place?"

Ranjoor Singh peered through the rain in every direction. At each corner of the clearing, north, south, east and west, he could dimly see some sort of ruined arch, and there was another ruin in the center.

"No," he said.

"This is the oldest temple ruin anywhere near Delhi. On some inscriptions it is called 'Temple of the Four Winds,' but the old Hindu who lived in it before we bribed him to go away called it the 'Winds of the World.' It is known as 'Winds of the World' on the books of the German War Office. I think it is really of Greek origin myself, but I am not an Orientalist, and the text-books all say that I am wrong."

"Lead on!" said Ranjoor Singh; and the German led them, swinging his lantern and seeming not at all afraid of being seen now.

"We have taken steps quite often to make the people hereabouts believe this temple haunted!" he said. "They avoid it at night as if the devil lived here. If any of them see my lantern, they will not stop running till they reach the sea!"

They came to a ruin that was such an utter ruin that it looked as if an earthquake must have shaken a temple to pieces to be disintegrated by the weather; but Ranjoor Singh noticed that the cart-tracks wound around the side of it, and when they came to a fairly large teak trap-door, half hidden by creepers, he was not much surprised.

"My God, gentlemen!" said Sita Ram. "That place is wet-weather refuge for many million cobras! If I must die, I will prefer to perish in rain, where wife and family may find me for proper funeral rites. I will not go in there!"

But the German raised the trap-door, and Ranjoor Singh took the unhappy babu by the scruff of his fat neck.

"In with you!" he ordered.

And, chattering as if his teeth were castanets, the babu trod gingerly down damp stone steps whose center had been worn into ruts by countless feet. The German came last, and let the trap slam shut.

"My God!" yelled the babu. "Let me go! I am family man!"

"*Vorwarts!*" laughed the German, leading the way toward a teak door set in a stone wall.

They were in an ancient temple vault that seemed to have miraculously escaped from the destruction that had overwhelmed the whole upper part. Not a stone of it was out of place. It was wind and water-tight, and the vaulted roof, that above was nothing better than a mound of debris, from below looked nearly as perfect as when the stones had first been fitted into place.

The German produced a long key, opened the teak door, and stood aside to let them pass.

"No, no!" shuddered Sita Ram; but Ranjoor Singh pushed him through; the German followed, and the door slammed shut as the trap had done.

"And now, my friends, I will convince you!" said the German, holding the lantern high. "What are those?"

The light from the solitary lantern fell on rows and rows of bales, arranged in neat straight lines, until away in the distance it suggested endless other shadowy bales, whose outlines could be little more than guessed at. They were in a vault so huge that Ranjoor Singh made no attempt to estimate its size.

"See this!" said the German, walking close to something on a wooden stand, and he held the light above it. "In the office in Delhi that the police have just sealed up there is a wireless apparatus very much like this. This, that you see here, is a detonator. This is fulminate of mercury. This is dynamite. With a touch of a certain key in Delhi we could have blown up this vault at any minute of the past two years, if we had thought it necessary to hide our tracks. A shot from this pistol would have much the same effect," he added darkly.

"But the bales?" asked Ranjoor Singh. "What is in the bales?"

"Dynamite bombs, my friend! You native soldiers have no artillery, and we have seen from the first the necessity of supplying a substitute. By making full use of the element of surprise, these bombs should serve your purpose. There are one million of them, packed two hundred in a bale—much more useful than artillery in the hands of untrained men!

"Those look like bales of blankets. They are. Cotton blankets from Muenchen-Gladbach. Only, the middle blankets have been omitted, and the outer ones have served as a cushion to prevent accidental discharge. They have been imported in small lots at a time, and brought here four or five at a time in ox-carts from one or other of the Delhi railway stations by men who are no longer in this part of India—men who have now been pensioned off."

"How did you get them through Customs?" asked Ranjoor Singh.

"Did you ever see a rabbit go into his hole?" the German asked. "They were very small consignments, obviously of blankets. The duty was paid without demur, and the price paid the Customs men was worth their while. That part was easy!"

"Of what size are the bombs?" asked Ranjoor Singh.

"About the size of an orange. Come, I'll show you."

He led him to an opened bale, and showed him two hundred of them nestling like the eggs of some big bird.

"My God!" moaned Sita Ram. "Are those dynamite? Sahibs—snakes are better! Snakes can feel afraid, but those—ow! Let me go away!"

"Let him go," said the German. "Let him take his message."

"Go, then!" ordered Ranjoor Singh; and the German walked to the door to let him out.

"What is your message?" he asked.

"To Yasmini first, for she is in touch with all of them," said Sita Ram. "First I will go to Yasmini. Then she will come here to say the regiments have started. First she will come alone; after her the regiments."

"She had better be alone!" said the German. "Go on, run! And don't forget the way back? Wait! How will she know the way? How will you describe it to her?"

"She? Describe it to her? I will tell her 'The Winds of the World,' and she will come straight."

"How? How will she know?"

"The priest who used to be here—whom you bribed to go away—he is her night doorkeeper now!" said Sita Ram. "Yes, she will come veree quickly!"

The German let him out with an air mixed of surprise and disbelief, and returned to Ranjoor Singh with far less iron in his stride, though with no less determination.

"Now we shall see!" he said, drawing an automatic pistol and cocking it carefully. "This is not meant as a personal threat to you, so long as we two are in here alone. It's in case of trickery from outside. I shall blow this place sky-high if anything goes wrong. If the regiments come, good! You shall have the bombs. If they don't come, or if there's a trick played—click! Goodbye! We'll argue the rest in Heaven!"

"Very well," said Ranjoor Singh; and, to show how little he felt concerned, he drew his basket to him and began to eat.

The German followed suit. Then Ranjoor Singh took most of his wet clothes off and spread them upon the bales to dry. The German imitated that too.

"Go to sleep if you care to," said the German. "I shall stand watch," he added, with a dry laugh.

But if a Sikh soldier can not manage without sleep, there is nobody on earth who can. Ranjoor Singh sat back against a bale, and the watch resolved itself into a contest of endurance, with the end by no means in sight.

"How long should it take that man to reach her?" asked the German.

"Who knows?" the Sikh answered.

"Perhaps three hours, perhaps a week! She is never still, and there are those five regiments to hold in readiness."

"She is a wonderful woman," said the German.

Ranjoor Singh grunted.

"How is it that she has known of this place all this time, and yet has never tried to meddle with us?"

"I, too, am anxious to know that!" said Ranjoor Singh.

"You are surly, my friend! You do not like this pistol? You take it as an insult? Is that it?"

"I am thinking of those regiments, and of these grenades, and of what I mean to do," said Ranjoor Singh.

"Let us talk it over."

"No."

"Please your self!"

They sat facing each other for hour after dreary hour, leaning back against bales and thinking each his own thoughts. After about four hours of it, it occurred to the German to dismantle the wireless detonator.

"We should have been blown up if the police had grown inquisitive," he said, with a shrug of his shoulders, returning to his seat.

After that they sat still for four hours more, and then put their clothes on, not that they were dry yet, but the German had grown tired of comparing Ranjoor Singh's better physique with his own. He put his clothes on to hide inferiority, and Ranjoor Singh followed suit for the sake of manners.

"What rank do you hold in your army at home?" asked Ranjoor Singh, after an almost endless interval.

"If I told you that, my friend, you would be surprised."

"I think not," said Ranjoor Singh. "I think you are an officer who was dismissed from the service."

"What makes you think so?"

"I am sure of it! You are too well educated for a noncommissioned officer. If you had not been dismissed from the service you would be on the fighting strength, or else in the reserve and ready for action on the front in Europe. And what army keeps spies of your type on its strength? Am I right?"

But then came Yasmini, carrying her food-basket as the rest had done. She knocked at the outer trap-door, and the German ran to peep through a hidden window at her. Then he went up a partly ruined stair and looked all around the clearing through gaps in the debris overhead that had been glazed for protection's sake. Then he admitted her.

She ran in past him, ran past him again when he opened the second door, and laughed at Ranjoor Singh. She seemed jubilant and very little interested in the bombs that the German was at pains to explain to her. She had to tell of five regiments on the way.

"The first will be here in two or three hours" she asserted; "your men, Ranjoor Singh—your Jat Sikhs that are ever first to mutiny!"

She squealed delight as the Sikh's face flushed at the insult.

"What is the cocked pistol for?" she asked the German.

He told her, but she did not seem frightened in the least. She began to sing, and her voice echoed strangely through the vault until she herself seemed to grow hypnotized by it, and she began to sway, pushing her basket away from her behind a bale near where the German sat.

"I will dance for you!" she said suddenly.

She arose and produced a little wind instrument from among her clothing—a little bell-mouthed wooden thing, with a sound like bagpipes.

"Out of the way, Ranjoor Singh!" she ordered. "Sit yonder. I will dance between you, so that the German sahib may watch both of us at once!"

So Ranjoor Singh went back twenty feet away, wondering at her mood and wondering even more what trick she meant to play. He had reached the conclusion, very reluctantly, that presently the German would fire that pistol of his and end the careers of all three of them; so he was thinking of the squadron on its way to France. In a way he was sorry for Yasmini; but it was the squadron and Colonel Kirby that drew his heart-strings.

Swaying to and fro, from the waist upward, Yasmini began to play her little instrument. The echoing vault became a solid sea of throbbing noise, and as she played she increased her speed of movement, until the German sat and gaped. He had seen her dance on many more than one occasion. So had Ranjoor Singh. Never had either of them, or any living man, seen Yasmini dance as she did that night.

She was a storm. Her instrument was but an added touch of artistry to heighten the suggestion. Prom a slow, rhythmic swing she went by gusts and fits and starts to the wildest, utterly abandoned fury of a hurricane, sweeping a wide circle with her gauzy dress; and at the height of each elemental climax, in mid-whirl of some new amazing figure, she would set her instrument to screaming, until the German shouted "Bravo!" and Ranjoor Singh nodded grave approval.

"*Kreuz blitzen!*" swore the German suddenly, leaping to his feet and staggering.

And Yasmini pounced on him. Ranjoor Singh could not see what had happened, but he sprang to his feet and ran toward them. But before he could reach them Yasmini had snatched the German's pistol and tossed it to him, standing back from the writhing German, panting, with blazing eyes, and looking too lovely to be human. She did not speak. She looked.

And Ranjoor Singh looked too. Under the writhing German, and back again over him, there crawled a six-foot hooded cobra, seeming to caress the carcass of his prey.

"He will be dead in five—ten minutes," said Yasmini, "and then I will catch my snake again! If you want to ask him questions you had better hurry!"

Then Ranjoor Singh recalled the offices that men had done for him when he was wounded. He asked the German if he might send messages, and to whom. But the dying man seemed to be speechless, and only writhed. It was nearly a minute before Ranjoor Singh divined his purpose, and pounced on the hand that lay underneath him. He wrenched away another pistol only just in time. The snake crawled away, and Yasmini coaxed it slowly back into its basket.

"Now," she said, "when he is dead we will drive back to Delhi and amuse ourselves! You shall run away to fight men you never quarreled with, and I will govern India! Is that not so?"

Ranjoor Singh did not answer her. He kept trying to get some message from the German to send perhaps to a friend in Germany. But the man died speechless, and Ranjoor Singh could find no scrap of paper on him or no mark that would give any clue to his identity.

"Come!" said Yasmini. "Lock the door on him. We will tell the general sahib, and the general sahib will send some one to bury him. Come!"

"Not yet," said Ranjoor Singh. "Speak. When did you first know that these Germans had taken this vault to use?"

"More than two years ago," she boasted, "when the old priest, that was no priest at all, came to me to be doorkeeper."

"And when did you know that they were storing dynamite in here?"

"I did not know."

"Then, blankets?"

"Bah! Two years ago, when a Customs clerk with too much money began to make love to a maid of mine."

"Then why did you not warn the government at once, and so save all this trouble?"

"Buffalo! Much fun that would have been! Ranjoor Singh, thy Jat imagination does thee justice. Come, and chase that regiment of thine, and spill those stupid brains in France! Lock the door and come away!"

CHAPTER XIV.

The crew of the Messageries Maritimes steamship *Duc d'Orleans* will tell of a tall Sikh officer, with many medals on his breast, who boarded their ship in Bombay with letters to the captain from a British officer of such high rank as to procure him instant accession to his request. Bound homeward from Singapore, the *Duc d'Orleans* had put into Bombay for coal, supplies and orders. She left with orders for Marseilles, and on board her there went this same Sikh officer, who, it seemed, had missed the transport on which his regiment had sailed.

He had with him a huge, ill-mannered charger, and one Sikh trooper by way of servant. The charger tried to eat all that came near him, including his horse-box, the ship's crew, and enough hay for at least two ordinary horses. But Ranjoor Singh, who said very little to anybody about anything, had a certain way with him, and men put up with the charger's delinquencies for its owner's sake.

When they reached the Red Sea, and the ship rolled less, Ranjoor Singh and his trooper went to most extraordinary lengths to keep the charger in condition. They took him out of his box and walked him around the decks for hours at a time, taking turns at it until officer, trooper and horse were tired out.

They did the same all down the Mediterranean. And when they landed at Marseilles the horse was fit, as he proved to his own brute satisfaction by trying to kick the life out of a gendarme on the quay.

Another letter from somebody very high, in authority to a French general officer in Marseilles procured the instant supply of a horse for the

Sikh trooper and two passes on a northbound train. The evening of their landing saw them on their way to the front, Ranjoor Singh in a first-class compartment, and his man in the horse-box. Neither knew any French to speak of, but the French were very kind to these dark-skinned gentlemen who were in so much hurry to help them win the war.

It was dark—nearly pitch—dark at the journey's end. The moon shone now and then through banks of black clouds, and showed long lines of poplar trees. Beyond, in the distance, there was a zone in which great flashes leaped and died—great savage streaks of fire of many colors—and a thundering that did not cease at all.

Along the road that ran between the poplars two men sent their horses at a rousing clip, though not so fast as to tax them to the utmost. The man in front rode a brute that lacked little of seventeen hands and that fought for the bit as if he would like to eat the far horizon.

In the very, very dark zone, on the near side of where the splashes of red fire fell, jingling bits and a kick now and then proclaimed the presence of a regiment of cavalry. Nothing else betrayed them until one was near enough to see the whites of men's eyes in the dark, for they were native Indian cavalry, who know the last master-touches of the art of being still.

Between them and the very, very dark zone—which was what the Frenchmen call a forest, and some other nations call a stand of timber— a little group of officers sat talking in low tones, eight Englishmen and the others Sikhs.

"They say they're working round the edge—say they can't hold 'em. It looks very much as if we're going to get our chance tonight. When a red light flashes three times at this near corner of the woods, we're to ride into 'em in line—it'll mean that our chaps are falling back in a hurry, leaving lots of room between 'em and the wood for us to ride through. Better join your men, you fellows! Oh, lord! What wouldn't Ranjoor Singh have given to be here! What's that?"

There came a challenge from the rear. Two horsemen cantered up.

"Who are you? What d' you want?"

"Sahib! Colonel Kirby sahib!"

"What is it? Hallo—there are the three lights—no, two lights— that's 'Get ready!' Who are you? Why—Ranjoor Singh!"

"Salaam, sahib!"

"Shake hands. By gad—I'm glad! Find your squadron, Ranjoor Singh—find it at once, man—you're just in time. There go the three lights! *Outram's Own!—in line of squadron columns to the right—Trot, March! Right!*"

Ranjoor Singh had kept the word of babu Sita Ram, and had managed to be with them when the first blood ran.

THE END.

YASMINI'S SONG

(OTHER VERSES)

The West Wind blows through the Ajmere Gate
And whispers low (Oh, listen ye!),
"The fed wolf curls by his drowsy mate
In a tight—trod earth; but the lean wolves wait,
And the hunger gnaws!" (Oh, listen ye!)
"Can fed wolves fight? But yestere'en
Their eyes were bright, their fangs were clean;
They viewed, they took but yestere'en,"
(Oh, listen, wise heads, listen ye!)
"Because they fed, is blood less red,
Or fangs less sharp, or hunger dead?"
(Look well to the loot, and listen ye!)

The North Wind hails from the Northern snows,
(His voice is loud—oh, listen ye!)
He cried of death—the death he knows—
Of the mountain death. (Oh, listen ye!)
Who looks to the North for love looks long!
Who goes to the North for gain goes wrong!
Men's hearts are hard, and the goods belong
To the strong in the North! (Oh, listen ye!)
Whose lot is fair—who loves his life—
Walks wide, stays wide of the Northern knife!
(Ye men o' the world, oh, listen ye!)

The Four Winds come, the Four Winds go,
(Ye wise o' the world, oh, listen ye!),
Whispering, whistling what they know,
Wise, since wandering made them so
(Ye stay-at-homes, oh, listen ye!).

Ever they seek and sift and pry—
Listening here, and hurrying by—
Restless, ceaseless—know ye why?
(Then, wise o' the world, oh, listen ye!)
The goal of the search of the hurrying wind
Is the key to the maze of a woman's mind,
(And there is no key! Oh, listen ye!)

Westward, into the hungry West,
(Oh, listen, wise men, listen ye!)
Whirls the East Wind on his quest,
Whimpering, worrying, hurrying, lest
The light o'ertake him. Listen ye!

Mark ye the burden of his sigh:
"Westward sinks the sun to die!
Westward wing the vultures!"—Aye,
(Listen, wise men, listen ye!)
The East must lose—the West must gain,
For none come back to the East again,
Though widows call them! Listen ye!

"Now a trap," said the tiger, "is easy to spot,"
(Oh, jungli, be seated and listen!)
"Some tempt you with live bait, and others do not;"
(Oh, jungli, be leery and listen!)
"The easiest sort to detect have a door—
A box, with three walls and a roof and a floor—
That the veriest, hungriest cub should ignore."
(Oh, jungli, stop laughing and listen!)
"This isn't a trap, as I'll show you, my friend."
But the tiger fell into it. That is the end.

(Oh, jungli, be loving and listen!)

Made in the USA
Coppell, TX
29 December 2020